interference

Michelle Berry

interference

a novel

a misFit book
ECW PRESS

Published by ECW Press
2120 Queen Street East, Suite 200, Toronto, Ontario, Canada M4E 1E2
416-694-3348 / info@ecwpress.com

LIBRARY AND ARCHIVES CANADA CATALOGUING IN PUBLICATION
Berry, Michelle, 1968–, author
Interference: a novel / Michelle Berry.
ISBN 978-1-77041-198-2
Also issued as: 978-1-77090-612-9 (PDF); 978-1-77090-611-2 (EPUB)
I. Title.
PS8553.E7723I58 2014   C813'.54   C2014-902587-4
C2014-902588-2

Editor for the press: Michael Holmes
Design: Rachel Ironstone
Cover photos: deserted playground by Benson Kua | www.flickr.com/photos/
  bensonkua/; slippers © zhekos/iStockphoto
Author photo: Abby Berry

Printing: Marquis 5 4 3 2 1
Printed and bound in Canada

The publication of *Interference* has been generously supported by the Canada Council for the Arts which last year invested $157 million to bring the arts to Canadians throughout the country, and by the Ontario Arts Council (OAC), an agency of the Government of Ontario, which last year funded 1,793 individual artists and 1,076 organizations in 232 communities across Ontario, for a total of $52.1 million. We also acknowledge the financial support of the Government of Canada through the Canada Book Fund for our publishing activities, and the contribution of the Government of Ontario through the Ontario Book Publishing Tax Credit and the Ontario Media Development Corporation.

For Heidi den Hartog
and especially for Stuart Baird.

IF GIRLS HOCKEY WAS EASY . . .
THEY'D LET THE BOYS PLAY WITH US

Slogan on the shirts for the
Peterborough Ice Kats Hockey League

fall

Dear Parents and Guardians,

This morning we became aware of an incident that occurred at another school earlier this week. We are forwarding this information to you, because we know you need to be aware of what is going on and we need to have an open dialogue between staff and parents. We have found that if we don't have this kind of discussion some of our parents get very upset. Last year's incident with the ice cream and the hermit crabs was just such an example of this.

Local police indicate that a man approached a twelve-year-old girl in front of our sister school, Markwell Elementary, on Lee Boulevard. Somehow avoiding the mother-monitors, this man was lingering around when the bell rang for dismissal. The student swears that she does not know the man, and when he asked her if she wanted a ride home she said no. He walked away and left the girl alone. He didn't seem to be in possession of a vehicle.

The man is described as "old" by the girl. We assume that means that he is somewhere between the ages of twenty and sixty. The girl also stated that he was a few inches taller than her — this would put him at around five feet, five inches tall. She said he had a small build and short, brown hair, balding on the top. He was wearing a dark green trench coat over a brown suit. He had a nervous manner about him and kept repeating himself. Police are continuing their investigation into this matter. They ask if any of you have information to please call Crime Stoppers.

We must all congratulate this anonymous twelve-year-old for her forward and rational thinking. Not only did she say no to the man when he asked her if she wanted a ride, but she also was aware enough to get a good look at him and report him to the police.

Safety among our students is always our top priority. Our staff will keep their eyes open in the schoolyard. They will be vigilant. We have ordered new walkie-talkies in order to communicate with the office if the teachers see anything out of order. Triple AAA batteries would be appreciated if you have any to donate. Please review all the safety rules you can think of with your children. This includes walking with another child and telling an adult immediately if someone makes them feel uncomfortable. Consider deciding on a secret word that only you and your child know in case someone says that you sent them to pick up the child.

Please feel free to call me with any questions or concerns.

Sincerely,

Marge Tanner

Marge Tanner
Principal, Oak Park Elementary School

1

Tom and Maria are busy raking the leaves. Tom is by the side of their front porch. Maria is out near the sidewalk. Their daughter, Becky, is playing across the street with her friend Rachel and the sky is full of white billowy clouds. The new woman who recently moved into the empty place beside Rachel's house pulls her car into her driveway, unbuckles her baby from the back and walks into her house. Tom stops raking to admire her blond hair, California-blond, bleached-out but still healthy looking, which is ironic. But isn't everything from California ironic, Tom thinks. Tom knows he'd never have noticed the hair, or at least the health of it, the blond of it, the irony of it, if Maria hadn't commented on it. They haven't introduced themselves to this new neighbour yet, but Tom and Maria watch her and Tom assumes, because of this, that they know a lot about her. The other neighbours have said things. Rachel's mother, Trish, has mentioned her. They know her name is Dayton. Dayton from California living now in Canada. The baby is Carrie, which reminds Tom of the Stephen King movie, of pig's blood and periods, of a hand coming out of a grave. That movie made Tom uncomfortable. Who would name their child Carrie? Someone named Dayton, he supposes. Tom sighs. Although that's such an old movie now, Dayton might not even know about it. She looks young. Early thirties? Late twenties? Or maybe it's just the hair. The name. Maybe she's older than Tom and Maria. Tom scratches his head and continues raking. There is a dog barking somewhere, but Tom isn't sure where. There are many dogs in the neighbourhood and they are often barking. This includes Tom's dog.

The swoosh and scrape of Tom's rake in the leaves, the smell of fresh dirt, the crisp chill air — all of this works to make him satisfied and still. After the week he had at the office, new clients, proposals to send out, the computers down for two hours on Thursday, raking up the golds and yellows and oranges, collecting all this colour, makes Tom take notice. Life might be better if he didn't have to work.

"Around the side," Maria says. He hears her out front. She has been raking the sidewalk and the sound has stopped, the grating sound the plastic makes when in contact with the concrete has ceased. Maria is talking to someone.

Tom moves to look around the side of the large front porch, dragging behind him a half-filled paper bag of leaves, carrying his rake in one hand. As he peers towards the street, the sound of Maria raking starts up again. Scratching at the near leaf-less sidewalk. He smiles to himself, thinking about how picky she is, always trying to get up every last leaf, every bit of soil, crumble, twig. She's like this in the house too, always bending to collect dog fur, dust clumps, stray fuzz and lint. No wonder she complains about lower back problems, all that bending. She says she does it for Becky, who loves a clean house, but Tom is sure Maria does it for herself too. Maria won't admit it, but Tom remembers that before Becky was born Maria would vacuum the house every day. She would mop the kitchen floor three times a week. It's funny,

5

but the fact that Maria won't admit it makes it not true. Tom questions his memories whenever they aren't the same as Maria's. Married for fifteen years, Tom remembers things from his past through Maria's eyes, as if he's in there, staring out. Like in the movie *Being John Malkovich*, Tom is in his own movie, *Being Maria Shutter*. Sometimes Tom closes his eyes and concentrates hard and tries to see his life a year, two years ago, but all he sees is what Maria has told him about his past. Even though he was there. She has erased all his mind. Tom's mother and father did this too. And Tom's brother. Everyone has always reinvented Tom. Tom would say, "Remember when I had that blue bike?" and his mother would say, "It was yellow, dear," and even though Tom knew, for sure, that the yellow bike belonged to his brother, Ted, and his bike was blue, and no matter how much Tom would fight it, she would insist that his bike was yellow, yellow, yellow, until, one day, Tom would remember his bike was yellow.

"Hello."

The word startles Tom. This happens all the time. Tom fading out, losing touch with reality. Thinking. A man is coming towards him, over the grass, around the corner of his house. Straight at him as he stands there, rake in hand, bag in other hand, staring at nothing.

Becky squeals with delight from across the street. She is twelve and everything makes her exclaim in high, loud screeches. Tom focuses quickly back to the present.

"Hello," Tom says, looking carefully at the man. Tom is immediately struck by the scar running down his face and he can't help but cringe. As if this man's face has been split in two by an axe, a thick, white scar from the centre of his hairline, directly below his widow's peak, straight through the centre of his nose, which is widened and lumpy, and down through his lip and stubbly chin. A wide scar, rough and jagged. A scar that is blatant in its violence. The scar doesn't move when the man says hello so that it looks as if each side of his face is portraying a separate, singular emotion. Like a clown's mouth, the two sides of his mouth turn up independently of each other.

Maria peers around the house at Tom, bends out into the open to catch Tom's sightline. Her eyes are wide and Tom remembers quickly what he loves about her. Even if she steals his past and cleans the house too often, she's still got that expressive, wild face. In one small moment he can read everything she wants to say in her arched eyebrows, those beady brown eyes, that full mouth. Tom collects himself and tries to smile at the man.

The scar-faced man is wearing coveralls, light blue, speckled with red and brown paint. His hair is straw blond. Thick. It's a shame, Tom thinks, the man might just be considered handsome except for the line that divides his face. The man is taller than Tom, and the muscles in his neck and forearms are prominent. Looking at him, Tom remembers something he hasn't thought of in years. His own memory. Not his mother's. Not Maria's. But his. Tom remembers finding a photo album high up on the shelf in his grandparents' basement. The album was full of postcards, placed within the plastic sleeves where photos should go. Each postcard was from a circus, and there were pictures on the postcards of the freaks from the circus: the half-man-half-woman, the fat woman, the bearded woman, the snake-boy, the gorilla-man, the sword swallower, the Siamese twins, the ugliest woman in the world. He remembers spending hours staring at those postcards — his grandfather collected them from flea markets, along with old photographs of farms and windmills and lighthouses and thimbles and spoons. Tom remembers being fascinated by the distorted faces and bodies. He would look at the pictures and then look away, ashamed at having caught himself staring. This is a sudden memory that is Tom's own. It belongs solely to him.

"Sorry," Tom says to the scar-faced man. "We had the house painted last year." He points to the man's coveralls. "I was told it would last a couple years. It's chipping up a bit on the porch, but I can do that next summer."

"Paint?" the man says. "Sorry?"

"He's here about raking," Maria calls out and then turns and heads back down to the street, dragging her rake behind her. It is obvious from her demeanour that she wants Tom to deal with this, that she wants nothing to do with this man in his coveralls standing in front of their house. She will have something to say later, Tom is sure, something to say about the way he handled the situation but, for now, she disappears into the distance.

"Raking?"

"Yes, raking. Can you use some help?"

"I can always use some help," Tom says even though he doesn't want any help. Even if he did want help, he knows he has nothing in his wallet to pay the guy. "But, sorry," Tom says quickly, regretting his words immediately. "I'm broke right now." He leans the rake on his hip and holds up his hands as if to show the man he has nothing in them. Not a cent. He flicks them. Waves them. Some small part of him wants to pull out his pockets, dangle the inside white lining, show the emptiness of them. Pull the lint out from the seams. A Charlie Chaplin or Buster Keaton move. Shrug a bit, hands in the air. Shuffle.

"I can help anyway," the man says. "Do you have an extra rake?"

"No, really. I don't have any cash."

The man smiles — half his face smiles, the other half is stiffer. It's disconcerting. Tom can hear his daughter across the street, bouncing a basketball on the neighbour's driveway. He can hear her shrill giggle. He hears her say, "Rachel, you're such a turd," and then they both bust up laughing so hard that Rachel has to sit down. She shouts, "Stop, I'll pee."

8

"You can owe me," the man says. "You can pay me another time." He begins to walk towards Tom and Tom uneasily steps back. Maria comes up from the sidewalk and around the side of the house.

"We need more bags," she says. "We are out of bags." She stops quickly when she sees the man still there. She looks curiously at Tom. He shrugs. "I can run to the store, I can get more bags," Maria says.

"I'll use your rake," the man says. "That settles it." He takes Maria's rake out of her hand and begins to work at the ground as if he's never done anything in his entire life but rake leaves. He is thorough and methodical. Tom watches him for a while and then lifts his face up to Maria again. She scowls at him. She looks frightened and angry — Tom should have handled this situation — but she scurries off towards the street and her car.

"I'll be back soon."

There is a large pile of leaves directly in front of Tom when the wind picks up. The leaves begin to scatter. The scar-faced man is in the backyard. Tom can hear him working away, he can hear the sound the rake makes as it snags his grass. He can hear his dog barking from inside the house — the dog down the street barking as well. In fact, it seems to Tom that all the dogs in the neighbourhood don't like this man.

Tom's whole life he's been surrounded by men and women who have no true physical deformities, nothing out of the ordinary — large noses, moles maybe, fat in the wrong places, but nothing horrible — and he thinks about how this is not normal. Much of the world lives daily with ugliness and suffering: amputated arms and legs, burns, disfigurement. Look at Sierra Leone. Or Rwanda. Or Syria. Iraq. But here, in his city, it's rare to even see a wheelchair. What Tom sees most of these days is the baldness and loss of eyebrows from cancer treatments. There are women at work. There is a man who works in the grocery store. That fuzzy-headed shape, bandana, wig, eyebrows drawn on with make-up, toques. Tom sees a lot of that these days. In fact, Maria likes to point out, "If it's not cancer, it's affairs," as everyone they know is going through one or the other. But in the past Tom knows his parents' generation saw amputated limbs from wars, scars from shrapnel, burn victims, circus freaks on postcards.

The wind picks up.

Tom puts his full bag of leaves on top of his blowing pile and also places his rake across it, trying to hold everything together. He would lie on the pile and wait for Maria to get back with more bags if he wasn't sure the leaves were littered with dog crap — he can smell it. Not his dog — Tom keeps close eye on where his dog shits — but the neighbour's dog. Early in the morning, drinking his coffee by the front window, Tom sees his neighbour's dog defecating on his front lawn. Every morning. In the same place. The neighbour never picks it up. Tom doesn't say anything. Maria gets angry but she doesn't say anything. Neither one of them wants to rock the boat. Neighbours are hard enough. Angry neighbours are even harder. That's another thing that is different in his life. Picking up dog shit. Not many people in the world do that. It's a luxury to own a pet, although, with a bag of dog crap dangling from his hand, it doesn't feel like a luxury. Tom's heard that in Paris no one picks up shit and they have street cleaners who wash the sidewalks early every morning, but he's never been to Paris and so he doesn't know if this is true. Like the leaves whirling around in front of him, Tom's mind is scattered. His concentration is off. Maria would say it always is. "Pay attention, Tom," she would say, snapping her fingers in front of his face.

It's just that there is always so much to think about.

"Dad." Becky is coming up the driveway with her basketball. Long-legged, stomach still protruding slightly, baby fat, a twelve-year-old approaching thirty-six, Becky gives off the air of nonchalance. She ignores the sound of the scar-faced man in the backyard. She purposefully looks away from the back of the house and focuses only on the front and the side. She bounces her ball carelessly and Tom knows she will lose it and it will roll into the street. A car will come. Tom is sure of it. "Hey, Dad. Who's that guy in the backyard?" Her voice quavers slightly.

"He's helping me rake."

Becky walks towards Tom. She places the ball against the house and stares at the pile of leaves.

"Don't jump in it," Tom says. "Dog crap."

"Eww." Becky studies her fingernails and then starts to bite them nervously. Tom knows that the thought of dog crap, of dirt, of anything unclean, unnerves Becky. Tom shouldn't have said anything, because there is no way Becky would have tried to jump in the pile and now, by drawing attention to leaves with dog poop in them, he has created a rift in Becky's mind. He can see her thinking and worrying. She wouldn't jump in leaves like a normal kid. Becky is obsessed with cleanliness and germs and it's only getting worse the older she gets. Tom worries about her constantly, but Maria says it's a stage, she'll grow out of it. Tom watches the loose basketball to see if it will roll down the driveway. Miraculously, it doesn't. It finds a groove and settles in.

"I can smell it." Becky shudders. She walks towards the back gate and looks at the scar-faced man. Squarely. She shivers. For some reason there seems to be no wind in the backyard. Tom can't figure it out. The man has made quite a few large piles of leaves throughout the yard and they are contained, not a leaf moving. Out front Tom is holding desperately to his one pile, which is shrinking now and is considerably smaller. The scar-faced man raises his head and nods at Becky. She ducks behind the gate, her face suddenly red, her eyes as wide as her mother's.

"Becky —" Tom starts.

"Oh my god," Becky whispers. "Oh my god, what's wrong with his face?" She shakes her arms about as if trying to get rid of what she has seen, as if what she has seen has clung to her body and she needs it gone. Now. Immediately. She shakes him off. "What's wrong with him?"

Maria comes back with the brown paper leaf bags, and Tom holds them open while the scar-faced man puts the leaves inside. It's an uncomfortable feeling being this close to the man, this close to his scar, but Tom makes a conscious effort not to pull away. In fact, the scar-faced man actually leans back, away from Tom, giving him space. Tom notices that he smells pretty good, a combination of wood and oil, a touch of deodorant warmed in the sun. They work silently and quickly. Maria goes inside.

"You know," the man says as he reaches down for another handful of leaves, "you couldn't ask for a better day."

"Yeah, I guess. Bit windy, though. But crisp. Clean."

"It's good," the man says, scooping the leaves and then using the rake as a shovel, filling the bags. "A good, still day. No wind."

"Well, I don't know." Tom looks at what used to be his pile. His rake. His half-filled bag, his demolished pile. He can see more of his leaves on his neighbour's yard than on his own. That's okay. Let him deal with the mess for once. Tom deals with the neighbour's dog crap. What goes around comes around, he supposes.

"Would you like lunch?" Maria calls from the side door. "I could bring you both out some lunch?"

The man nods. "That would be nice," he says. Tom watches his face when he talks. There are two sides to this man. Two-faced. One side of his face says one-half the words. Tom looks up at the clouds and notices someone on a roof about four houses down the street. Saturday chores. He suddenly hears the hammering that goes along with the man. Another neighbour farther up is on a ladder cleaning eavestroughs. Scattered throughout the street there are people raking. His daughter has gone back to playing basketball with Rachel across the street. Tom wonders if this scar-faced man would have joined the circus in the old days — shown his face to scare people, to excite them. He wonders if his grandfather would have bought a postcard of this face and if the caption would have been "Cut in Half With an Axe" or "Sword Fight Gone Wrong." Tom doesn't know why his grandfather kept postcards of freaks in his basement in a photo album and, until today, until he remembered, Tom never really thought about it. But now he sees it was odd and there was no reason for it. It's insulting, in fact. And slightly racist. Or, if not racist, then appearance-ist.

"Becky," Tom calls out. "Lunch."

"She's in here with me," Maria says. "We're already making it."

Tom looks towards the basketball net and, yes, it's the neighbour's child, Rachel, shooting baskets, not Becky. Tom loses track of his daughter. Girls at this age are like shadows. They flit in and out of his mind. Like a blind spot on his eye. And this frightens him. What if he permanently loses his daughter? What if one day he can't catch her reflection anymore? Every time he sees her she has somehow changed. She has grown taller or wider. Her hair changes colour with the sun. The style of clothes moves in and out of fashion. One day she is Becky, the next day she'll be someone else. Or she'll be somewhere else. She'll be gone.

After sandwiches and a beer the man stands up from the bottom of the porch step where he has been sitting and wipes his hands on his paint-splattered coveralls. Tom has been curiously watching him eat, but pretending to look across the street at the squirrels shooting up and down the huge oak tree in front of Trish's house. He admires the squirrels and then watches Rachel shoot baskets on her own. When the man drank his beer he held the bottle against one side of his lips, took a swig sideways. When he took a bite of the sandwich he took it full on, directly in the middle. But he chewed on one side or the other. One cheek would masticate while the other would remain frozen. Another bite — the opposite cheek. It took everything Tom had not to say anything, not to ask. And the man didn't offer any explanation for his disfigurement. He simply chewed, drank, swallowed, joined Tom in watching Rachel. Now he is standing with his hands on his hips and looking at the last pile of leaves on the front lawn. They have worked hard, Tom and the man, and have accomplished more than Tom thought he would for the day. When Maria went inside to make lunch, she didn't come back. Tom assumes she has used the extra hand as an excuse to get on with other things: maybe brushing the dog, doing laundry, starting a soup for dinner. Tom can smell something cooking every time she opens the door to hand him beer, napkins, sandwiches and finally cookies and fruit.

The man is grateful for the food. Tom can tell. The way the man stands there, relaxed and satisfied, with his hands on his hips, and admires all the work they've done. Tom counts fifteen bags of leaves at the front sidewalk. Except for the scar dividing his face into two, the man would be just fine. A nice working companion. Very helpful and quiet. In fact, Maria, when Tom works with her putting leaves into bags, ends up talking so much that he finds he has to pause in order to react. And, of course, when she talks he thinks. And when Tom thinks too much things don't get done quickly enough. Tom wishes he had $40 to give the man. He wishes he had something. He wishes he had asked Maria to go to the bank machine when she went to get more leaf bags. Why didn't he think of that? For all the time he spends thinking Tom knows he can be very thoughtless. After all, Maria tells him as much.

Becky comes out of the front door with a cookie and her basketball. Tom watches as she glances at the man standing there with his hands on his hips. He is turned from her, offering only half his face, and Becky quickly looks elsewhere. Tom sees wet wipes in her back pocket. For after the cookie, he assumes.

"Going back to Rachel's," she says and skips off the porch, heads across the street — looking before she crosses — and into Rachel's driveway. Tom and the man admire them. The girls shoot hoops for a bit and giggle and look across the street at Tom and the scar-faced man. The girls whisper. Then they shout. They argue. There is a small pile of used wipes beside the base of the basketball net. Tom didn't notice them before. But now that he's seen them he's having a hard time noticing anything else.

The weird thing is that the scar-faced man doesn't acknowledge the girls at all. He doesn't blush or look nervous. He is aware that they are looking at him — and, Tom reasons, he must know why they are looking at him — but it doesn't seem to faze him one bit. In fact, it's as if he isn't even aware of his disfigurement, as if his split face is nothing out of the ordinary. Tom is beginning to feel comfortable around him, almost as comfortable as the man himself feels around Tom. Who's to say Tom's face is perfect? Who's to say Tom himself is easy to look at? We can't account for other people's tastes. In fact, being with this man makes Tom feel better about his past, about sitting on the floor of his grandfather's basement, sneakily gawking at those postcards. Tom was never sure if what he was looking at was good or bad, allowed or discouraged. Was this some sort of pornography? Why would his grandfather place the album in the basement? Up high on the shelf? Why did no one in the family ever mention them?

If everything else that happened later hadn't distracted him from this lesson, Tom would have looked back on the day and remembered that he learned something about beauty and ugliness and about judging others. He would think that he learned something about what was right and what was wrong and about how to react and interact with people who are different from him, and finally, perhaps, that he learned something about his grandfather. If things had gone better, that is.

"Only three more bags, I'd say," the scar-faced man says, beginning to work again. Becky is hollering across the street and Rachel is doing cartwheels carelessly near the road. Tom stands up from his position on the porch and walks down to stand next to the man. The difference between Rachel and Becky is absurd — one wiping her hands, the other rolling on the grass between the sidewalk and the road.

"You never told me your name," Tom says.

"And you never told me yours," the man says. Tom and the scar-faced man laugh. The man's laugh sounds wheezy, as if it's caught somewhere between the cut through his lips.

"Tom Shutter," Tom says.

The man nods, and begins to work again. "Hold this bag for me, Tom." He bends to pick up more leaves from the last few piles, and when he does Tom sees the back of the man's neck when his collar rides down with the stretch from his coveralls. There is a tattoo on the man's neck, and Tom strains to make it out but the man turns and catches him staring. The man stands quickly and adjusts his collar, as if ashamed. It looked like a cross to Tom, but he couldn't be sure.

"Stop it, Rachel," Becky shouts. "Dad, Rachel won't clean her hands and they are all dirty."

"Becky's a neat freak." Rachel laughs.

"Work it out, guys," Tom shouts back, looking nervously from the man to his daughter. As if he has to impress the scar-faced man. His daughter's cleanliness, her strangeness, compared to his scar-face. Tom starts to walk across the road to mediate the argument. When he turns back he sees the man standing near the bottom of his porch, holding a rake in one hand, a pile of leaves pressed against his chest in the other. The man is staring up at Tom's house, up at the second-floor balcony, up to where Becky's room is. He is tense, stiff, still — like the leaves, like the died-down wind, like the autumn air around him. Tom shivers. It's a warm Saturday afternoon in early November but Tom senses winter is near.

Becky and Rachel make up. Rachel wipes her hands on her shirt and this, for some reason, is good enough for Becky. They sit on the curb on their sweaters and watch the scar-faced man work. He works on the bags, filling them. Becky's hair shines bright in the diminishing sun. Nothing like the new neighbour's gold California hair, Tom thinks, but still, it's pretty. Tom watches her as he helps the man bag the last leaves. His daughter is so pretty. Twelve years old and already a heartbreaker. Tom's heart breaks every time he looks at her, every time he can see her, his vision of childhood being what it is.

Maria opens the front door. She signals to Tom, crooks her pointing finger. The dog barks from inside the kitchen. Tom can see him down the hall. He doesn't rush at the front door anymore, like he used to, but he still likes to bark. He likes to let himself be known. He likes to prove to everyone that he is still useful even though they've been yelling at him for years not to bark.

"What are you going to pay him with? Do you think he'll take a cheque?"

"Not sure," Tom says. "I could go to the store and get cash. It would only take me a minute."

Maria studies the man on the front lawn. "I'm not sure I feel comfortable with you going," she says. Her hands are crossed across her chest. "What about if I go and get money? I should have done that before, when I got the bags. You should have told me to get money. I just never carry money around anymore."

Tom nods. Maria pulls on her coat and heads out to her car again. "I'm just going to the store," she tells the scar-faced man. "I'll just go get something at the store."

The man nods. Maria makes her nervousness obvious. She doesn't need to justify everything she is doing to this man. Just go to the store, Tom thinks. And then come back. Pay the man.

"I'm just going to get you some money. You've been such a help today."

"No," the man says. "I can come back tomorrow or another time. You don't have to go now to get money."

"It's no problem, really," Maria says. "Just to the store. The cash machine. No problem at all." She climbs in her car.

"Mom," Becky calls out from across the street. "Where are you going?"

"Just to the store," Maria says, her window open to the warm air. "I'll be back soon."

The man has finished the leaves and he sits on the bottom step of the porch, watching Maria drive away for the second time that day. Tom drags the last bag to the sidewalk and wipes his hands on his jeans. With Maria gone the day seems awfully sad suddenly. As if she has driven out of their lives. Tom looks at Becky, who is standing at the base of the basketball net, across the street, clutching the ball to her chest as if it's her child. Rachel is running in circles around Becky, poking her with a stick.

"The rain held off," Tom says.

"Was it supposed to rain?"

"That's what they said." Tom studies his lawn. It's almost perfect. Not a leaf anywhere. His neighbour's lawn, however, is a mess. Tom knows that with a stiff west wind all those leaves next door will be on his lawn again and he'll have to start all over. The man never cleans up leaves, never shovels snow, never picks up his dog shit. He's really not a great neighbour. Although he's quiet. Stays inside. Tom never has to talk to him. That's a huge bonus. Trish, Rachel's mom, is over all the time, worrying Maria with every little detail of her life. "I really appreciate your help," Tom says. "Even though I didn't think I needed it, I sure did. My wife, well, she ends up talking so much I never get anything done." Tom laughs. A throaty laugh. It comes out funny because Tom feels guilty the minute he laughs. He feels as if Maria can hear him. The man nods, smiles with half his face.

"It was no problem at all," the man says. "I like raking."

"And painting?" Tom says.

"Painting?"

"Your coveralls. All that paint. You must be a painter."

"No, that's not paint," the man says. He wraps his arms around himself, huddles in as if trying to protect himself. "That's just rust and such."

"Cars then?"

The man shakes his head, shrugs.

"You work on cars?" Tom asks.

"No," the man says. "Not on cars. Not really."

"Well, I'm going in to wash my hands. Can I get you something? A lemonade? Coke?"

"That would be nice of you," the man says. "I'd like a Coke, if you have one."

Tom walks around the man, still huddled on the bottom step, and enters his house. He leaves the door open and the screen door bangs shut behind him as he meanders down the hall. The dog is overjoyed to see him. Wiggles his hips until his body is bent in half. The tail whaps on the floor like it's beating a drum. Tom bends to pat him. He then pours himself a glass of water and washes his hands at the kitchen sink, scrubbing hard under his nails and up his wrists where the dirt from the leaves has travelled. Even though he was wearing gloves most of the time he still managed to get dirty. Becky would be horrified if she could see her father's hands. This is something he doesn't get in an office, dirt under his fingernails. This is the feeling of hard, simple work, not frustrating computer-controlled work. Afterwards, Tom pulls a Coke from the fridge and pours it into a glass for the man. He adds ice and thinks for a bit about adding a lemon slice but then realizes that the man might think he's weird. A nice face; a nice house; a nice family; a nice, clean, leaf-free lawn and then a lemon slice. It might just be too much.

As he steps over his dog and carries the glass of Coke to the front door, down his long narrow hallway, he hears Maria's car pull up to the curb. She comes into the house just as Tom reaches the front door.

"Here you go." Maria hands him some $20 bills. "I figure we should give him about $40, or even $60? What do you think?"

"I think $40 is fine. He was here only two hours and we didn't ask him to help out. Plus we gave him lunch."

Maria stands in Tom's way. "You want lemon in that Coke?"

"No, it's not for me, it's for him."

"What do you think happened?" she whispers. "His face?"

Tom shrugs. "Doesn't matter, I guess. He's a hard worker."

"Must be difficult, though, to be judged all your life for that face."

"Maybe it just happened. Maybe he hasn't had long to deal with it." Tom knows, when he says this, that it isn't true. The man has lived most of his life with that face — it's in the way he moves, the way his eyes take you in when you talk to him, the way he approaches the world. And, if this is the case, it means that whatever happened to him, happened when he was just a boy. Maybe Becky's age.

"Still," Maria says. "I can't imagine." She touches her face thoughtfully. She stands there in front of the door, blocking it.

"I have to get past you," Tom says. "Give him his drink and the money."

"He isn't outside," Maria says. "He's not out there. I thought he might be in here with you. Maybe he's using the washroom?"

"What do you mean?" Tom pushes around Maria, almost spilling the Coke, and looks out the screen door. The scar-faced man isn't on the bottom step anymore. Tom goes outside and looks up and down the street. He walks around the house and looks in the backyard. There is no one in sight. It's strange for anyone to leave before getting paid. The man worked hard. He knew Maria was getting money for him. He didn't slack off once today. Why would anyone work like that for nothing? And why would he leave without saying goodbye? Maybe he will come back tomorrow. Maybe he'll come back tomorrow and get money from Tom and Maria and they can ask him what happened to his face and wish him well. Tom wants to know about his face. Tom wants to say something to him. He doesn't know what, but this kind of leaving isn't right.

"Tom." Maria is calling from the front door. Tom heads back to the front, still holding the glass of Coke. "Tom." Her voice is insistent and shrill. "Tom?"

"What? Is he there?"

"Tom?" Maria is standing on the front porch, looking out across the street. She is holding herself just like the scar-faced man held himself when Tom asked what the stains on his coveralls were, hugging, arms wrapped around her chest as if she were holding her ribs in. She is holding herself just like Becky held the ball. Tom suddenly notices the silence. No ball bouncing, no bickering girls. "Tom, where's Becky? Where is Becky? Did she go with Rachel's family when they left? They were going out for dinner, Tom. Did they take Becky? Tom? Where's Becky?"

Tom just stands there, holding the glass of Coke, looking at the empty basketball net in the driveway of Rachel's house. Listening to the stillness. He counts the bags of leaves on his front sidewalk as if reassuring himself they are all there. Eighteen bags. Then he turns towards his wife, his mouth ajar, and even though he is not religious, he offers up a silent prayer. Please, Tom offers up, please.

"Tom," Maria cries again. She is shaking. "Where is Becky?"

"I'm here," Becky says, thumping out the door and onto the front porch. Chewing gum. Snapping it in her mouth. The smell of sweet watermelon follows her from inside. The dog sneaks out with her and stands tall, tail wagging, sniffing the air.

"Oh god," Maria says. She puts her hand on her chest and laughs. The laugh is like a bark. The dog looks up at her and woofs softly.

"What's going on? What happened?"

Maria grabs Becky and hugs her. "Where were you?"

"Rachel left," Becky says from the centre of Maria's chest, her voice muffled. "I came inside. Let go. You're squishing me."

As Becky scrabbles out of her mother's grasp the wind picks up and Tom turns away from his family to watch, his heart still beating furiously, as all his neighbour's leaves fly towards him in mini-cyclones. Sometimes, Tom thinks as the dog chases the leaves, thrilled to be free, you think the world surprises you when, in fact, it's not the world, it's you. You who surprise yourself. And then Tom stops thinking because thinking gets him nowhere and instead he puts down the Coke and picks up his rake to start again on the leaves and the bags in the cold autumn air.

MYTHS ABOUT BREAST CANCER:

MYTH: Abortion and miscarriage cause breast cancer.
MYTH: Antiperspirants/deodorants cause breast cancer.
MYTH: Breast implants cause breast cancer.
MYTH: Bruising the breast causes breast cancer.
MYTH: Men don't get breast cancer.
MYTH: Cell-phone use causes breast cancer.
MYTH: Radiation by mammography causes breast cancer.
MYTH: Thermography is an effective breast-screening tool.
MYTH: Wearing an underwire bra causes breast cancer.

2

There was a time when Claire didn't have cancer. A time she woke up in the morning and didn't think about the day ahead, about her life ahead, about that thing inside of her that is growing and mutating, that alien monster, and instead thought only about coffee and cereal. There was also a time when she had friends who would call and ask her to do things, call to check up on her. Now no one calls. They are afraid of her — as if cancer is contagious — afraid of what they should say and what they shouldn't say and what they want to say and what they don't want to say. Besides, Claire's not fun anymore. She's a freak. Who wants to be around someone who has cancer?

Claire understands this. Just two years ago, when Lise was sick, she felt the same way. Claire dropped off a bunch of flowers on Lise's front porch and scurried down the street as if Lise had the plague. Once she called her. Once she saw her in the grocery store and smiled and waved and tried to look rushed. Once she said, "How are you?" but realized she shouldn't have asked that, that it was a stupid, stupid question, and besides, she didn't want to hear the answer.

Lise is okay now. In fact, Lise moved so Claire isn't really sure if she's okay or if she just moved away from here. Scrambled into the country, like an animal hit by a car — off into the bushes to die. Or to live. Claire isn't sure.

Death.

Claire is walking death.

But we're all walking death, Claire thinks. In fact, any one of her friends could easily die before she does. Car accident. Heart attack. Tripping down the stairs. Anything could happen. An airplane could fall out of the sky onto a house. It's happened before. No one knows. No one thinks about that. Claire, though, with this huge C looming over her head, thinks about it all the time. She thinks about the grim reaper, about heaven and hell and god and nothingness and decay. She thinks about it until she can't breathe and then she turns her mind to something useful, like laundry or groceries or just sleeping. Claire sleeps a lot. Depression, she thinks. And radiation. The radiation exhausts her. Especially after the chemo and, before that, the operation. Her body has taken a beating and now it needs to rest.

Before Claire had cancer she worried all the time about getting it. In fact, the cancer diagnosis was almost a relief. "Well," she thought. "I can finally stop worrying about getting it." Not really a relief, but Claire tries to think of the positive as much as she can. There has to be two sides to everything. Even cancer?

It's the loneliness that bothers her the most. Even when she is surrounded by people — in the mall, at the hospital, with nervous friends, with her husband, Ralph, or her kids — even then, she is lonely. All on her own. You come into this world alone, and you leave the same way. This thought terrifies her. What, then, is the point of anything?

The cancer defines her now. Claire used to think of herself as a wife, a mother, a school teacher. But now she's walking, talking cancer. People at the hospital tell her that she's new to this game, they tell her that she'll get used to it, that the anger, the sadness, the fear, will go away. But Claire can't imagine getting used to this all-encompassing disease. She can't imagine going about her day lightly again — ever again. She can't imagine the small snake at the back of her mind, the one hissing, "Cancer," shrivelling up and disappearing.

So when Mrs. Rathbin shows up at her door the third Tuesday of her two-month-long daily radiation treatments, the beginning of October, a cold snap, Claire is resigned, preoccupied, consumed, worried, angry, depressed. The nearest hospital with a radiation department is an hour away and the cancer society sends volunteers to drive patients there and back. The first few weeks Ralph would drive her. He would take time off work. But after the first couple of times he was so anxious and upset about the situation — about the people smoking outside the hospital, about the wait times, about the loudness of the TV in the waiting room — that Claire asked him not to drive her anymore. She told him he would be much better off at work. He seemed discombobulated at the hospital, forgetful and agitated. And his worry seeped into Claire until she felt it pressing down on her chest, burning her — even more than the radiation. Then came Mr. Manuel, an older gentleman who spoke so quietly and so infrequently that Claire mostly slept on the long rides to the hospital and back. Mr. Manuel has a cold, though, and doesn't want to infect Claire. And so Mrs. Rathbin comes into her life today, barrels into her front hallway, bursting in, her large behind sashaying through the door. She is short and wide — in fact, she may be wider than she is tall. She is dark-skinned and white-haired. Her lips are painted a striking, shiny purple and she is wrapped in an oversize orange knitted shawl that sparkles when it catches the light. There is a smell that follows her in — foot odour and lilacs. She is wearing boots and they are untied and the laces drag behind her.

"Well, lookee here," Mrs. Rathbin bellows into Claire's front hallway.

Claire tenses. She doesn't know why they call themselves Mr. and Mrs., these volunteers. Mrs. Rathbin can't possibly be more than ten years older than Claire, even with all that white hair. But Claire guesses that it gives the drivers some sort of professionalism, or else creates needed distance. Perhaps they don't want to be too familiar to patients who could very well be gone tomorrow. Another way for them to disconnect from the situation. But Claire isn't being fair. After all, these people volunteer their time to do a lot of driving. And Claire needs a driver because she's so tired and tense and scared most of the time that she knows she'd drive off the side of the highway into a ditch.

"You've got kiddees." Mrs. Rathbin points to the portraits of Jude and Caroline on the walls.

"Yes."

"Well, that's really special," Mrs. Rathbin says. "Little ones around the house."

"Oh, they aren't little anymore," Claire says. "Jude is fifteen and Caroline, she's seventeen. Those are old pictures."

Mrs. Rathbin pulls herself up and stands on tiptoe to look closely at the pictures. "Is that fellow here a girl or a boy? Jude, you say? What is that? Judy? Judah?" Mrs. Rathbin snorts.

Jude does look slightly feminine in that picture. Claire never noticed it before. "A boy," she says. "Jude. Just Jude. Like Jude Law, I guess."

"Who?"

"An actor." Claire searches through her purse for her keys. "Although we didn't know about Jude Law until after."

"After what?"

Claire looks at Mrs. Rathbin. "After we had Jude."

Mrs. Rathbin nods. "Now that's an interesting name. Jude. I wouldn't have thought of naming a child that." She scurries around behind Claire and helps her with her coat. The woman has to stand on her tiptoes to reach Claire's shoulders and Claire is average height. When she reaches up to help with the sleeves Claire smells more lilac and something else, cinnamon? Claire's sense of smell is heightened these days. Like an animal sensing danger, she supposes. Her hearing is better too. She's fully self-aware, always. It's disconcerting. "Off we go," Mrs. Rathbin shouts, "on a one-horse open sleigh." Mrs. Rathbin's open-laced boots have left puddles from the brief morning rain on the floor. Claire sighs. Wonders if Ralph will notice or if he'll step into the puddles in his socked feet. She pictures him doing this, wandering the house in those wet socks, not bothering to change, leaving footprints behind.

Claire finds nothing funny these days and she knows she's in for a long ride with this woman. In the old days she might have thought Mrs. Rathbin was humorous — a strange, large, bustling, weird woman. Someone to study. But right now this fat, busy, opinionated, loud woman is too much. Claire couldn't have imagined she would ever miss the silent Mr. Manuel. But then there are a lot of things she can't imagine these days. Like the future. Like what it's going to feel like at the end. The last seconds. Where will she be? What will she be thinking? Will there be pain? Will she remember things about her life? Will things flash before her, will there be a white light? Will she fight it? Accept it? Scream? Cry? Go silently? Claire has so many questions that she knows will remain unanswered. For a while yet. And by the time they are answered it won't matter anymore.

Claire wipes her eyes.

Sometimes, at night, she sits straight up in bed because she can't breathe. She can't breathe as she imagines the end — her end.

Sometimes she hyperventilates, rushes to the bathroom before she wakes Ralph. This can't be it, she thinks. This can't be all there is.

The worst thing about all of this is that Claire didn't even feel sick. Not even for one minute. She was at her yearly physical exam. The doctor sent her for routine tests. She felt great. And then he sat her down, in his office — a room she had never been in before — and he said, "You have cancer." The second he said that — "You have cancer" — Claire began to feel awful. As if her whole body decided to shut down at once. She felt overwhelmed and sore. Her breast — the evil one — ached. She felt exhausted. And then the operation, the chemotherapy, the radiation, everything conspires together to make you feel so sick you take this disease seriously. But at the very beginning, before she knew, she felt the best she ever had. Yoga classes in full swing, coffees with friends, working just the right amount, her kids fun and independent. Life was good. Sometimes Claire wonders what would have happened if the doctor hadn't told her. Would she have gotten sick? Maybe she would have gone on indefinitely? Maybe it's the knowing that makes you sick?

Claire rubs her head. Now that she's done the chemotherapy she's starting to grow peach fuzz, but it's sharp and itchy. If she wears a hat she can't stop scratching. But if she doesn't wear a hat she feels naked and exposed and cold.

Mrs. Rathbin is struggling with her boots, tripping over the untied laces, fiddling in her large bag for her car keys.

Claire studies Jude's picture. He's eight in the photo. He doesn't look like a girl now. Not in the least. His voice is so low she can barely hear it — a growl — and there is a small dusting of soft hair on his upper lip. Claire has to be careful changing his bedsheets or taking out his garbage. Balled up Kleenexes everywhere. Wet stains. The juices of a fifteen-year-old boy. He looks at her with sorrow in his eyes. Horrible sorrow. She can feel it leaking from him. He doesn't know what to say or how to react. His mother's breast is sick. Her lymph nodes are gone. Just sliced out. And her hair fell out. She has no eyebrows or eyelashes. Eczema on her skin.

Ralph says that she needs to talk to Jude. Ralph says that Claire should sit down with him and make him cry. "Make it come out, Claire," he says. "Make the boy release everything that is inside of him. If you don't he'll keep it bottled and one day he'll explode."

One day. When Claire is gone.

Ralph has cried. Caroline can't stop crying and shouting. Angry Caroline. So mad at the world. But Claire likes Jude's quietness, his uncertainty. She likes that he hasn't collapsed around her yet. Like a faithful pet, he studies her and takes her in. He waits with her. She feels honoured by him.

"You got your keys?" Mrs. Rathbin says, holding up her own keys. "Got your hat? It's getting cold out."

Claire and Mrs. Rathbin leave the house. Claire studies the woman's car. A dumpy looking thing, rusty and dented. It looks as if it was once dark blue. It is now covered in wet mud and is a greyish-brown.

"Not much of a car," Mrs. Rathbin says, giving it a little kick, "but it'll get us to where we want to go."

Claire wants to say, "Hawaii? Will it get us to Hawaii? Or the moon? Can we go to the moon?" but she remains silent as she tries to climb into the front seat. Mrs. Rathbin first has to remove several bags of items — what looks like knitting, wool — and a box of cat litter. It's as if Mrs. Rathbin didn't expect her to actually get in her car. Maybe she thought I'd be dead by the time she got here. The back seats are full of junk too, so it's not like Claire was expected to sit back there.

"Just a little rearranging and then off we go."

Claire settles in. Adjusts her coat. Takes off her itchy hat. Sighs. She looks out the window at her house, at the line of Christmas lights left up from last year, dull in the daylight, at the place the wreath will go on the front door in a couple of months. Looking at her house, she notices that she left the light on in the hallway. Caroline and Jude will be home from school soon and then all the lights in the house will be blazing. Claire sighs.

Sometimes Claire wonders about dying in a car accident. She thinks about how ironic it would be — dying on the way to get radiation treatment to stop her from dying. Lying motionless in the road, thrown headfirst through the windshield, bleeding to death, her cancer seeping out of her body, finally impotent. Take that. Claire thinks of her cancer as a fuzzy, germy creature crawling quickly through her body. As if it's a centipede — those huge ones that come out in spring in the basement and scurry away so fast that there is no way you can step on them. Or whenever Claire sees those commercials on TV for Scrubbing Bubbles — some kind of shower stall cleaner — those little cartoon bubbles with eyes and tentacle feet, scrubbing the shower — she thinks they look exactly like the cancer she imagines. Scrubbing away at the walls of her internal organs. But instead of getting things clean, these cancer bubbles are spreading the grime and dirt everywhere. And there is nothing Claire can do about it.

Quick death on the road on the way to radiation seems like a solution.

"But you could have a long time left, Claire," Ralph says all the time. "You don't know for sure. There are always new discoveries. There can always be hope."

The uncertainty will kill her before the cancer does. Stay positive, they all say. But how do you stay positive in the face of it all? It's laughable, really. If Claire could laugh.

"So," says Mrs. Rathbin, clearing her throat. The car shakes and rattles as they head off down the highway. "Do you knit?"

"No." Claire closes her eyes.

"I knit."

"I can see that." There are knitted doilies hanging from the rear-view mirror. There are bags of yarn in the back seat now. There are, in fact, knitting needles resting in the little compartment in the door and poking Claire in the thigh. She stifles the urge to take them out and stab Mrs. Rathbin in the eyes. The image comforts her.

When she was diagnosed, Claire thought about all the things she wanted to do in her life. She developed one of those bucket lists. And the first thing that occurred to her, the first thing on her list, was murder. She wanted to get violent, attack someone, kill. She wanted to torture Paul Bernardo. Or Charles Manson. She wanted to slice the neck of a serial murderer or a pedophile. Claire imagined choking someone evil or slashing her nails across the eyes of Hitler. All these people who are and were allowed to live, instead of all these people who are forced to die. Claire would lie awake at night, staring at the ceiling and conjuring up the most gruesome deaths. It wasn't a good thing, but it made her feel some sense of control or, at least, some sense of the beauty of revenge. An eye for an eye kind of thing.

When Claire told Ralph, jokingly, about her thoughts, he said it wasn't like her to talk like this. He said she was depressed. And then he took her to the doctor, who put her on antidepressants. Now she doesn't think about killing people. Not that much. Sometimes Jude will turn on a video game for her — where she can shoot people — and this makes her feel better. If only for a minute or two. The anti-depressants make her feel like a shell. She's full of emotion for only a second. Her shell has holes. The emotion leaks out quickly. One minute she is close to tears, the next minute something distracts her and she feels nothing. Not happy. Not sad. Nothing.

"Not a mean bone in your body, Claire," Ralph says. "You couldn't even kill a fly."

Little does Ralph know that Claire has killed many flies. And ladybugs. Centipedes. She has killed spiders and worms and roaches and ants and she once actually hit a black cat with white feet in her car and didn't stop to see if it was okay. She drove on. She's really not as nice as he thinks she is.

See? These are the things she will leave behind. A vision of herself that isn't correct. And this worries Claire, makes her nervous.

The antidepressants also make her unfocused. She can't concentrate for very long on one particular thing. They make her feel like she's on antidepressants instead of making her feel like she's normal. Claire moves in and out of thoughts. She watches things flash in her mind and then they disappear. Nothing stays for long. This worries her — when she remembers to worry. Because if nothing is staying put in her mind then she's missing out on a lot of things that she needs in order to live the rest of her life. She wants to be heightened and aware and alive to the world around her. But she also doesn't want to be depressed.

"I knit hats for cancer patients," Mrs. Rathbin says. "Would you like one?" She reaches back, swerving slightly on the icy road, and grabs a hat from a box in the back seat. Like Mrs. Rathbin's shawl, the hat is orange and fuzzy, tiny bits of sparkles in the yarn. Claire is holding onto the dashboard.

"Oh, thank you," Claire says. "That's very kind of you." She puts the hat on her lap and pets it like she would a small cat. It's one of the ugliest hats she's ever seen. It's lopsided and looks like it would fit a giant.

"I used to knit hats for newborn babies, preemies," Mrs. Rathbin says, "but then I got to thinking about chemotherapy and figured that people like you, well, they aren't used to being bald. A baby is used to it. A baby is born bald. But you, well, you haven't been bald since you were born and so your head must be mighty cold."

Get me out of this car, Claire thinks.

What surprises Claire the most is that she thought that the way she observed the world would change. She always thought, when she contemplated eventually getting cancer, that she would say to herself, "Well, at least it will make you grateful and appreciative and patient and kind," and all that crap. She thought that, being sick, she would see the world through rose-coloured glasses. Perhaps be more willing to donate to charities or help people across the street, or be more caring. Love her neighbours, her annoying friends. Instead, Claire feels more impatient, more ornery and angry. Because her time is running out, she has no desire to waste a precious minute with anyone she can't stand. It's hard to be polite when you have cancer. The other day her old friend from one block over, Trish, phoned and started rambling about her life, about her kids and her handcrafted teddy bears, about Rachel's habit of eating in the living room, and the new neighbour who has moved in. And something about a man with a scar on his face. Silly, unimportant things. A neighbourhood party they had in the late summer, a woman whose husband left her for another woman, what she had cooked for dinner that night. She was blathering away quickly, without pause, and Claire couldn't stand it. Not for one second more. Claire knew that Trish was uncomfortable, unsure of what to say, merely trying to make conversation, only trying to distract her, but Claire had had enough. So she hung up on Trish and hasn't spoken to her since.

The strange thing was Trish never phoned back. So, Claire reasoned at the time, in the long run she thought she did them both a favour. She gave Trish the release she needed; she hung up so Trish didn't have to finish what she was saying. It was over.

One less person at my funeral.

Now she thinks she should phone Trish back. She also knows, deep in her heart, that Trish will be the first one into her funeral.

35

That's the kind of woman she is. Annoying and clueless, but kind and patient with other people's faults.

"You can take a hat for your girl. Or even for that boy of yours," Mrs. Rathbin says. "I bet they'd both like a nice warm hat. This winter might be a doozy." She starts to reach into the back seat again.

"I'll get them," Claire says. "Watch the road."

The car slides into the on-coming traffic lane and Claire holds her breath. But Mrs. Rathbin adjusts herself and the wheel and gets the car back safely. Given a quick choice everyone wants only to live.

"It's an innate kind of thing," Mrs. Rathbin says.

"What?" Claire has her body twisted into the back seat. She is rummaging through the box of knitted hats. Every colour under the rainbow. Blue, black, green, yellow, orange, pink, red, purple, white. What would Jude like? She smiles, imagining Jude's expression when he sees one of these hats.

"Knitting. It's like I was born doing it. I don't even have to think about it. Do you know?"

"Do I know what?"

"What it's like?"

"What what's like?" Claire is confused. She's not really listening to the woman. Or, at least, not taking it in. Mrs. Rathbin's thoughts have slipped out the holes in her shell.

"Oh dear," Mrs. Rathbin says, looking over at Claire. "I've overwhelmed you, haven't I? I do that."

"Do what?"

Mrs. Rathbin laughs. "What were you born doing, Claire?"

Claire pauses. Wonders what they are talking about. Born doing. Claire remembers nothing about herself before she was married and had kids. She can't remember how she felt, thought, moved, talked. She can't remember being anyone but who she is now. And what is that? A mother. Mostly a mother. Sometimes a wife. But a mother. With cancer. Was she born being a mother? Not possible. A teacher? No, she could take it or leave it and, in fact, had to leave it — early retirement — when she was diagnosed. Too much to handle teaching and cancer at the same time. Jude, Caroline. Claire defines herself by her kids. What will they do without her? What will she do without them? How will she be able to let them grow up without her?

"I am fifty-nine years old," Mrs. Rathbin says loudly. "I may look older, but that's how old I am." Mrs. Rathbin pauses to breathe. Claire is astonished. Mrs. Rathbin does look a lot older. "I can't eat Brussels sprouts. They are good for you but they make me vomit. They are ugly and they take a long time to decompose in the compost. And they attract aphids like crazy, so are hard to grow without pesticides. I hate to drive. I have been in several accidents. Once I had my license taken away. But I got it back. Everyone I've ever met says I talk too much. Lots of people say I overwhelm them. But I can knit a hat and that," she pauses and looks at Claire, "that makes all the difference."

Silence in the car. Claire swallows.

"Your turn!" Mrs. Rathbin shouts.

They've parked the car and entered the hospital. Mr. Manuel used to let Claire out at the front entrance and go ahead and park the car, but Mrs. Rathbin insists on parking and then coming inside with Claire. This means Claire has to walk through the parking garage and into the hospital entrance and down the stairs to the radiation department with a huffing, puffing Mrs. Rathbin.

"A little exercise will do you good," she says, as she sweats and breathes heavily, rolling her bulk towards the hospital.

Me? Claire thinks.

Mr. Manuel would wait in the hospital cafeteria. He would do the crossword puzzle in the newspaper and drink hot water. Mrs. Rathbin comes right down to the radiation department with Claire, ignoring Claire's suggestion that she wait somewhere else.

A woman in the waiting room with Claire last week told her that she was burned by the radiation and that her breast swelled up to the size of a cantaloupe. She broke out in rashes. The woman was scared to get the radiation again. But there she was. "What else can I do?" she had said, shrugging her thin shoulders.

Mrs. Rathbin settles into a chair in the waiting room. Directly across from Claire. She pulls her knitting needles out of a bag she has hidden under her bulky shawl. There are many baskets of yarn placed all around the room for people to knit scarves while they wait, but Mrs. Rathbin has her own ball of yarn, her own needles. Mrs. Rathbin begins to organize her hobby all over her lap and on the seat beside her. She hums. Her plastic bag crinkles. Her knitting needles clack. Claire watches the TV in the corner, on mute, the news racing past, scrolling words under images. Snowstorms and fires and highway accidents, traffic and politicians and stock markets and shootings. A boy has fallen through the ice while skating. They've left his body there, under the ice, until it is safe to retrieve. Claire tears up, wipes at her eyes. Mrs. Rathbin clicks away.

Sorrow. There is something about that word — the sound of it, the look of it on a page, the feel of it in her heart. Jude's sorrow. Caroline's sorrow. Ralph's sorrow. Claire owns that word now. It belongs to her.

"Stop that," Mrs. Rathbin says. She points her knitting needle at Claire.

"Pardon me?" Claire looks around.

"Stop crying. It won't do you any good."

Claire opens her mouth to say something but nothing comes out.

"Honestly. I know." Click click go her knitting needles. Another hat. The nurse at the front desk looks up from her computer and smiles shyly at Claire. Claire looks again at the TV. Then she looks back at Mrs. Rathbin and sets her jaw.

"How dare you tell me how to feel?" Claire says. Her voice shakes.

"That's right," Mrs. Rathbin says. "Yes. Much better. Get angry."

"Angry?" Claire shouts. "I've been nothing but angry since April."

"A world of good," Mrs. Rathbin says to her knitting. "It'll do you wonders."

"You're crazy," Claire whispers.

The two women sit in semi-silence. Claire glaring. Mrs. Rathbin knitting and humming.

On the ride home Claire is uncomfortable. She is bone-tired. Mrs. Rathbin is singing along to music on the radio.

When Claire was the sickest with the chemotherapy she could almost understand not being afraid of death. She was so ill she wanted to die. "Put me out of my misery," she said to Ralph as he held her hair back while she vomited. But even then, when Jude or Caroline came home from their world, when they sat near her on the sofa, wrapped themselves in her afghan, pressed their large, warm bodies against her cold one, even then, no matter how bad she felt, Claire really didn't want to die.

"You've got only two choices," Mrs. Rathbin says. She flicks off the car radio. "You eat those Brussels sprouts or you throw them in the garbage. That's all there is to it."

Don't they screen these volunteers? Shouldn't they have to take a competency test or something? A psychological examination?

"Or," Claire sighs, "you could not make them in the first place. In fact, you don't even have to buy them. You could pass right by the Brussels sprouts container in the grocery store. Buy asparagus or broccoli." Claire looks straight at Mrs. Rathbin. "So there."

"So there." Mrs. Rathbin smiles. "Right you are."

Claire is home. Jude is beside her on the sofa. They are watching *Ellen* on TV and trying to laugh at everything she says, even if it isn't funny. Forced laughs. Jolly laughs. Claire tells Jude about Mrs. Rathbin. She hands him the knitted hat. She has picked an orange one for him. He takes it. He puts it on. It's bulbous and horrible. They laugh some more.

In bed that night Claire relives her final few minutes with Mrs. Rathbin. The woman had pulled up in front of Claire's house, her hubcaps scraping on the curb. She had turned her large bulk slightly and looked Claire directly in the eyes. For all her craziness there was a kindly twinkle in those eyes. Claire had felt a tiny bit ashamed.

"Mr. Manuel will be back tomorrow," Mrs. Rathbin had said.

"Good. Thank you." Claire had moved to get out of the car, but Mrs. Rathbin laid a hand on Claire's leg.

"Let me tell you something, Claire," she had said.

And here it was. Claire had been sure Mrs. Rathbin would say something that would sum it all up — cancer, love, family, death. She would answer the question she had posed earlier as to what Claire was born doing. Mrs. Rathbin, with her orange knitted shawl, her purple lips, would be one of those gurus, Buddha-like, who would put it all together. Like the moral at the end of a story. Mrs. Rathbin would be Claire's Happily-Ever-After. This, she would say, is what you will learn from this horrific experience in your life. Claire couldn't help herself. She was actually waiting for the lesson, her mouth slightly open, her eyes wide.

"Brussels sprouts aren't that easy to ignore," Mrs. Rathbin had said. And then she squeezed herself out of the car, she went around to Claire's side and she helped Claire out. Mrs. Rathbin had walked Claire up to her front door, she had made sure Claire got in safely, and, finally, she had left. Claire had stood in the front doorway watching her drive off, haphazardly, down the street. Mrs. Rathbin had beeped once.

"Brussels sprouts," Claire says now, in bed, Ralph beside her listening. "Brussels sprouts. I don't get it."

But that's okay, Claire thinks, because when Claire told Jude what Mrs. Rathbin had said, Jude didn't get it either. And neither did Ralph.

To: dayton22@hotmail.com
From: puckbunnybrady@pik.com
Subject: Parkville Ice Kats

Dear Dayton,

Congratulations on taking the first, most important step —
signing up with the Parkville Ice Kats! A wonderful decision
you won't regret. I guarantee it. By submitting your form on
our website you have now officially registered for the Senior
Ladies Leisure League. Games will be on Wednesday nights,
from October 25th until March 7th. Because we know you ladies
are busy and running around doing everything around the
house — kids, housekeeping, jobs, dinner — we have tried to
book ice time for anytime between 7 p.m. until 10 p.m. You
will only have to play two or three late games throughout
the season. A holiday schedule (Christmas is coming) will be
sent to you at this email address. We end earlier in March
this year because of all the absences in the last games due
to those amazing vacations you all take with your hubbies
and kids during the school break. Wish I were so lucky.
Your deposit has been recorded. Please send the remaining
outstanding balance to the address below. We do not accept
credit cards or PayPal. Hard enough to figure out the website
— you know what I'm talking about, don't you? Please note:
there will be an end-of-season party sometime in March for
all the Ice Kats teams. Be there or be square.

Remember: hockey is a game that requires competition but also
fair play. There will be no checking allowed. Attached is
your personal injury waiver. Please sign and return with your
payment.

Enjoy the season! Go Ice Kats Go!

 Tina Brady
Parkville Ice Kats
Co-ordinator Extraordinaire

P.S. Dayton, you are on the White Team — such a great group
of girls. We have also placed your neighbour, Patricia Birk,
on this team as per your request.

3

It's the first game of the season.

There are six of them on the ice, if you include the goalie.

Two forward, one centre, two defence.

And three of them are new to hockey. They don't really know what to do.

The puck is dropped and Dayton looks at it. She takes a poke at it with her stick but misses touching anything, even ice. In fact, the stick pulls her forward and she almost falls. The ice is slippery, freshly Zambonied, if that's a word. Dayton feels sick to her stomach and she's hot from the equipment and her heart is beating so loudly she believes she can hear it until she realizes that the noise is the other team banging their sticks on the boards. The last time she felt this way was in the airport with her daughter, Carrie. Holding onto her little body tight and going through customs trying not to look or sound scared. Trying not to be suspicious.

She rushes forward. All Dayton can do is skate. The blades swish on the ice. Trish skates past her, shouting, "Woo hoo," without humility. Trish's stick is so high in the air that Dayton is sure she's going to take someone out. Are you allowed to hold the stick that high? Dayton wonders.

"Stick on the ice, stick on the ice," someone shouts from their bench. Everyone looks the same in their equipment and so Dayton can't tell who said that. Even if she could tell, it wouldn't matter — she doesn't know anyone else on the team yet but at least she was right about how high you can hold the stick.

The other team shoots. The puck ricochets off the goalie's stick. Dayton stands still, watching, until she realizes that she can get involved. She forgets, sometimes, to move. Caught up in the speed of the game, in the back and forth of it. Someone shouts, "Skate, skate." It's not often Dayton wants to move forward and take control. She tends to hang back and watch. That's the kind of person she is. Only once in her life has she pushed forward and taken control. But here, on the rink, she does it again. Moves forward. Skates. Dayton attempts to hit the puck away from the net but misses. Trish lends moral support with another "woo hoo."

Dayton just moved to town from California. Six weeks ago, late summer, she climbed on the airplane, carrying her daughter and a diaper bag and as many of her things as she could get out of the house and into three suitcases. Clothes, passports, birth certificates, toys, a photo album, her mother's cookbook. The beginning cold, the trees turning colour, the rush of leaves under her feet, the fall, strikes her every time she goes outside. Knocks her down almost. It is the end of October, Halloween next week, and Dayton can see her breath in the air. She left palm trees and cactus and sweet warm breezes. She left green and blue and came into orange and brown, and now she is into the beginning barrenness of winter, trees beginning to tangle together, limbs empty. Now she is playing hockey because Trish asked her to and because she couldn't think of a reason not to. Trish's twelve-year-old daughter, Rachel, would babysit Carrie, Trish said. Trish herself would

44

drive and lend Dayton equipment. Trish's husband's old stuff is too big and threatens to fall off. Dayton has to wrap tape around her hockey pants and there is a smell coming off the equipment that wasn't there when she first tried them on. She assumes she is heating them up with her sweat. It all made sense. Trish said the neighbours across the street, Tom and Maria, would be home in case anything went wrong. Oh, and Frank, he'd be home too, but Trish said he sometimes falls asleep in front of the TV and can't be woken up. Some kind of narcolepsy, she thinks, or just old age. But Tom and Maria are always available. Trish said they rarely go out. "In fact," she said, "their bedroom light is often off at ten."

"I go to bed at ten," Dayton said, looking at the clock over the stove. 9:45.

"Senior Ladies Leisure League," Trish laughed. She was holding open a pamphlet and had her laptop there to sign Dayton up. They were in Dayton's kitchen and Trish was waving her glass of wine around dangerously over the laptop and Dayton was trying hard not to be nervous. The solid tile floor of her new kitchen busts glass like a bomb and Dayton didn't have the energy to get the vacuum cleaner out. Besides, the laptop might burst into flame if Trish's wine spilled. Carrie was asleep upstairs. Max, the new kitten, was sitting in Trish's lap. Max is Dayton's poke at normalcy — "get a kitten," she thought, "life will be good." But Dayton forgot about the cat litter, the incessant meowing when she finally got Carrie to bed, the desperate need for attention. Two empty bottles of wine on the table between her and Trish. Pinot grigio for Trish — "That's all I'll drink," she had said. "That and anything red." Trish snorted — she laughs loud, talks loud. Dayton was drinking red, only because she had only one bottle of pinot grigio in the house. Except for Trish and her booming, echoing voice, everything was quiet in Dayton's house.

"We aren't seniors," Dayton said. "I'm forty-three."

"I'm forty-eight," Trish said. "I'm way more senior than you. But still, I find it extremely insulting."

"What's even more insulting is calling us ladies." The women laughed. They typed their information into the laptop, registering for the league.

"Any ailments?"

"What does that mean?"

"Heart issues? High blood pressure? Diabetes?"

Dayton thought about it. "Nope, nothing."

"What if I write 'overweight,'" Trish said. "Do you think that's an ailment?"

"You're not overweight."

"Pleasingly plump?"

Trish swore she had never played on a team before, but she had watched the game at least. Her son, Charlie, plays, as does her husband, Frank. And occasionally, Trish confessed after she pressed Submit on Dayton's form, occasionally she plays shinny on the backyard rink her husband builds every year. Because Charlie plays hockey, Dayton assumes Trish must, at least, know the rules, she must know something about the game. "Dayton," Trish laughed loudly. "You think I actually watch the game when I go? I catch up with the other moms. No one ever watches their kid play hockey. I couldn't even tell you what position he played."

"There are positions?"

"Sure, I signed you up for defence."

Dayton nodded.

In California hockey was occasionally on TV in the bars when Dayton went for a drink after work. In the old days, before she had Carrie and stayed home alone most nights, she remembered watching hockey on TV in the bars. She had maybe glanced at it on the news while washing up the dishes after dinner. John had said he played once upon a time — Dayton can never be sure of what is the truth when it comes to John — but Dayton never paid attention to hockey. Not really. Men moving fast. Skating hard. A puck you can't even see on TV, sticks everywhere. It was cold on the TV and Dayton was warm in sunny L.A. Beach volleyball, now that's something she watched as she strolled the boardwalks with Carrie in a Snugli.

"Do you have to wear a costume?" Dayton asked.

Trish snorted her wine. "Costume? We're not playing dress-up, Dayton, we're playing hockey. Costume. Oh, that's too funny. It's called equipment. I think. That's what I think." Trish was getting drunk. Dayton smiled shyly.

But now, here they are, on the ice, and Dayton is pretty sure it is all about the dressing up. It took her a serious, confusing, complicated forty-five minutes to figure out how to dress herself in this equipment, this armour. That's only, Trish told her, because Dayton put everything on in the wrong order. Dayton will remember, next time, to plan it all out, to concentrate — her jill, then her shin pads, socks, shorts — and THEN put the skates on. She was lucky she didn't rip Trish's husband's expensive padded shorts trying to squeeze the sharp blades of the skates into them. Someone should have made her practise getting dressed beforehand. The other new woman on the team tells Dayton she practised in her living room. Someone should have given her a lesson ahead of time. Life is like that — no one helps anyone out ahead of time but everyone seems ready to give advice after. To chide you. Laugh at your mistakes.

A jill — now that was something new. Every little piece of Dayton's body is protected, even her groin. Trish said, "I've had my babies," to the young guy in the sports store, "I don't need to protect anything down there." He laughed, shrugged, blushed a bit. Old ladies, he must have thought, buying hockey equipment, protecting their old lady parts. Dayton could almost see him swallow down the bile. What's next? The end of the world? Senior Ladies Leisure League.

After the skates you put on the shoulder pads, neck guard, elbow pads, jersey and helmet. Trish and Dayton drew a line at the mouth guard. "How am I supposed to talk or cheer with that thing in my mouth?" And now Dayton's out on the ice, watching the puck slide quickly past her goalie and into the net, listening to the board-banging other team, and wondering about it all. About playing the game of hockey. About women — some mildly old, some young, some in between — gathering together at 9:00 on a work night, their kids in bed, to slide around with blades on ice and whack at this little, hard puck using sticks. And why is the puck so hard? What's it made out of? Even through her padding Dayton felt the smack of the puck when it hit the back of her leg.

"Off the boards, off the boards," someone shouts. Dayton has no idea what that means. She skates away from the boards, thinking maybe she is too close to them.

Ever since she left John, Dayton has tried to do things differently. Her first thing was to move away. That was different. Not like her. And she didn't just move down the block either, but to a new country, to a city she'd never heard of, a small town, really. The second thing she tried to do differently was to make friends. She didn't have any friends in L.A. who weren't John's friends first. So when she needed help there was never anyone there for her. Dayton had no one. And now she's playing ice hockey. ("You don't call it ice hockey," Trish said. "It's just hockey. If you call it ice hockey, people will know you've never played." "But I've never played," Dayton said. "I know that, Dayton, and you know that, but you don't want anyone else to know that, do you?") That's her third different thing.

The tree outside the window of Dayton's new house reminds her, late at night, of the one that sucked that kid into it in the

48

movie *Poltergeist*. Dark and huge and thick, its limbs reaching out to her, scratching ominously against her window. Carrie's snuffles on the baby monitor echo through the house. John is somewhere back in California, probably out at the bars with another tanned, breast-implanted woman. After all, what other kind of women are there in California? How stupid Dayton feels to have believed him. To have married him. To have stayed with him when he did the things he did to her. "How stupid am I?" she asks the tree each night before she falls asleep. But Dayton knew she couldn't get away. Not without completely disappearing. John doesn't like to lose anything — his car keys, a dime, his sunglasses, his wife. Losing is for losers, he says.

"Dayton, puck," Trish is screaming at her, and Dayton sees a break in front of her and rushes in to take a swipe at the puck. Again, she misses. She can't seem to connect that small black dot with her long wooden stick. It seems easy, but for some reason it isn't. But she can skate. Dayton knows she can skate — all those figure skating lessons as a kid paid off — if only she could hit the puck. Someone skates past her so quickly that Dayton can feel the wind. She looks at her stick as if it's the stick's fault. But, in fact, the stick has kept her standing. She realizes she is using it as a crutch. Balancing herself with it. Leaning on it. Heavy.

It's such a typical story — the Husband and the Buxom Blond. It happens all the time. Trish waved her hands around her head when Dayton told her and said, "Oh my god, can't men do something new once in a while? Can't they surprise us?" Dayton smiled then because John was full of surprises. Surprises Dayton could predict but that still surprised her. Angry, shouting, predictable surprises. She liked Trish immediately. Trish who has been married to the same quiet guy for twenty-three years. Trish who has a house full of kids and dogs and cats and goldfish, a messy, lived-in, disorganized, happy house. Trish who makes teddy bears for a living. Sewing on button eyes and sparkly ribbons. "Buxom," Trish said. "Now that's a word I haven't heard since before I was born." She held up her wine glass to toast the word. She laughed loudly. The kitten, Max, moved slightly on her lap. "Buxom."

Dayton skates to the bench. Two minutes off. Two minutes on. The sweat is rolling down her nose, her temples, her neck. She feels as if she is wearing a sauna.

"I'm dripping," she says to Trish. "Especially my hands." Dayton holds up her gloves, looks at them. "Why are my hands so sweaty? And my elbows. And my neck."

"This is way too much fun," Trish says. "Don't you think this is fun?" Trish is panting beside her. They watch three other women skate out and take their positions. There is another woman standing with them behind the boards but they don't know her. Trish smiles and the woman smiles back and says, "Woo hoo," and Trish grins. The woman says, "All I keep saying out there is 'shit shit shit' every time I miss the puck. 'Woo hoo' is much better."

They all laugh.

Dayton tries to remember the last time she did something like this. She thinks it was grade seven, volleyball, that was the last time she played a team sport. After that it was all jazz dancing and ballet and gymnastics and swimming and figure skating and aerobics. Stuff girls do for themselves, not for a team. It feels good to be present with a bunch of women and not have to talk about anything much, not have to serve wine or worry about saying the right thing. Not have John hovering over her, watching everything she does, everything she says. And who cares about what you look like under all this equipment, under this costume? Who cares if you are buxom or flat-chested? Who cares if you are blond or brunette? Your bruises and scars don't show underneath all of this padding.

The worst thing that ever happened to Dayton was when John came home from work and told her. After all she had put up with. Weeks they'd been fighting. Years, it sometimes seemed. Before their rushed marriage, before they told anyone Dayton was pregnant, they fought about everything and anything. Any little thing. What kind of toothbrush to buy, where to shop for curtains, whether to even get curtains or get blinds. Everything. They both knew they shouldn't have married, of course they shouldn't have. But they did. Because they thought it was the right thing to do. Because John was transferred from Toronto to California and Dayton needed a reason to follow him. But then he came home one day and everything was still and quiet, Carrie was sleeping, and he came right out with it. For no reason other than the sudden quiet of their home. They weren't arguing. Or talking. They didn't even say hello first. He laughed. Dayton knew, of course she knew. John was John. Sometimes home, sometimes not home, always distant. Mostly angry. Shouting. Mostly selfish. Mostly self-absorbed. Dayton thought, later, that if he hadn't said anything, if he hadn't said, "I'm seeing someone else," she would have gone on with life the way it was and she probably wouldn't have changed anything. Carrie was brand new, California was new. Life was new and John could have done exactly what he wanted, like he always did, if he just hadn't told her. Most of the time Dayton is mad at him not for having the affair, but for telling her about it. For making it come out in the open, making her feel more ashamed than she already did. If he had only kept his big damn mouth shut.

And Dayton knows that when she thinks this way she sounds exactly like her mother. Ignore the obvious. Push your problems away. Get on with life no matter what. The sick thing is that Dayton grew up watching her mother make mistakes and promising herself she wouldn't make the same ones. Here she is, though, now in the same position as her mother.

Buxom. Implants? Really, John, really?

Maybe men can't surprise us, but we sure can surprise them.

He never, for a moment, saw it coming. That fact Dayton is sure of.

Stepping out of the bench and onto the ice, Dayton sails towards the puck, towards the net. She takes her stick back as far as she can without hitting anyone and she whacks at that little black thing and suddenly her team is roaring. She hit the puck. She actually hit the puck and it slid wildly, out of control, straight into the net.

Later on, in the change room, Trish says, "Hey, Dayton, it doesn't matter that it went into our net, it just matters that you hit the damn puck. You really hit it." And everyone laughs. Someone has brought beer and they all sit there on the change-room benches half in and half out of their equipment, and some of them drink a beer. Just one. Someone starts talking about the weather and Dayton quickly realizes that she has no idea of the winter that is to come even if she grew up in Toronto, that she can't predict the future any more than she can justify stealing Carrie away from John and leaving California.

He'll find her someday soon. Losing is for losers. John does not think he is a loser. Someday John will show up on her front doorstep. He'll look at that big honking tree in front of her house reaching out to grab him and eat him, and he'll take Carrie back with him and things will never be the same. He always does this kind of thing. He surprises her with his predictability and Dayton is sure that his next surprise will be huge, and destructive.

But, for now, it's Dayton 1, John 0. Dayton scored a goal. Who cares, she thinks, if it was in the wrong net?

Build-Your-Bear ™

Your way is the right way . . .
Come Build, Come Play, Come Love.
Your Bear.

Dear Ms. Patricia Birk,

We are writing to inform you that we are considering serving you with a Cease and Desist order regarding your line of specialty bears. Here at Build-Your-Bear™ we take pride in our uniqueness. Your "The Bear Company" has trod all over our brand. Are you even trademarked? The variety of clothes you offer — everything from tutus to three-piece, pin-striped business suits — the custom-made Career Bears, including Astronaut Bear and Plumber Bear, even the line of Sports Bears, were all original creations of Build-Your-Bear™. We are aware, of course, that you cannot possibly be operating on the scale of our company, but it has come to our attention that there are several similarities with your bears that are simply too close for us to ignore. How many other people have thought to make a Lady Gaga Bear, for example? Or a Dick Cheney Bear? We can understand your Obama Bear, but a bear based on Richard Nixon seems unlikely to be an original idea without the backing of the major advertisers that we have.

At the moment we will not serve you with papers. However, if you do not prove to us that your ideas are original AND cease making these bears, we will be forced to take legal action.

Build-Your-Bear™ goes back many years. We were founded in 1997. We are proud of creating original bears for young girls and boys that, when combined with certain clothes and accessories, make each bear someone highly recognizable. Besides, we had to pay for permission to create look-alikes of the famous celebrities. Why shouldn't you?

Sincerely,

Maisy Crank
CEO and Head Bear of Build-Your-Bear™
Madison, Wisconsin

4

Is it any wonder, Trish thinks, that I'm always yelling? This morning, for example, the candy bar wrapper on the front-hall bench, the rotting apple in the lunch bag, the gym clothes on the kitchen table. And Rachel's basketball rolling at her feet. Every morning she trips on the damn thing. Plus the dog. He's underfoot all the time. Trish finds herself leaning over him to fill up the kettle in the sink. It's easier to bend over him, as he lies there on the floor like he thinks he's the kitchen rug, than to tell him to "move it" every fifteen seconds. Trish gets tired of saying the same thing over and over. He slinks back. That's the problem: he leaves — at least he listens to her at first — but suddenly he is there again, always underfoot. She didn't want the dog but she's the one who has to deal with him. And he latched onto her as if she were his long lost mother. Everyone else gives him love, walks him, feeds him, Trish does nothing, but the damn dog is always following her around, sticking to her like glue.

They all look at Trish as if she's crazy. Her daughter, Rachel, rolls her eyes. Her husband, Frank, ducks out of the house quickly, desperate to go to work. Charlie, her youngest, ignores her. They rush around, creating chaos, and then they leave to school, to work. And they create chaos at work and school. Charlie with the hermit crabs last year. Rachel knocking the boy flat on the playground: "I learned how to punch from my father," she said. Trish was beside herself. Looking at everything from beside herself. A siamese twin. One Trish loud and confident and in control, the other squirming and terrified, huddled up like the crabs Charlie released that got into the electrical system. Who knew hermit crabs could move so fast? Who knew it was ice cream day? Who knew one hundred boxes of the stuff had been delivered to the school, put in the freezers, waiting for recess? Who knew soggy ice cream could go bad that quickly? And most of all, who could possibly have known the kids would eat it? Trish separates herself most days and is left to clean it all up, to try to get her life, her house, back together. Trish needs order to get any work done. And she can't have order when everyone is home. That's the thing about her, she has to touch everything, even it all out, move it around, in order to make it hers again. This, Trish knows, takes about an hour. An hour to feel that her family are truly gone and she is safe from their wildness, so silent she can hear the house creak, and alone. It's not the house that's hers, she tries to tell Frank, it's the freedom to hear that quiet creak in the stair, the feeling that once again she is something besides mother and wife and problem-solver. She is herself again.

Frank always sighs when she complains. She knows he doesn't understand, she knows he doesn't care. It's not that he doesn't love her and treat her well and respect her — although sometimes Trish wonders if it's more like he puts up with her — but she knows that deep inside he thinks, Women. Just that. Women. With a little internal *phew*, or even *pfft*, attached to it. That says it all for Frank, Trish is sure of it. "Women." Deep inside he's a bit sexist.

He got it from his dad, nothing he could do about it. Trish's father-in-law is all blistering machoness. Even at age eighty-two. "Get me my cane, girl," he shouts. "What's for dinner?"

So this morning, when the knock on the front door comes, Trish does the only thing she knows how to do, she ignores it and hides. There is no other option. Her hour of getting herself together is already up. She has done her straightening, she has re-wiped the kitchen counters, she has put the hair clips on the hall table, ready to be carried upstairs — by her, of course, who else? Trish has opened the curtains and wiped the dog's nose prints off the back glass door. The morning is hers again — the world is hers — and she's not letting anyone destroy this peace she has made. Trish refuses even to answer the phone during the day. Instead, she listens to the answering machine and picks up only if she feels the need.

The neighbours often call. Maria, across the street, panicking about whose turn it is to drive the girls to band Tuesday mornings, or Tom, Maria's husband, wanting Frank to help him carry something from his car into the house, something heavy that Maria can't help him with because of her back problems. Their daughter, Becky, comes over every morning to pick Rachel up for school or to drop off the eggs her mother borrowed or to give back the sweater Rachel lent her. In fact, this neighbourhood is a constant flow of back and forth, everyone walking across the street many times a day, dogs rambling around together in back or front yards, phones ringing, people calling out for their kids to come home, get ready for bed, get in the bath now. Now. Get. In. The. Bath. The cats fight in the dead of night and howl in the spring. The man in the house beside Tom and Maria hammers, working on his attic, until midnight. Even the new woman, Dayton, has recently begun knocking on Trish's door, ever since they have started playing hockey together. She taps lightly, as if afraid Trish's glass door will break, and she is quiet and nervous, as if she doesn't want to bother Trish. It's nice, this neighbourhood. Trish is the last person to complain about the friendliness between neighbours. But not in the morning. Not when she needs time to decompress.

Last night Charlie, who is only eight, pulled Trish's face down close to his mouth while she was kissing him goodnight and said, "Will I ever be as old as you and Dad?" Trish suppressed the urge to hit him, to laugh, to cry. Instead she said, "I hope so, honey," and he looked disappointed and miserable. For a brief second Trish hoped she had given him nightmares.

Except that he always climbs into their bed when he has nightmares.

She's forty-eight years old. How did that happen?

The knock again. Trish is hiding behind the sofa in the living room. If she wants to get up the stairs to her sewing room she has to pass the window in the front door and whoever is knocking will see her. Maybe she shouldn't have opened the curtains? Trish could always wave and continue on up the stairs. She could hold up a small sign, created just for this purpose, that says, "I'm working, go away." She could give the person the middle finger or just walk past as if she's blind and deaf. The last idea is the most tempting, and Trish would probably do that if she had a white cane for support. In high school Trish played the part of Helen Keller in the end-of-year play. She kept her eyes open and unfocused every night for three shows. Tapping with a white cane. She rarely stumbled. An impressive performance. One of the highlights of Trish's life.

Behind the sofa, down here, Trish begins to notice the lint on the rug, the crumbs from where Rachel was eating her cereal and her stale muffin, feeding chunks of it to the dog. The dog will eat large things — muffin chunks — but not crumbs. He won't touch a crumb. As if it's not worth his time. He won't vacuum the carpet for Trish and that is why she got him in the first place.

In fact, other than making her feel guilty for not taking him for a walk, her dog does very little but get in the way. And the cats. The goldfish. Don't get her started.

When Trish was small all she wanted was to be an actress. She wanted to take Broadway by storm. She wanted to be admired. What kid doesn't? The high school drama teacher actually told Trish that she had potential. Sure, some years she just sewed costumes, but sometimes she got a good role, like Helen Keller. Or she was a background actor and would walk across the stage in a crowd scene for *West Side Story* or caw as a crow in *The Wizard of Oz*. And Trish has used what she learned sewing costumes for her business, so joining the drama club wasn't a waste of time, no matter what her mother said. Now Trish owns a small (she's the only employee) business making bears. The Bear Company. Specialty bears. In her sewing room. Upstairs. Past the glass front door. Past the person still hovering on her porch. She's not an actress. And, according to her eight-year-old son, she's very old. Plus, she may be sued by Build-Your-Bear™.

"Knock knock."

Trish can't believe the person at the door actually says that. "Knock knock." As if the physical knock on the door isn't enough. She wonders if she should say, "Ding dong," when she goes over to Dayton's house and rings her doorbell, or shout, "Tinkle tinkle," when she enters the corner store and the bell goes off. Or "tinkle tinkle" when she pees, which is more appropriate, "growl growl," when she's hungry. "Moan" in bed with Frank. Trish grimaces. Tries to snicker. It's too early in the morning to make herself laugh. She just can't do it.

Here she is, on the floor, crouching, feeling sorry for herself. Surrounded by her family's mess and her pets, wanting only to get to work, knowing her time is limited, and her business may soon be limited, and the kids will be home by 3:15 p.m. She is stressing about it. While next door Dayton and Carrie have nothing but each other. And a cat. They left everyone they knew in California and came here to start afresh. Trish feels for her sometimes. Even though she has lovely blond hair and a slim figure. Sometimes Trish envies her. Dayton only has to pick up after one person, a baby. How hard is that? Plus she left everyone behind. Sometimes the idea of that appeals to Trish more than it should. Sometimes her daydreams consist of seeing herself gone, away from home, watching everything collapse without her there, watching her family say, "Wow, Mom did do a lot around here. We miss her." Sometimes she conjures this kind of dream when she's having sex with Frank. Lying there, helping him a bit, he's working hard above her, she sees herself turn at the front door, wave, and disappear. Gone.

"I can see you in there," the voice says.

Is it start fresh, or start afresh? Trish wonders. What is afresh? More than fresh? Fresh again, she supposes.

"Damn." She begins to stand. What more can she do? Trish puts her hands on her large hips. Isn't the fact that she's hiding enough? Can't he get the hint?

"Just a minute of your time?"

Trish sees his shape at the door but can't see his features. The light is dim, the shadows fall around him. Maybe he's delivering bear parts: button eyes; little bow ties; shiny, sparkling shoes and dresses? But no. Trish filled out her newest order online only yesterday. It takes at least a week for delivery. Maybe he's serving her with those cease and desist orders from Build-Your-Bear™?

"It's about your children," the man says, and Trish pulls herself straight into standing. Her legs have fallen asleep. No matter how much they drive her crazy, no matter how much she sometimes wishes they would just grow up and leave home, no matter how much she often wishes she could leave everyone behind, her children are her blood, her soul, her heart. Anyone mentions them and Trish melts a little into her shoes. Her legs give out. She limps to the door and flings it open.

"Yes? What?"

He is a little man. Bald at the top of his head, hair in a ring, as if he's one of those monks from the old days. He reminds Trish of someone. She feels she should know him, that she does know him, but she can't place it. His brown suit aids that monkish look. If he had a rope belt Trish wouldn't be surprised. She thinks about creating a Monk Bear. That might be fun. Build-Your-Bear™ couldn't claim she stole that idea from them. Could they?

And then she remembers that man Tom told her about, the one with a scar down the middle of his face, and she is glad that this man is small and brown-suited and monkish. Not large and split in half. She still shivers when she thinks about what Tom said, about how he didn't take money for his work, about how he watched the children play basketball.

"What about my children? What's wrong?"

"Why were you hiding?"

"Excuse me," Trish says, "what about my children?"

"Not *your* children in particular," the man says. He clears his throat as Trish stares straight at him. She's a big woman, not fine-boned in any way, and he's a small, bald man. He pushes his glasses up on his nose with his middle finger. One push right between the eyebrows. He squinches his eyes and purses his lips. Trish notes his lips are dry, cracked, scaly. White spittle stuck in the corners. She recoils slightly.

"You don't have to be rude."

"Me?" Trish shouts this a little. She can't help herself. "I'm obviously busy —"

"Busy hiding?"

"I am obviously not wanting to be disturbed —"

"Yes, but —"

"And you come pounding at my door —"

"I knocked politely. I even said, 'Knock knock.'"

"Talking about my children —"

"Not *your* children, just children in general. You see, they aren't safe —"

"Excuse me? Excuse me?" Trish is shrill. But this is what you get when you disturb someone after she has finally had her hour, put her mind back together, formed herself afresh. Frank often says not to mess with her before she's had her coffee, but this, this is even worse. Trish tries to shut the door but the little man has his shiny shoe stuck in the doorway and no matter how many times she jams it with the door, he doesn't move. In fact, he shouts, "Ouch, ouch," but doesn't pull his foot back. He's a sucker for punishment.

"Get your foot out of my door."

"But I have to tell you about the children." The little man looks down at his foot as if he's checking to see if it's still there. "I don't like Mondays," he says, as an aside.

"But it's Tuesday." Trish pushes a little more at the door, at his foot, but it's wedged inside tight. He's not moving it.

"Here, just take this." A pamphlet comes towards her. She takes it. A natural thing, she thinks later, when going over this scene in her mind. Her hand reaches out automatically. Trish figures she can take the pamphlet and shut the door and go upstairs to her sewing room and make her bears. But first she will need to give herself another hour — perhaps drink another coffee, fiddle with the curtains, maybe have some dark chocolate — in order to put her world back in order. The man looks sad, crestfallen. He looks like he's going to cry. Trish is a sucker for criers, but this man is not melting her heart.

"What?" Trish says. "I took your pamphlet." She shakes it at him. "I'm not into this religious stuff. What more do you want?"

And then he does cry. He starts to sob. His foot stuck in her door, his brown suit dull, his sad, bald little head. He sniffs loudly. "But think of the children."

"Oh, for god's sake." And, against her better judgment, Trish opens the door a little wider.

The man stops crying immediately and steps in, one shiny foot in front of the other.

Sitting in the living room Trish and the little man stare each other down. Trish still has the pamphlet in her hand but she hasn't looked at it. The whole situation is absurd. Trish has four bears to do this week and that includes delivery. One of the bear owners lives an hour's drive away. Where will she find the time? She's being harassed by Build-Your-Bear™ and she needs to get things done in case they come at her. She needs to get her bills settled, deliver her goods. Even before they started threatening her, there was always the worry that Build-Your-Bear™ would take her business away from her. With their fancy bear-stuffing machines and their mall location and their fake bear doctors, who are really just teenage kids wearing medical garb, pretending to fix your bear's boo-boos. How can Trish compete against this bear extravaganza? And it might seem silly to someone on the outside looking in but, to Trish, it's her work. It's her sanity. It's the only thing she has for herself.

Trish looks at where she was hiding behind the sofa and now that she's been up close to it, she knows exactly where the cereal/muffin crumbs are and it is as if she can see them from across the room. Why does Rachel eat the muffin with her fingers, tearing it apart over her lap? "What? Do you want me to use a fork?" she says, when Trish asks her. Saucily. She's become saucy and sarcastic. Trish is a little proud of that, but also annoyed. After all, Rachel's only twelve. It will get worse. Actually, why does Trish's daughter eat in the living room anyway? What's wrong with the kitchen table? Trish makes a mental note to have it out with Rachel tonight. Tell her to clean her room too. And take the dog for a walk for once. Do something besides make a mess.

As if summoned by her thoughts, the dog enters the room, bored. He sniffs at the little man. Then he lies down and goes to sleep. Some guard dog. Some watchdog, Trish sighs. The only things he barks at are the squirrels. Or Tom and Maria's dog. They bark at each other as if they're debating or chatting or passing on messages. Charlie loves it. Shouts, "Calling every pup and hound, the Dalmatian puppies have been found!" But nothing else gets the dog excited in the least. Trish guesses she should be grateful. There are some dogs that bark all the time. She can hear them at night, across the neighbourhood. Maybe Charlie is on to something, maybe they are communicating with each other. Their owners never seem to notice, either. No one tells their dog to shut up. No one brings their dog inside on hot summer nights when the rest of the people on the street are trying to sleep with their windows open for the breeze. Just because they have air conditioning and can't hear their dog doesn't mean the rest of the neighbours can't. Trish's mind is a whirling mess. Maybe she's lucky she isn't working on her bears right now. Maybe she wouldn't be able to concentrate. Ever since the letter from the Build-Your-Bear™ Head Bear, well, she's been distracted.

Trish supposes that her neighbours let their dogs bark because no effort to be polite is made when you get comfortable with people. That's why new relationships are so compelling. Take, for example, Dayton. She's new. That's why Trish invited her to sign up for hockey. And Trish doesn't regret it in the least. It's a blast. Dayton has really improved in the last couple of weeks. So has Trish. But Trish knows that Dayton will take her for granted soon.

She'll get comfy with Trish and soon Trish will be over taking care of Carrie while Dayton goes on dates.

The man is looking around her living room as if he is the queen come for tea.

"What can I help you with?" Trish attempts to be patient, she tries to take the edge out of her voice, but she finds it hard. Her voice is hard.

"You don't have to get snippy," he says, pouting. "This thing I do, it's daunting."

"Daunting?" Hold it in, Trish. Hold it in. Trish imagines pounding him on the top of his little bald head with the dictionary Charlie has left out on the coffee table. She imagines picking him up by the back of his muddy brown suit and kicking him out the front door. She imagines cutting him up and feeding him to the dog. And somehow, even though that's a violent image, there is no blood involved.

"The sooner we get this over with," she says, teeth tight together, lips barely open — and she wonders why her jaw always aches — "the sooner I can get on with my day."

"Sigh."

Did he actually say "sigh"? Trish isn't sure, but she thinks that's what he said.

Knock, knock. Sigh. He's a sound effects man.

"We got off on the wrong foot," the man says. In fact, he bends down and rubs his foot, draws attention to it. Punctuates his sentence with the physical. The foot that was caught in the door. "Literally." He laughs as if she didn't get it. One laugh, one "ha." And his laugh is like a shot. It rings into the living room and startles the dog from his nap on the floor. The cat, slinking by, takes off like her tail is on fire. Trish shivers.

The phone rings.

She doesn't move to answer it.

64

"Aren't you going to get that?"

"No."

"But —" the man stops talking and looks at her, curiously.

The answering machine kicks in. "Trish? Hi, it's Mary, from the school. Your Christmas wreaths are in. Give me a call and we can arrange a time to pick them up. Or Rachel can bring them home. If she can carry them. I'd give them to Charlie but, well, you know how he is. Anyway, call me when you get a chance. It's Mary."

"Beep," the man says. He says it in time with the beep on the machine.

Trish almost expected him to do that.

"At least I'm not the only one you ignore." He laughs again. That bark. "Ha." Trish, her pets, they all jump slightly and then settle themselves quickly.

That's when Trish looks down at the pamphlet. That's when she sees what she has in front of her, what she's holding in her hands. And she almost drops it. She gasps.

"Get out of my house." Standing now. The man looks up at Trish and smiles. Trish can feel her heart beat in her neck.

"Seriously, you really have to stop being so difficult. People will turn from you. People will turn their backs on you and walk away. These boots," he says, pointing to his shiny shoes, "are made for walking."

Trish moves fast towards the kitchen, meaning to pick up the phone. She waves his pamphlet in the air. Furious. "I will call the police. I really will."

"But think of the children. Laugh, laugh."

"Get out."

Her dog barks. Once. A squirrel outside.

The man stands from the sofa and follows Trish into the kitchen. His shiny shoes tap-tapping on her floor.

"I thought you meant my children. And then I thought you meant children in general. Like poor children or sad children or starving children or children who don't get Christmas."

"I meant all those things. Children."

"What do you mean?" Trish's hand is on the phone. "What do you mean?" Shrill now. "This," she throws the pamphlet down on the floor as if it has burned her, "this is disgusting."

The man bends to pick up the pamphlet. "Sigh," he says again. And he begins to cry. Little tears squeeze out from the corners of his eyes. He's working hard at it.

"You're crazy. I'm calling the police. I'm phoning 9-1-1."

He turns and begins to walk quickly out of Trish's house. Down the hall, past the dog, past the cat rolling on the floor, digging her claws in the hall carpet, and out the front door.

"Wait. You can't leave." Trish's hand is on the phone. Her heart in her throat. "You can't pretend this doesn't exist."

"You never think about the children," he says. He turns and says this to her. "Bang," he says, as the door slams shuts behind him. "Clip clop," he says as he starts down the wooden steps. "Whoosh," he shouts as he starts to run up the street. Trish is on the front porch now, watching him rush away. A little bald man who looks like a monk in a brown suit. She doesn't even have one of his pamphlets anymore. He took it with him. If she phones the police she has no proof he even exists. Now Trish understands Tom's dilemma about the scar-faced man, his hesitancy to call the police. Tom didn't have anything to go on but the man's horrific face. And the fact that the man spent all day raking his leaves for free. That wouldn't have impressed the police. But Tom didn't see what Trish has seen. There were things in that pamphlet, in the second it took Trish to look at it, that she will never forget. She will close her eyes at night and those pictures, those children, will haunt her. They are imprinted on the backs of her lids. Trish will tell the police, she will warn them, they will write everything down in their little books, but still those images will cloud her vision, blacken her dreams.

Sometimes you forget just how vulnerable you are. You move through the world, taking things for granted. Just last spring her friend Claire was diagnosed with breast cancer. Just last spring. One day she was laughing about something, going on about her life, the next day she visited her doctor and then suddenly saw her future a little too clearly. She told Trish she had no symptoms, no lumps. No warning. And now there is a small man out there holding tightly to his sick pamphlets, rushing headlong down the street, towards the rest of the city, towards the rest of the wide, wide world.

Although Trish often feels unbalanced and unsafe in her life, there sometimes comes — full-force — those crisp mornings when the world moves quickly off-kilter and presents her with a new way of seeing things. A new way that isn't an act, that isn't part of the stage, the drama of life. A reality that crashes into existence. Those cold mornings when what little time Trish has taken to straighten up her life and get on with it really doesn't matter anyway.

Dear Parents and Guardians,

As you may have noticed, it is getting close to Christmas. Our halls are decked, our mistletoe is hung — just kidding! Can you imagine what would happen if we hung mistletoe? — your children are trying hard to be good. Santa will soon be here. It's a magical time of year and nothing, absolutely nothing, can dampen our joy. Please don't forget, during this beautiful season, to think about decorating your own houses. Order your special Christmas wreaths soon. They are selling like hotcakes — or candy canes! Large wreaths are $40, medium are $30 and the very small, to decorate your dog's house, perhaps, or maybe even your side doors, are $15. All proceeds go to the Abernackie Men's Shelter on Braithwaite Drive. Remember, these poor souls aren't as lucky as we are. They need warm clothes for winter, and hot plates for their rooms. They need good cups of coffee. So share your Christmas spirit! Don't hesitate to order your wreaths.

Please phone Mary in the office or send your cheque in a letter with your child. We will call to let you know when you can pick up the wreaths.

Merry Christmas one and all,

Marge Tanner

Marge Tanner
Principal, Oak Park Elementary School

P.S. Of course, Happy Hanukkah and Kwanzaa to those of you who don't celebrate Christmas. Please visit the special room in our school, room 401, that is dedicated to your traditions.

Build-Your-Bear ™

Your way is the right way . . .

Come Build, Come Play, Come Love.

Your Bear.

Dear Ms. Patricia Birk,

Are you serious? A Monk Bear? What were you thinking?

We have — as I am sure you are well-aware — a Priest Bear, a Buddha Bear, a Muslim Bear, a Sikh Bear, a Jewish Bear, a Hare Krishna Bear, etc. We have them all. Even a Good Samaritan Bear. This is your last warning. We will not hesitate to pursue legal action.

Maisy Crank
CEO and Head Bear of Build-Your-Bear™
Madison, Wisconsin

5

Becky listens to Rachel. Rachel says she has been kicked out of the house because she was eating a muffin on the couch in the living room. "Can you believe how unfair that is?" Rachel says her mother scooted her out, told her to get some "air." "Air? It's freezing out here." Rachel says it's not fair. Her brother, Charlie, gets to stay inside, but she has to go out and it's cold and miserable.

Rachel moves on to bad-mouthing Charlie. She's always on about him. He's eight years old and a pain in the butt, she says. Becky shoots hoops and tries to avoid stepping in the torn-up grass, in the dirt around the basketball net. She doesn't have a brother so she doesn't wonder about Rachel's brother, Charlie. She has a dog. But Rachel has a dog too. And Becky's dog is nothing like a brother, even if he is the same age. Eight. Which is old in dog years.

Rachel says, "You aren't paying attention, Becky," and quickly steals the basketball from her. She shoots and sinks it. Then she runs around in circles, whooping and waving her arms around, and then she falls in the dirt.

"Why'd you do that?" Becky says. "I was on a roll. Five more and I would have made thirty."

"Blah, blah, blah," Rachel says and rolls around.

"Dog poop," Becky says, staring at Rachel. She holds the ball close to her chest. "You're probably rolling in dog poop. You're an idiot."

Rachel smiles up at her. "Wouldn't you like that? You'd like that, wouldn't you?"

"Yeah." Becky turns to the hoop and shoots. "It'd be great."

"That's my net, you know," Rachel says. "I don't have to let you play if I don't want to."

Even though Rachel is wrong, it's Charlie's net, not hers, Becky doesn't say anything. Becky has no idea why they play together. They have nothing in common except living directly across the street from each other. Nothing else. Rachel is spoiled and bossy; she doesn't even like basketball. In fact, the only thing Becky likes about Rachel is Charlie. He's quite nice. Shy and calm and clean. Which is odd because Charlie and Rachel's house is so messy.

Becky likes clean. She likes orderly, organized, tidy houses. She likes to vacuum and dust her room every day. And even though she loves her dog, she won't let him lie on her bed.

Across the street Becky's parents are putting up the Christmas decorations. The wreath from school, the lights, the reindeer that lights up and moves its head up and down. Becky stops shooting and watches her father. He looks strange from over here. Becky isn't used to seeing him from afar. He looks like someone she doesn't know. A stranger. Stranger Danger. Like that guy that she thought she saw hanging around the schoolyard last week. The one with the black hoodie with the word "Falcons" on the chest, the hoodie that covers his face, that puts his features in shadow. Becky thought she saw him watching the girls play hopscotch but by the time she'd found a teacher on the playground to tell he was gone and she decided that she'd probably just imagined him. After all, the police have been coming to her school all week, giving lessons on being safe, on being aware of your surroundings. Becky wondered if she might have been a little afraid because of this — maybe she was just hallucinating him. Overreacting. Like Annabel Hunter did when she ran into Mr. Berton, the janitor, down in the washroom. He was only cleaning, something Becky is pleased about. She is amazed, actually, as she didn't think those bathrooms ever got cleaned. Annabel acted as if the janitor was a murderer and ran screaming up and down the halls until the principal put her hand over Annabel's mouth and led her directly to the office.

Then there was the whole boring assembly about overreacting. About being "aware" but not too paranoid. Becky doesn't know how you balance it. Annabel really did see the janitor in the girls' washroom and he *is* freaky looking.

Becky's molar is chipped slightly, and Becky stands there worrying her tooth with her tongue. She doesn't want to tell her parents about her chipped tooth — she isn't sure what happened, it was just chipped one morning when she woke up, probably from grinding her teeth — because she hates the dentist. Really hates him. More than she hates dirt. And she's not overreacting. He pokes at her gums with little metal tools and always seems to hit a nerve. She's told her mom that her teeth are sensitive but her mom says she has to get them cleaned anyway. The chip is annoying and is cutting into her tongue and she can't help playing with it. Becky takes off her hair clip and puts it in her mouth over the chip so she won't bother it. She sucks on the clip. The hair clip tastes like summer, like chlorine and sweat. It smells like mould. A bitter, earthy smell.

Becky's father is still there, plugging in the lights which sparkle in the dimming light. Her mother is nowhere to be seen. Becky remembers that man awhile ago who helped her dad rake.

That scar-faced man. Becky feels shivery. Even though he wasn't wearing a "Falcons" hoodie, Becky wonders if he could be the same person hanging out at her school. There was something in the way that man stood, his hands in his pockets, his face covered. Becky isn't sure. All men look the same to her. Even the scar-faced man looks the same as every other man. They are all tall and big and featureless.

"You have to pass the ball, Beck," Rachel says. "Or I won't play with you anymore."

"We should have two balls," Becky says. "Why don't we have two balls so we can each shoot."

"That's not how you play, stupid."

"You can play any way you want to play. I don't want to pass the ball when your hands are probably covered in dog poop."

Rachel's mom comes out looking for Charlie. She looks frazzled. She's holding one of her bears, half dressed.

"He's in the house," Rachel says. "You let him stay inside. You made me come outside. To freeze to death."

"Charlie," Trish goes back inside, calling him. Then she pops her head out again and says it's time for lunch, and her head disappears again. Then the bear comes out, held by her outstretched hand, and it says, "Now!" The girls stare at each other. Rachel glares.

Saturday is often like this. Becky goes over to Rachel's. They play inside or outside. They fight. Becky heads home and hangs out in her room with her dog. Cleans a bit. Tidies up. Sometimes her parents take her out for dinner. They go to the pizza place or the fish and chip shop. Sometimes they just pick up food — rotis or burritos — and come home with it and eat it in front of the TV.

Tonight Becky had Mexican, and now she's in her bedroom

watching some shows on her laptop while her parents watch their own movie downstairs. She can hear her mother laugh every so often. She's loud when she laughs. There are a lot of things that bother Becky about her mother. Her laugh is just one of them.

Becky wonders if the guy with the Falcons hoodie was staring at her. She's not sure. He just stands there and stares. The guy who was raking with her dad that day kept looking at her. He had such a freaky face, Becky can't even describe it, sliced in two, a giant scar. Even though he worked hard, raking, Becky was sure he kept looking at her. And he put a spin on her dad. He made her dad nervous, Becky could tell. Maybe it was his face. Becky thinks a face like that would make anyone nervous. After the guy left that day there was a lot of whispering between Becky's mom and Becky's dad, but she doesn't know why. Maybe because the man up and left without taking any money for his work. Even Becky thinks that's weird. Why would you do anything without getting paid for it? Becky's mom said he would be back the next day for money. But he never came back.

Becky spent the drive to the Mexican restaurant telling her dad all about Stranger Danger. He listened carefully. Becky likes how he always listens. In fact, he connected what she was saying with the raking man. Somehow he connected it. Even though Becky said nothing. Her dad said he didn't want to make her nervous. Ever. He said he was sorry he panicked when he couldn't find her after the man with the weird face left that day. He said she shouldn't worry about that man, have nightmares or anything, but by saying this he made Becky scared. She wasn't really afraid of the man until her dad said that. But then thinking of that scarred-up face, that weird half-face — well, now she is scared. And her tooth is bothersome and there is a bit of Mexican food stuck in it, where it's chipped, and Becky is digging at it now in front of her laptop in her room.

Bringing up that man made Becky want to watch something really tame. She picked from all the old DVDs they have in a box in the living room. She thought about a Christmas movie. It was almost time to start watching those: *The Grinch*, *It's a Wonderful Life*, *Scrooge*, *A Christmas Story*. But instead she chose a DVD of old *Hannah Montana* episodes. They aren't taking her mind off anything. Becky has no idea why adults would want to frighten children. It seems that everyone Becky knows is a little more worried these days. Before the police started talking to everyone at her school Becky felt like a kid. Now she feels like an adult. She feels as if she has a responsibility to do something, but she doesn't know what.

And even though she's mad at Rachel, right now Becky wishes Rachel were here. Watching a DVD with her. Becky's eight-year-old dog isn't proper company. He falls asleep quickly and snores as loudly as her mother laughs. Outside Becky can hear Rachel's mother goofing around with Charlie in the driveway and talking loudly to the new neighbour. She can hear Charlie bouncing a ball in the dark and Rachel's mom says something about hockey and the new neighbour says something back. Her little baby, Carrie, who is really cute and sweet, makes a loud squealing noise and everyone over there, in Rachel's driveway, laughs.

For a while, after the raking man came, Becky's father started driving Becky, Rachel and Charlie to school even though he never usually did that. He drove them up to the schoolyard and then he sat in the car until they were safely in the fenced area. He did this for a couple of weeks and then he stopped, and Becky, Rachel and Charlie walked together again like they used to. Rachel complained. She liked the rides to school. The warm car. She blamed Becky and Charlie for everything. She said it was their fault Becky's dad had stopped driving. She said it was Charlie's stinky feet and the way he always cleared his throat.

Each day is getting colder and darker. The leaves are all off the trees. Becky notices this when she walks home. She has nothing more to scuff along in. Christmas can't get here fast enough. Becky has asked for a rechargeable DustBuster, among other things. She figures she can hang it in her closet and use it to suck up dirt anywhere in the house. Her mother thinks this is funny. "What twelve-year-old wants cleaning supplies for Christmas?" Becky heard her say to someone on the phone the other day. "What about jewellery? An iPad even?" She laughed.

Ha ha, Becky thinks. I'm a joke. If she had a daughter who wanted to keep her room clean she'd be a pretty happy, lucky mother. What's wrong with people? Becky worries her chipped tooth. Besides, Becky knows that her mother is just as clean as she is. Becky has caught her vacuuming the same rug three times in one day. She is aware that her mother wipes counters obsessively.

For the last couple of days the guy in the hoodie has been standing outside the schoolyard looking in. He's back. Becky has seen him. She has pointed him out to her teachers, but whenever they look the guy is gone. The teachers have begun to ignore her. One of them, Mrs. Spruce, even mentioned the boy who cried wolf. She told Becky to calm down, to stop "overreacting." But he is there. After a while he appears wearing a down jacket. She can't see his face clearly with his heavy jacket on and a scarf and a toque, but Becky knows it's the same person. He has this casual way of standing, like he's happy to wait there for the rest of his life, like he doesn't ever need to move. Most people move from one foot to the other, they shift their weight, but this guy stands like a statue and watches the schoolyard. Same way the guy who raked the leaves stood. Becky has, however, come to the conclusion that he isn't there to see her. Because when she runs back and forth he doesn't move his head to follow her movements. She isn't sure who he is looking at. Maybe he has his eyes closed, Becky can't tell.

And every time she draws attention to him, every time she tries to point him out, he isn't there anymore. He is gone.

Because of Annabel's "overreaction" to the janitor in the bathroom, the kids in her grade seven class have to go to the bathroom in pairs. Girls with girls. Boys with boys. Down the long hallway, down the long staircase, to the basement of the school. Becky has been forced to pair up with other girls in her class even when she doesn't have to pee. She wouldn't pee at school anyway, not even if you paid her. The toilets are disgusting. No one bothers to flush. And the floor is wet and sticky with toilet paper. Becky usually stands just outside the door to the washroom and tells whomever it is she's escorting that she'll wait for her there. Becky won't even lean against the wall while she is waiting. She stands stiffly, trying not to touch anything. Her tongue bleeds where she rubs it against the chip on her molar.

Sometimes she has a stomach ache from holding her pee in all day, but Becky knows that a stomach ache is better than all of the things she would catch if she used the bathroom.

The nightmares Becky has been having for half her life — since she was six — are getting worse. She used to wake crying only once a week — these days she's up most nights, clutching her pillow. But because she is twelve, Becky doesn't bother her parents anymore. She stays in her clean, tidy room, trying to stop her heart from exploding out of her chest, trying to remember what it is that is scaring her. She doesn't know. Becky can't remember her nightmares anymore than she can remember to feed the dog before school. When she wakes up sweating, the visions disappear as quickly as the guy standing outside of the schoolyard fence. As it gets closer to Christmas the visions stop, to be replaced by dreams about the Grinch and Santa and angels and bells. She remembers these ones. One night Becky dreams about eating an entire turkey on her own, just grabbing the meat off it as it sits on the kitchen table. Scarfing it down. When she wakes up, her stomach growls fiercely and when she goes downstairs for breakfast, she throws up in her bowl of cereal.

"You'd better stay home today," her mother says, feeling her forehead. "You're sick."

Becky slumps back up the stairs and into her room. She disappears under her duvet and, feverishly, sleeps until noon.

"I've got soup for you." Becky's mother places a bowl of soup on the bedside table. "How are you feeling?"

"Uh."

"Uh as in better? Your fever has gone down." Becky's mother takes her cool hand off Becky's forehead. "Would you be okay if I went out? I have some errands to run. I'll take my cell phone. Or you can call Dad at work if you need anything."

Becky nods and falls back into her pillows. She doesn't care where her mother is, as long as she can go back to sleep.

When she wakes up, Becky hears nothing. Silence. The house is still. Her mother is gone. Becky knows, in her feverish state, that if she stands and walks over to her bedroom window and looks out she will see the guy. He will be standing there, staring at her house. And even though it's only mid-afternoon, his face will be in darkness. She doesn't even have to get up to know this. She can feel him there. She can also feel her tooth. Her tongue. Becky wonders if the chip will eventually be worn down by her tongue, worn to a soft surface. Maybe, if she waits long enough, she will fix her own tooth with her tongue. When she looks in the mirror she can't see anything wrong with her tooth. But when she touches it with her tongue it feels like a huge, sharp, spiky, pointy thing. It feels enormous in her mouth.

The front door slams. Becky jumps. Her mother is home.

The principal has called Becky's parents into her office. She has called Becky in as well.

"We seem to be having a teensy bit of a problem with old Becky in the schoolyard," the principal starts. Becky hates how she talks. Like everything is just peachy keen. Okey-dokey. "Becky, do you want to tell your parents what's going on?"

Becky shakes her head.

"Beck," her father says, "is something bothering you? What's up, kiddo?"

"He is," Becky says. "The guy out there. He's bothering me."

"She seems to think that there is a person watching the schoolyard," the principal says. She shakes her head. She cackles. "But no one else sees him. He's invisible."

"You don't look in time," Becky shouts. "You never look in time to see him."

"Calm down, sweetie."

"Inside voices," the principal says. "Okey-dokey?"

"But you never look in time. No one looks in time and then he's gone."

"She had a fever a few days ago," Becky's mother starts. "It could be after-effects —"

"Maria," Becky's father says. "I'm not sure that's possible."

"No, this has been going on since we had the police in to talk to the grade seven kids about Stranger Danger. I think," the principal says, "she's overreacting just an eensy-teensy bit to the messages the police delivered. It's nothing new. Several other kids have been having similar problems. We think we might have to rethink these police visits."

"I'm not overreacting."

"Becky, keep your voice down," her mother says.

"It's the same guy who raked our yard," Becky whispers, but her mother is talking over her. "I know it is."

"We'll talk about this at home," her mother says. "Thank you so much for your concern, Mrs. Tanner."

"Oh, no problem at all." The principal rises and shakes Becky's parents' hands. "You can go back to your class now," she tells Becky. She puts her hand on Becky's head and there is a spark.

You stole my electrons, Becky thinks.

"In the meantime, Mrs. Shutter, can I interest you in another wreath? I know you purchased one, but wouldn't another one look lovely on your side door?"

At home Becky can hear them talking. She crouches on the stairs and listens. Her dog tries to lick her face but she pushes him away.

"There's something wrong with her," Becky's mother says. "I mean, seriously, Tom, someone watching her? And her cleaning. Have you noticed how much she cleans?"

"That guy who raked our yard in the fall scared me too," Becky's father says. "I don't blame her for being a bit worried. And you clean all the time, Maria."

"Don't be silly."

"You're too hard on her."

"She wants a freaking DustBuster for Christmas. A DustBuster."

"So what? She's just a little different. There's nothing wrong with being clean."

"Rachel wants a docking station for her iPod. Charlie wants a new basketball and some hockey equipment. Every other kid in the whole world wants something other than a DustBuster. I'm clean, Tom, but I'm not psychotic."

Becky can hear her father moving around the kitchen. Her parents' voices move in and out as they walk. Becky feels a buzzing in her head. It's from her tooth. It's killing her. And her tongue. A permanent canker sore. Giving her headaches.

"I've seen that guy downtown." Becky hears her father clearly.

"What? Where?"

"He was walking down the street. I was driving. I couldn't stop."

"Why would you stop?"

Pause. A dish clinks. Becky can hear something being poured.

"To pay him, I guess. I figure we owe him some money."

"Don't be ridiculous. It was his problem that he left. We were going to pay him. He left. That was so long ago."

"I just feel like we owe him something."

"We don't owe him anything, Tom. Don't be stupid."

"I'm not stupid, Maria. I'm just nice. You might want to try it sometime."

Becky stands, stretches her legs — her knees crack — and heads back up to her room. She isn't imagining him. He does exist. Her dad saw him too.

Christmas morning and Becky's DustBuster works great. She has to charge it, but the little bit of charge that was in it directly from the packaging worked to suck up some of the dog fur on the carpet beside her bed. When she is busy with her DustBuster she forgets about her tooth. But when she has to put it back in the charger her tooth feels horrible. A pounding sensation. A boiling. It feels as if her gums are on fire. Becky is still not sleeping well. And the tooth makes it worse — every time she falls asleep she starts to grit and grind and she wakes instantly from the jagged pain. It's a pain that shoots through her mouth, her jaw, her ear and up to her forehead. It makes her eyes water. And it bothers her that she can never remember what she is dreaming about. Not even if she concentrates as hard as she can.

After Christmas vacation it is too cold to play in the schoolyard. Becky and her classmates go stir-crazy inside and end up in trouble most days. Lunchtime seems endless. They want to run and jump and play. Instead they are told to sit at their desks and do puzzles. The teachers refuse to stay in the classroom. Supervising during lunchtime is not in their contract. So the kids go wild and the classroom becomes worse than messy with cream cheese and butter and sandwich meat stuck under the desks and rubbed across the floor. One kid puts a piece of bologna in a heating vent and it rots and the room smells like death for weeks. Becky gets more nervous — the messiness is bothering her. She stands at the window most lunch hours and watches the schoolyard, wiping her hands on her jeans over and over.

He is always there. Standing still. Just outside the fence. Beside the tree. Now you see him, now you don't.

One day Rachel and Charlie are sick. They have the flu. Becky is forced to walk home alone. She knows the guy is right behind her but she doesn't want to turn. If she doesn't turn she won't see him and he won't be there. Becky makes it home and bursts through the front door.

"Hey, what's your hurry?" Becky's mother is standing in the

kitchen, apron on, washing cookie trays. "I got off work early and thought I'd make cookies. Becky? Don't slam —"

Slam.

"— the door."

Becky collapses and lies on the floor, lifeless.

"Are you okay? What's wrong? The floor is dirty, get up. Take your boots off, Becky."

Becky leaps up. Of course the floor is dirty. She brushes herself off. She steals a glance at the front door but sees nothing through the tempered glass. There is no one there — or if he is there, he's continued on down the street.

"Oh god," Becky's mom says. "What happened to your mouth?"

In the mirror Becky sees blood covering all her teeth. As if her teeth have been painted pink. And she can taste it. A sour, metallic taste. When she fell to the floor she must have bit her canker sore. Her tongue is ragged. Becky's mother gets her to rinse in the sink and then puts ice on Becky's tongue. She calls the dentist. She makes that dreaded appointment. She says, "You should see her tongue. And her tooth. It's horribly chipped. I think she's cut her tongue on it."

Becky spends the evening sucking on ice chips and drinking smoothies. She gargles with salt water. Tomorrow morning she has to go to the dentist and "get that chip looked after." She is terrified. If there is one thing that scares her more than the guy in the schoolyard, more than her nightmares, more than dirt, it's going to the dentist.

It is 8:30 in the morning and Becky is furiously Dust Busting. She has sucked up the dust on her dresser, her desk and most of the floor. Her mother stands at the door of Becky's room and watches.

"Okay, are you ready?"

They leave the house and get in the car. Becky is terrified. She is so scared that she doesn't look for the guy. She is so afraid of the dentist that she almost wishes the stranger would just get it over with and kidnap her right now. Because that's what he's going to do eventually, right? Kidnap her and murder her and probably sexually assault her before he murders her. That's what they do. To girls.

But she doesn't really mean this. She doesn't want to get kidnapped. It's just that the idea of someone putting their hands in her mouth — even with latex gloves on — makes her stomach ache, makes her lose the ability to keep her hands still. She is shaking wildly.

"It's just a dentist appointment, Becky. No need to worry. He'll fix your tooth for you."

Becky burps up a bit of her morning cereal. She stares out the window of the car, not seeing anything. In the parking lot at the dentist's building Becky's mother has to take her hand and lead her out of the car and into the lobby. Up the elevator. Across the hall, turn the corner and they are there. Becky's mother sighs. The waiting room is crowded. Becky's mother looks at her watch. Becky sits quickly on a plastic chair. She ignores the sign that reads "Please Take off Your Boots" but Becky's mother doesn't and after she has taken her own boots off she pads over in those little sock-covers to Becky and takes Becky's boots off. Even with the blue sock-covers on Becky can still feel the germs, the warts, the dirt, creeping into her toes through her socks. Athlete's foot, fungus. Does her mother know that athlete's foot is the same thing as jock itch? Becky read that the other day on the internet. The pictures that went along with the site made her gag. Even now, thinking about them, Becky feels ill.

In the dentist's chair Becky is shaking so hard that her mother and the assistant have to hold her down. The dentist wears a mask and picks at her teeth. He tells her that she has an infection. He tells her that she'll have to get that tooth capped, that she'll have to go on antibiotics for the gum and tongue infection. He tells her everything she doesn't want to hear and she shakes wildly and Becky's mother asks about a sedative.

Hours later Becky is led up the front porch into her house. She is wobbling slightly and has a headache but her tooth feels fine. The temporary cap is slightly higher than her tooth but Becky actually likes the feel of it, soft and smooth, on her sore tongue. She feels giggly and dizzy. An eensy-teensy bit nauseous. She laughs.

"Into bed little girl," Becky's mother says. "I'll bring you up some soup in a bit. We'll wait until the sedative and the freezing wear off or you might bite your tongue."

As Becky walks towards her bed, she glances out her window and sees Rachel, her face red from fever, in the window of her house. Rachel sees Becky. They wave. Rachel holds up a bear, one of her mother's creations. Becky can't make it out, but it looks like a Doctor Bear. It has a white coat, something hanging from its neck. Becky wishes her mom made bears. She gives Rachel the thumbs-up. And then they both look down into the front yard. There is no one there. No person with a big coat. No guy with a hoodie even. No guy with a toque and scarf. No scarred man. No one. Rachel points to the ground. Becky points too. Then Becky points at her tooth and gives Rachel another thumbs-up. Rachel points to her forehead and gives Becky a thumbs-down. Becky smiles. When she sleeps she dreams about basketball. And when she wakes up she remembers her dream.

Her tooth is better. Her tongue feels great. There are some warmish days now just before winter really sets in. Those warm days, her parents say, deceive you. The calm before the storm. Blah blah. Becky refuses to listen. Instead she kicks around a soccer ball in the frozen dirt of the schoolyard. The snow will come soon, they've already had dustings, but for now it's staying away. Becky spends hours each evening polishing and cleaning her cleats just in case spring really is around the corner. Her dad says she's crazy. "We've got many months left, honey," he says.

The person is gone. She hasn't seen him in a while. Becky listens each day and each night to the adults around her, watching the news with her parents, just waiting to hear something — a child missing, someone arrested. But she hears nothing bad. Only the regular things — break-ins and carjackings. He's gone, this person.

And, although it takes some time, Becky tries so hard to forget about him that she almost does. She almost forgets about Stranger Danger and the police. Her classmates are allowed to use the bathroom on their own again. Even Annabel goes down to the basement bathroom by herself. Which is good, because Becky can't stand the filth.

winter

To: puckbunnybrady@pik.com
From: puckbunnybrady@pik.com
Subject: Robbery!

Hey Ice Kats!

Yes, as you can tell from the subject line, we've had our
first locker room robbery of the season. Someone's purse was
stolen from room 4 last Wednesday night, January 10th. I know
what you are thinking: "You told us not to bring our purses
into the room so it's the fault of the girl who brought her
purse in." But think about this for a minute — a robbery
committed against one of our teammates means a robbery
committed against us all. If we, as a team, don't feel safe
in the locker room, where can we feel safe?

If anyone knows anything about this or if you saw anyone
leaving locker room 4 last Wednesday night when the team
was on the ice, please let me know. From now on keep your
valuables in your car and LOCK your car. You wouldn't believe
how many times I have to say that to people in this town —
lock your house doors, your car, your bicycle too. Parkville
may be a small place, but we still have thieves. Of course
you'll have to bring your car keys into the locker room but
how about taking them to the bench with you? I know some of
you moms bring your cell phones to the bench too, just in
case your kids wake in the night. What I'm saying is: do
everything you can to protect your valuables.

Get yer game on!

Tina Brady
Parkville Ice Kats
Co-ordinator Extraordinaire

6

There are three males watching this game. One fat guy who keeps jumping up and doing the wave. One quiet guy, head down, over in the corner on his BlackBerry, thumbing in a message to work, the mistress or the kids. And then Jude.

The fat guy does the wave, the BlackBerry guy endlessly texts, and Jude buries his head in the hood of his jacket to keep warm, his hands in the pockets, the zipper done up to his chin. He sinks down into his seat and rests his wide feet on the back of the seat in front of him. His legs are gangly, his body growing so rapidly it even surprises him. At times he catches himself knocking into things, whapping things with his long arms, tripping on things with his long legs. It's all he can do not to fall. Some days his knees look twice as big as his thighs. Other days he feels proportioned. It is cold in the arena. The ceiling heaters aren't on. Jude supposes that the heaters are saved for paying customers, not husbands or boyfriends, not the teenage kid in the stands.

Jude watches the action on the ice. His eyes peer out darkly from under his hood. His teeth chatter. His nose feels wet and cold.

Like a dog's. The women on the ice are beginning to improve. Jude is impressed. When he first started coming to these games in the fall it was like watching kids out there, large kids who couldn't skate fast or pass the puck. It was like watching that game Jude used to play in elementary school, hot potato. Each time the puck came at one of the women she would flick it quickly away, as if it burned her stick. Now, though, he is suitably content with their game. He feels like he's watching something now, something more important, not just a game. He has to hold in his breath so that he doesn't shout when things are going well.

Hot potato, dodge ball, who's got the bone. Jude has distinct memories of each of these games, of how he felt playing them, of how they made him feel. Telephone — when everyone sat in a circle and passed the message around until it became so wildly skewed that it had no connection to the original.

It's the white team he cheers for. It's the white team he watches. There are three players who have obviously never played before and he likes to be there to silently cheer them on. They are awkward and funny, often having as much trouble skating as playing the game.

At the beginning he watched the grey team, but now it's the white team he's taken with. There's something about their hair under their helmets, the way it comes mostly past their shoulders and is all different — curling or straight, ponytail or loose. Their hair is nice to watch, but he also likes their laughter. Peeling. Ringing. High-pitched laughter. Their camaraderie. The way they high-five each other, or pat each other with their sticks. Jude loses himself in these nights, forgets all the things he wants to forget, concentrates on the ice.

Late in the fall Jude was walking out from the rink one night on his way home. He had been sullenly watching the grey team — they weren't impressing him. Too competitive, too angry. But then he heard the laughter coming from the change room and he stopped and listened. Like bells. A few gruff snorts. Cackles. That's when he decided to watch the white team. To forget about the grey team and focus instead on the white. When their laughter rang around him and sent a shiver up his spine. They sounded like they were having so much fun and Jude wanted to be a part of it — in some way — he wanted to share in the laughter. So he checked their schedule on the internet and he hasn't missed a game since.

Now Jude's watching the game and he feels as if he can smell them out there on the ice. He can smell their femaleness, their sour, fishy smell, like his sister in the morning when she comes down for breakfast, her hair sticking up, her breath reeking. He can smell their shampoos and deodorants and perfumes. And he swears to himself that he can smell the white over the red team. He sighs and lowers deeper into the seat. The seat in front of him bangs open — his foot has slipped — and bangs shut again. A white player looks up. Jude turns his head away from her quickly.

Sometimes he wonders if there is something wrong with him. Sometimes he wonders if he's normal. He is never quite sure. Jude knows, though, that none of his friends spend Wednesday nights watching women's hockey. He is certain of this. So if this makes him different, then he is different. Not good different or bad different, just different.

He isn't interested in them sexually. He doesn't want them or lust after them or think about them in any way like that. Jude is interested in them mainly because they fill something that is empty inside of him. When he's here, in the arena, he feels full. When he goes home, he feels empty. But when he leaves the rink on Wednesday nights he doesn't think about them again until the next Wednesday. They don't come into his dreams. If Jude were to run into them on the street he wouldn't even recognize them or make the connection. When he's here, though, on Wednesday night, his mind and body feel satiated.

"What do you mean you didn't get the files?" The BlackBerry man is frantic on his phone, holding it up to his ear to talk and then thumbing as quickly as possible in his lap.

Another fat-assed wave from the other guy. Jude smiles to himself. He's pretty funny. The women on the ice laugh when they see him bounce up and down.

The one Jude's watching tonight, and it always changes, is the newest player, the one who obviously knows nothing about hockey. She is tiny and has long blond hair. She shouts, "Shit," when she falls. Fiery, he thinks. Energetic. She looks younger than she probably is — he cannot guess anymore how old women are. Anywhere from thirty to fifty. As old as his mother or younger or older. And how old is his mother? Nowadays she looks older than she is. She used to look young. Women are such mysteries to Jude. But he knows this woman has a young baby — he has heard her mention it when he passes by her in the parking lot — and so he thinks she must be closer to thirty than to fifty.

Every Wednesday Jude concentrates on one particular woman on the team. He stares hard at that one, willing her not to get hurt, willing her to have fun, willing her to smile. Most of the time he's satisfied. Sometimes his woman will fall. No one has ever been hurt.

Jude shifts in his seat again, careful not to bang the plastic seat in front of him. His legs ache. Sometimes it drives him mad. His mom calls them growing pains. Sometimes Jude feels as if his legs have been sliced in half and there are maggots worming their way through his wounds. Sometimes it hurts to stand up. At night he tosses and turns in bed. He feels as if he has to run. He lies there in agony, trying to still his running legs.

Jude is growing while his mother is shrinking. He is growing bigger and stronger while she is getting weaker and smaller. She lost her hair, but his hair seems to grow so fast he can't keep up with it. And then the hair on his arms, his legs, his chest, his face. There's hair everywhere now. And nowhere. Bodies, Jude thinks, interfere with everything — they mess things up as they grow and change and morph and fail.

But she's only weak for now. The radiation will have worked. The chemotherapy. The operation. Everything will work. Jude is sure of it. How could it not work? How could his mom not be around anymore? That's not something that is even in the realm of possibility. Even though he's aware this could happen, she could die, there is nothing about this fact that makes any sense or even seems to penetrate his brain. Not. Possible.

One of the larger women scores a goal. Everyone shouts. The white team on the bench bang their sticks against the boards. "Woo hoo," shouts a woman, and this sound makes Jude's head ache until the rest of the team laughs and the bell-like sounds wash over him. Jude's woman skates hard, playing right wing, and crashes into the boards but she doesn't fall. She rubs her shoulder as she skates back, though, and he immediately thinks about the bruise that must be forming on it. It is blue and purple; it is darker around the edges. It is a small bruise, the size of a coin.

And then he shakes his head and focuses on the game again. The BlackBerry man looks up from his device, straight at Jude, as if he knows what Jude is thinking, and he nods. Jude hides his face further into his hood and nods back.

Most of the time he doesn't think about his mother. Or about women. Or even about girls. When he's alone he barely registers anyone but himself. But when he's near the hockey team, or when someone looks at him straight on, he is always startled to feel the emotion well up in him. His need for her, his mother. His ache.

Another cheer, more banging of the boards, and then the game, as quickly as it began, is over. The women shake hands with the other team, bump fists, "nice game, nice game," and skate off, talking. The woman he is watching tonight is the last to leave the ice. She looks reluctant, as if she doesn't want to go home, as if she doesn't want the game to be over. He knows what she is feeling.

Jude lingers at the pop machine in the hallway and imagines them in the change room, peeling off their sweaty equipment, laughing. He tries to imagine their faces mostly, because he can't see them behind the cages of their masks. He thinks about their eyes and what colours there are. Multiple colours in the change room. Blues and greens and browns. Hazels and greys. So many eyes. Red lips, pink lips, pale lips. Freckles and pimples and birthmarks and scars. Scars. They have scars, each of them, all the women on the white team. He is sure of it. Scars on their faces, on their legs and arms and stomachs, on their asses. Bruises. Purple and black and red. Like his mother, they aren't completely healthy. They aren't perfect.

Jude straightens a little and watches the women start to leave the change room. The fat man who was doing the wave, jolly in a stereotypical way, picks up the bag for a woman and puts his arm over her shoulder. The BlackBerry man says, "Good game," to a petite blond and helps her manoeuvre her hockey bag out the doors. He doesn't offer to carry it. His BlackBerry is in one hand, her hockey stick in the other. She looks annoyed with him, her little mouth sucked in. She is chewing on her lower lip.

Jude waits awhile for the woman he was watching tonight. When she finally emerges from the change room she is with a friend. This is disappointing. The two women walk together out the door, into the night, talking and smiling, the larger woman laughing loudly. Jude thinks he knows the other woman, but he can't figure it out. He follows behind. Like a dog. He didn't see his woman's eye colour because she was looking down when she passed him, but he will see it eventually. He knows this like he knows many things, like he knows that his mother will survive. Next week Jude will have another woman to focus on, and then another week another woman. Jude follows the hockey players out to their car and then, when they get in and turn on the ignition, he moves sideways and he tilts his long legs, his arms, his torso, his gangly body around a corner and he disappears into the night.

To: dayton22@hotmail.com
From: johnnyman@cresscompany.com
Subject: Bitch

Dayton,

You stole my daughter. I found you. It was pretty easy. I
know where you are, where you live, what you have done. You
stole my money too. I'm so fucking mad you wouldn't believe.
How do you think it felt for me to come home from work and
you were gone? Carrie was gone. Her toys, your passports,
our fucking money in the bank, everything was gone. But you
used a credit card to buy your plane tickets. You're such
a moron. How many times have I told you to watch some TV?
If you had bothered to watch TV or movies instead of always
reading your goddamn books, you would know that you can be
traced by using your credit cards. So I know where you are.
I've put a stop to all your credit cards, but you've figured
that out already I assume. When are you coming back? Are you
coming back? Do I care? You really piss me off. Like I'm so
mad I feel like I'm going to explode. How could you do this
to me? Do you know what this looks like for me? What will
my friends think? I know it's taken me a couple months to
write to you, but I was so mad before that I couldn't think
straight. Now I can. Now I know what I'm going to do. I'm
going to get Carrie back. I don't want you back, Dayton, but
I'm going to take Carrie away from you. You've hurt me so
now I'm going to hurt you.

John

...

To: johnnyman@cresscompany.com
From: dayton22@hotmal.com
Subject: Re: Bitch

John, please don't act rash. Think it over. I will be in
touch with you through my lawyer. You should note that I am
keeping all threatening emails or correspondence. Carrie is
fine. Please wait until we can figure something out legally.

Dayton

...

To: dayton22@hotmail.com
From: cresscompanysecurity@cresscompany.com
Subject: Re: johnnyman@cresscompany.com

Your email has been returned to you. The person you are
trying to contact no longer works at Cress Company. Please
change your files accordingly.

Cress Company Finances
California, USA

7

They meet for the first time at the grocery store and have no idea that they have so much in common. Claire lets Dayton take her spot in line because Dayton's baby is grumpy and whining, sitting in the front of the cart with her legs dangling down, kicking her mother over and over. Shouting. Claire says, "You go first," and helps push the cart into the lane, both women avoiding the slushy, kicking winter boots.

Claire remembers those times — not fondly. If someone had let her go ahead, just once, it would have made a difference. Jude would kick her; Caroline would be pulling things off the shelf. Claire would end up buying them candy to shut them up, or cookies, or chips, or something awful.

"Thank you." Dayton stands in the lane, staring down at the groceries in her cart. "You would think they could have devised a better way to do this."

"Pardon?" Claire itches her head. The wig is horribly scratchy.

"Grocery shopping. Seriously, think about it." Dayton starts unloading her cart but continues talking. Her daughter keeps kicking and Claire keeps her distance. The line behind them gets longer.

"First you take the groceries from the shelf," Dayton says. "Then you put them in your cart. Then you take them from your cart and put them up on the checkout thingee here," Dayton signals the conveyor as it moves slowly carrying her canned tuna with it. "Then you put your stuff in a bag. Then take the bag to your car. Then carry the bag into your house. Then unload your groceries into your fridge and cupboards. What is that?"

"What is what?" Claire says. This woman is attractive in a thin, awkward way. Her long, blond hair swoops in front of her face. She talks with her hands. Waving the oranges around, boxes of granola bars. She pauses all the time, between words, as if she's trying to remember what it is she wants to say.

"That's six times."

"Six times?"

"Six times that you hold whatever you buy and transfer it from one place to the other. Six times."

Claire says, "I never thought about it that way." But she's right. This woman is absolutely right. It's ridiculous. Like most things in life.

"Think about it." Dayton stops and turns towards Claire. The man behind them in line sighs and rolls his eyes. The checkout woman calls for a price check on the oranges. "If someone would invent something. Say . . ." Dayton thinks. "Say a little do-hickey that might scan the item. No, wait. What about if we had a do-hickey —"

"A scanner?" Claire is watching Dayton's hands as she mimes what she means. It's like playing Pictionary. Claire thinks, I haven't played Pictionary in a long time. She wonders if Jude and Caroline would want to play sometime or maybe they are too old now. There is a small amount of time, between the age of this little baby in the cart and Jude and Caroline's age, a tiny time where your kids want to do things with you, where they actually enjoy your company.

"Yes. That's right. If we had a scanner, each of us," Dayton waves her hands around the store. "And maybe there is only one of each item on the shelf. So you'd save retail space too. The stores could charge less for the products —"

"And then we scan it."

"Yes. We scan it, enter it into our own little scanner. Whatever we need." Dayton's daughter stops kicking and watches her mother's animated face. She giggles. She picks at her nose, which is leaking.

"That's $232.50," the checkout girl says. She cracks her gum. There is a loud pop. Claire marvels that the girl can chew gum with braces like that. And what's wrong with the girl's braces? They are greenish in colour.

Dayton hands over her credit card. "We could bring our scanners to the counter. Then pay and go wait outside and —"

"And someone from the back would have put our grocery order together and would be there loading the bags into our cars. Oh," Claire claps her hands together. She can't help herself. "I really like that idea. I'd shop at that store." Claire beams.

Dayton signs her receipt and looks pleased with herself. She goes to the end of the line and starts packing her groceries into the bags she has brought from home. The man behind Claire clears his throat and sighs again. Claire enters the checkout line and begins putting her items — soy milk, organic broccoli, yogurt — onto the counter. She watches Dayton as she puts all her items in her bags. She doesn't care about the order. Eggs go on the bottom. Bread squished under bananas. She is distracted and chewing her hair. Her daughter is chewing and sucking and generally making a mess of a granola bar she has ripped open out of the box. Claire joins

Dayton at the end of the conveyor belt and begins loading her own few groceries into her bags.

"I'm Claire," she says, "by the way. And I like your idea a lot."

"I'm Dayton. This is Carrie."

Both women look at Carrie. Carrie smiles. There is a huge piece of granola bar rolled in her cheek. She looks like a chipmunk. Dayton reaches out and sticks her finger in Carrie's mouth and pulls it out. She breaks off a small piece of the mush and gives it back to Carrie. Carrie gurgles and smiles. Then Dayton pops the rest of the gooey mess in her own mouth. Claire feels slightly ill.

"I have a daughter named Caroline. We wanted to call her Carrie as a nickname, but she never let us. She always wanted to be Caroline."

"Carrie is Carolina. But I just call her Carrie. Carolina is where my husband, my ex-husband, is from."

"My Caroline is much older than this little one." Claire feels sad saying that. "Seventeen."

"Really?" Dayton smiles. "They grow up so fast, don't they? Sometimes I wish it was faster," she pulls more granola bar from her daughter's mouth, eats it, "sometimes not. It was nice to meet you."

"You too."

The women leave at the same time but Dayton moves faster than Claire, who tires easily these days. The Tamoxifen she's on doesn't have the side effects of the chemo, but the whole process, the whole way of life, of living with knowing, of living like this, well, it makes her tired. Claire's wig is itchy because her hair is finally growing in. She imagines the hair pushing against the inside of the wig, trying to get out. Soon she won't wear a wig anymore. She only wears it when she goes out. And only because she hates the looks of pity she gets from everyone. Not because she cares about what she looks like. She'd go completely bald all day if people would just stop touching her arm, smiling sadly, giving her brave smiles.

In the parking lot Claire and Dayton are parked side by side.

"What a coincidence."

"Yes," says Dayton.

They get in their cars and drive opposite directions so when they meet up again at the dentist's office in the afternoon they are both surprised.

"Are you following me?" Dayton says.

Claire is taken aback but then realizes it's a joke. "Checkup?"

"I chipped a tooth playing hockey," Dayton says. She points to her teeth. There is a small chip out of one of the front ones.

"Oh dear. Playing hockey?"

"I'm in this ladies' leisure league. It's really fun. I moved here in the fall and my neighbour introduced me to the game. I should really wear a mouthguard."

"I have a woman friend who plays hockey. Trish Mantle. In fact, her husband, Frank, plays hockey with my husband, Ralph."

"Trish? She's the friend who got me to play. She's my neighbour."

"Small world. You live on Edgewood then? I'm right around the corner, a couple blocks away."

The women laugh.

"What a coincidence."

The street is iced over and it's hard to walk. The trees crack above her. Caroline walks clutching her homework to her chest. Friggin' cold, she thinks. The cold makes her eyes water. She has to pee. She always has to pee when it's cold outside. Although she wants the money, she kind of wishes her mom didn't tell this woman she would babysit. Caroline has a lot of homework and is feeling stressed all the time because her English teacher keeps piling on the projects. There's *Othello* now. And an Independent Studies Unit. There's something wrong with him, her teacher. He's angry all the time and takes it out on the class. One day he made a girl stand up in class and he tore her essay in half in front of her. She started to cry and the teacher said, "Don't be a sissy." Caroline was shocked. Caroline needs to do well in all her courses this year so that she's set for applying to universities next year. Seventeen years old and she feels already as if she's had enough — she's worried all the time, angry, anxious, losing weight. There's just too much going on in her life right now.

Dayton meets her at the door and ushers her into the warm house.

"That's a huge tree," Caroline says. "I walked past it every day going to school when I was a kid and I guess I never really noticed it."

Dayton looks out at the tree and nods. "Sometimes we don't notice things if they are always in front of us."

With the mood Caroline is in, with the sadness that always seems to follow her these days, the stress, Caroline thinks that this woman in front of her, this Dayton, is incredibly perceptive and, in fact, brilliant. Caroline gets a little teary and blushes. Everything makes her feel emotional these days — huge waves of highs and lows. Ever since her mother has been sick.

Dayton shows Caroline around the house. They tiptoe past little Carrie's room but Dayton doesn't take her in and instead shows her the sleeping child on the video baby monitor. Caroline has never seen one of these monitors before and she marvels at it.

"You can watch her all night long," Caroline says. "Look, she rolled. Look, she's sucking her thumb."

Dayton heads out the front door, clutching her hockey stick and bag. The bag is so big that she has to turn sideways but still she gets stuck. Caroline gives her a little push. They laugh.

"Thanks so much for doing this. I'm so glad I ran into your mom the other day. I won't be too late." Dayton takes a step down the stairs then turns and says, "Oh, I forgot about Max. The kitten. Don't let him out. There he is. Watch it —"

A kitten sneaks up behind Caroline and she uses her foot to stop him from going outside. He looks up at Caroline. A snobby look. As if he knows who the boss is. She looks down at him. He walks back towards the kitchen, tail in the air.

Caroline watches as Dayton meets up with Trish next door, one of her mom's old friends from before the cancer, and they load their bags and sticks into Trish's car. They beep as they pull out. Caroline waves. They drive off. Caroline still watches. She watches the tree. It's so huge, it takes up the entire sky. How could she never have noticed it before? She's never seen anything so large and scary. If this tree fell, it would definitely kill someone. In fact, it would probably take out quite a few houses. Caroline thinks about how her mom doesn't have many friends anymore and how she used to have lots of them. The before-cancer friends and no after-cancer friends. It's weird. You'd think that after cancer is when you'd need your friends the most, but Caroline's mother doesn't seem to want to do anything with anyone other than Caroline's dad. She turns back to the baby monitor and watches that. Soon she gets bored and turns on the TV to watch instead. Her homework lies open on the coffee table in front of her. Her English essay. Her ISU book. A book about war because that's what the mean English teacher said he wanted her to read. "But it's independent study," Caroline had said quietly, "shouldn't I pick it on my own?" And he exploded at her, shouted something about being a feminist. She teared up. Rushed out of the classroom. Now she's reading a book about war. And hating it.

When the phone rings it startles her. In the video monitor she sees little Carrie stir. The last thing she wants is for the baby to wake up. Caroline likes kids, but she really doesn't want to have to deal with tears or diapers right now. Besides, Carrie won't know who she is and might be startled.

"Hello?"

There is a sound. Like wind. Like wind in a tunnel. And then a shout. Click.

"Hello?" Caroline shrugs and hangs up the phone. A shout. A man's shout or a woman's shout? And would she call it a shout or a scream? Or just background noise, as if the caller was in a busy place? Caroline wraps her sweater tighter around her torso and looks around the big living room. She looks at the blackened windows. She looks at the front door. Did she lock it?

Caroline shakes her head. Wrong number, she thinks. In the video monitor little Carrie flicks off her sheets and rolls to one side of the crib. Caroline can see her breathing, that's how good the video is. Caroline turns back to the TV and then, suddenly, she begins to cry. Caroline's fear is palpable. She is seventeen years old and her mother is dying of breast cancer. Her mother had no hair, no eyebrows, no eyelashes even. It's growing back now, the hair, but still. Caroline sobs quietly. She stares straight ahead and just lets the tears roll down her cheeks. Her eyes hurt all the time. If they aren't actually swollen from crying they are tingling and she is about to cry. She wakes up with exhausted eyes. A headache. Dryness. As if she's leaked out all the water inside of her. Her chest and stomach hurt constantly. Caroline thought it would get better, that she would get used to this, but she hasn't. Her mother has been operated on, she has had chemo and radiation. Now there is peach fuzz on her head. And Caroline continues to cry.

The phone rings again.

Max chirps and jumps into Caroline's lap.

She startles and knocks the video monitor off the table.

"Hello?"

The same thing. A sound. Like wind. Coming at her from within a tunnel. A shout. Male? Female? Click.

"Fuck," Caroline says and continues to cry. Max turns twice in her lap, his small claws digging into her jeans. They are sharp and they hurt. He settles himself and begins to purr. And then Caroline hears another sound. A howl that starts low and reaches higher into the air — a pitched, anxious howl. She looks around. What could it be? Then she sees the monitor on the floor and there it is, that's where the sound is coming from — the baby crying from upstairs. Caroline wipes her eyes and places Max on the other side of the sofa. He sticks to her and she has to wrench him off. He meows, annoyed. She reaches down and picks up the video monitor from the floor and looks at it. Little Carrie is standing in her crib, staring straight at the screen, straight at Caroline. Her mouth is a round, gaping hole. Her eyes are wide and ringed with tears, terrified. Caroline drops the monitor and rushes up the stairs.

The phone rings again.

Caroline doesn't answer it.

There is a knock on the door. A voice. "Knock knock," the voice says.

Caroline doesn't hear it.

In the baby's room Caroline reaches down into the crib to pick little Carrie up but the baby doesn't know her and screams even louder when she sees the older girl's arms coming in. There is a sudden smell in the air. Caroline stands there, seventeen years old, her mother dying, an essay on *Othello* due, a fucking war book to read, and a baby shrieking so loudly she can't hear herself think. There is the smell of shit in the air and someone crank-phoning her. Caroline resumes crying. She joins the child.

Both cry. One loud and wailing and uncomfortable. The other with shoulders shaking, big, loud gulps of air. Until finally the baby stops crying and studies the older girl. She moves over to the far side of her crib and curls up in the corner, one eye open on the big girl who is still sobbing, and she sniffles once, twice, closes her eye and falls asleep. Her soiled diaper looks huge, warm and wet.

Downstairs there is a knock again. A quiet tap, tap, tap.

Caroline settles down on the floor of the baby's room and looks around. There are bears and dolphins and dinosaurs and princesses — toys everywhere. There are books in a large pile in the corner. A closet door is open and Caroline can see small, wildly coloured dresses hanging in a row, a laundry bag on the floor. Caroline doesn't remember when she was little, but she remembers her brother, Jude, when he was young and how their mother would bend into the crib to take Jude out when he cried. How she would soothe him by blowing on his neck until he giggled. Caroline would say, "Now me," and her mother would lean down and blow on Caroline's neck and the warm breath would turn cold quickly and Caroline would shiver and laugh.

How is it possible, Caroline thinks, to lose your mother? She's not even gone, and I've lost her. Once her mother bent down to blow on her neck, now Caroline is taller than her mother and her mother will never blow on her neck to make her giggle again.

They didn't tell Caroline or Jude about the cancer until it was confirmed and there was no turning back. So there were a couple months where the siblings knew something was up, where they could feel it in the air, which seemed thick with sorrow. Caroline thought her parents were getting a divorce. She assumed, from the way Jude was acting, that he didn't think anything. He just waded through the liquid air sluggishly and came and left the house silently and with skill. He wouldn't talk to Caroline about it. Caroline complained a lot: why was everyone so quiet? Why was everyone ignoring her? "Why," she asked one night, "is everyone being so nice to each other?"

Her mother. The operations. The chemotherapy. The radiation. Her nails cracked and fell off. Her hair fell out. Her eyebrows and eyelashes disappeared. Her mother's skin was covered in rashes. Her cheeks red and scaly.

Sometimes, still, Caroline catches her mother crying in the bathroom. The door is locked but Caroline can hear the deep, guttural sobs.

And all she can think, all the time, is *it's not fair*.

"Life isn't fair," her father says. "Get used to it."

But Caroline can't understand that. Or she doesn't want to understand that. It doesn't make sense to her. I'm only seventeen, Caroline thinks. For some reason I thought life was fair.

Max pushes open the door and comes into the room. Caroline stands, bends to scoop him up before he meows and wakes the baby, and carries him with her into the hall. The fresh air in the hall hits her. She really should have changed the baby's diaper.

The diaper reminds Caroline of the story circulating around her high school these days. Jude says it isn't true, but Caroline is sure it can happen. Liquid Leonard is what they call him now, all the kids. Left to die in his reclining chair. Left there for four months. Leaked straight through to the basement.

But the most disturbing thing about this story, Caroline thinks, is that his wife lived there with him. She kept taking in the dinner, left it there on his TV tray. She gave him the TV guide. She sprayed him daily with Raid to keep the flies off. When they found him, the story goes, he had that week's TV guide right beside him. And his dinner was only a day old.

"Can you imagine the smell?" Jude says.

Caroline thinks of him, Liquid Leonard, slowly sinking into the recliner. She thinks of his wife, not being able to handle his death, wanting to ignore it, thinking it isn't fair that he died before she did. She gags a little, there on the stairs at Dayton's house, a small gag as the imagined smell combines with the leftover diaper fumes from the baby's room. Max hisses and jumps out of her arms.

A door slams downstairs. Caroline jumps.

The phone rings again.

Dayton stands outside on the front porch, watching Caroline walk quickly down the dark sidewalk, trying not to slip on the ice, towards home. Strange girl. She looked stoned. Her eyes were all red. But Dayton supposes Caroline is a more appropriate babysitter than Trish's daughter, Rachel, who is only twelve. Even if Caroline might smoke pot.

Still, Dayton wishes the girl had got a ride home from her mother. Claire tried to pick her up. Dayton could hear her on the phone arguing. But Caroline wanted to walk and Claire didn't seem to have the will to fight her.

The hockey game went well tonight even if they lost again. Dayton is getting the hang of it. She's able to throw her small weight around a little more. She takes chances now. She trusts her equipment to protect her. And, even if it doesn't, she trusts her teammates to save her from harm.

Inside, the phone rings again. Caroline mentioned there were a lot of prank calls. Dayton wonders if it's John. She wouldn't be surprised if he was calling and hanging up. A grown man. It seems so childish. But Dayton doesn't know exactly what he is capable of — after all, Dayton took his daughter and disappeared. Dayton turns to go inside, to answer it, when she sees something in the mailbox. As she reaches for it, a pamphlet, something moves outside under the tree in the shadows. A person? A little man? A boy? She swivels quickly back to see what it is, but there is nothing there. Forgetting the pamphlet, Dayton goes inside and shuts the door. Locks it. The phone stops ringing. She leans back on the front door. She wonders when she will stop worrying about John, about the fact that the emails stopped, that he seems to have lost his job. When will she stop worrying? Is that even possible? When will she feel safe inside her house, or even outside of it? When will she be okay?

When Dayton stole Carrie out into the night, whisked her away from California, away from John, she didn't think it all through properly. She felt she had reason to leave. John's affair. John's verbal, emotional abuse. She was worried for herself. Worried for Carrie. But stealing your child in the dark of night, escaping through the air, lying to the customs officers, renting a house with cash and fake identification, and settling in as if nothing will hurt you, that's just plain crazy. What was she thinking? Dayton sinks down to the floor and takes Max into her lap. Was there no other option? What else could she have done? What if she had gone the normal route — divorce — and John had retained custody of Carrie? What if she couldn't see her baby ever again, or only on weekends? John, after all, had the job. Dayton had nothing. Except an old bottle of Prozac she is ashamed of, hidden in her underwear drawer. Prozac John could easily use against her.

"She is depressed," he could say. "She needs to take pills."

But Dayton hasn't touched the bottle of Prozac in years. Even when she feels she really needs to start taking it again, she doesn't touch it.

Dayton tortures herself with questions like this.

And what happens when the money she stole runs out? She has no credit cards anymore. He stopped those.

What happens when John comes after them? Because he will. She knows this.

Max purrs happily. His small spine curls and he is a ball of black in her lap, his tail wrapped up to his nose, sleeping. Dayton can smell herself. Her sweat, the salty, garlic smell of it. Her hair smells stale and mouldy, like her hockey equipment. She imagines that this is what Trish's husband, Frank, must smell like. The equipment Dayton wears is, after all, his. She can hear the wind pick up outside and the tree branches tap, tap, tap the side of her house.

Just now, when Dayton watched Caroline head home down the empty, dark street, she wished, with all her heart, that she was as lucky as Claire. Claire has it all: Ralph, her kind husband; two nice children; a safe, easy home for her daughter to head towards. Claire has everything. Even the little argument she had with Caroline on the phone about picking her up. Even that was done well. It's not fair, Dayton thought.

Dayton wishes that she had that scanner she was talking about in the grocery store. She would scan everything she wants in life, just bleep things into the hand-held device and, at the end of it all, she would drive her car up to the back of a store and load everything into it: a father for her baby, a house, a job, money, the legal right to live here, her groceries, even clothes, everything. Maybe she'd even scan another cat to keep Max company. Bleep.

Upstairs Carrie begins to cry. Dayton sighs and stands. She brushes the fur off her lap, makes sure the front door is locked, turns off the lights in the hall and downstairs, and climbs the stairs to see what Carrie needs. The smell hits her when she reaches the landing.

Outside, the tree taps. The pamphlet blows out of the mailbox. Outside, Caroline is almost home.

Outside, he waits under the gigantic tree, a smallish figure, and he watches the house. Then he ducks out from behind the tree and catches the pamphlet as it blows past.

And, further on, Claire stands, arms crossed on her chest, her fuzzy scalp shining, in her front window, waiting for her daughter to come home.

To: tomshutter@prestige.com
From: art@abernackieshelter.com
Subject: Followup to phone call

Tom,

I'm sorry I wasn't originally able to help you find the
man you were looking for. However, shortly after our phone
conversation I ran into him! What are the chances of that? I
knew he was not part of our shelter system. I was certain of
that. I am also certain that he has never used our shelter.
So I figured you were out of luck. Then, just this morning, I
ran into him. Literally. My car even bumped him a little. Let
me explain: he works at the full-service car wash on Braid
Street. My windshields were a bit steamy and I touched him
slightly with my front fender as I drove into the area where
they dry your car down after the automatic washing. They
use really soft towels. It's actually quite a good service.
Anyway, I didn't mean to bump him. It was an accident. All
of this doesn't matter and he took a grand tip from me, the
point is — he works there. You can'find him now. Just go
down to Braid Street and get in that god-awful line of cars
needing to be washed. I'm sure this is your man — 100% sure —
how many men sport scars like that? I've never seen anything
like it.

Hope this helps you. I think it's great that you want to pay
him for helping you rake. I can understand that completely.
Please don't hesitate to visit our Men's Shelter anytime you
are in the area — we could use men like you volunteering!

Cheerio,
Art Spack

Abernackie Men's Shelter
Braithwaite Drive, Parkville

8

It's Lego in the basement with her brother, Charlie, or reading by herself in her room or helping her mother wash up the lunch dishes or watching her father watch sports on TV. That's all there is. So when Becky knocks on the door and asks Rachel if she wants to hang out, Rachel decides that's the best option or alternative. Rachel doesn't particularly like Becky but she hates Sundays even more.

Option and alternative were two words on this week's spelling test. Two words she got wrong. Now her mother is making her use them at every opportunity — which was another word on the test. Rachel has no idea how using a word will make her spell it correctly. But she has no option. Or optian? Altarnetive?

"What do you want to do?" Becky asks. She is leaning in the doorway, letting all the cold air in. Rachel won't let her into the hall. She never lets Becky in. Becky is sick of it. "Let's hang out at your house. My house is too messy."

Ridiculous, Rachel thinks — which is one of last week's words — Becky's house is spotless. "You just don't want me to mess up your bedroom."

"Yeah, well," Becky says. "It's true. You always make a mess."

Rachel shrugs. "Let's go up to the school then." ·

Becky looks behind her, out into the street. "I guess."

"Shut the front door," Rachel's mother calls from the kitchen. "You're letting all the cold air in."

Rachel rolls her eyes. It's always "you're letting all the cold air in" or, in the summer, "you're letting all the hot air in." Rachel wishes her mom would make up her mind.

It is crazy cold. Becky runs home to put on her snow pants and boots, her hat, scarf and mittens. Rachel begins the process of suiting up. It's like getting ready for deep-sea diving, her grandpa always says. Rachel snorts when he says it, as if it's funny, but she's sick of him saying it. Every damn time she sees him he says it, "deep-sea diving." She thinks he got it from a movie. It's not even his own line. But she humours him, because he's old. And because he's her grandpa and he gives her great gifts. And she loves him. That too.

Rachel doesn't know why adults think they are so funny. Her mother is always cracking jokes that make no sense. Her father laughs loudly at himself. Even her teachers think they are hilarious.

"You certainly woke up on the wrong side of the bed this morning," her mother says, coming out of the kitchen and drying her hands on her thighs. "You've been muttering to yourself all morning with a nasty scowl on your face."

"So?"

"Just mentioning it. Don't shoot me." Rachel's mom holds her hands up as if she is under arrest and backs into the kitchen. "Have a nice afternoon. Don't freeze to death." She laughs.

Hilarious, Rachel thinks.

The girls pass the new woman, Dayton, getting out of her car. She isn't dressed for winter. She isn't even wearing mittens or a hat but she has great leather boots on. High ones. With a bit of a heel. She's from California, Rachel thinks, so she has an excuse. And she has fashion sense. Rachel wishes she were from California. Actually anywhere else than here. Rachel's sick of winter. She also wishes she had fashion sense. She looks down at her snowsuit and sighs.

Becky thinks Dayton is stunning. When she gets older she's going to live alone with her own baby daughter and wear boots like that. Becky is certain of this. Her house will be spotless, her baby won't even drool. Everything will be perfect.

"Hello, girls," Dayton says as she bends into the back seat to get her daughter.

She is thin and lovely. Rachel babysits for her occasionally (there is no way she's getting that word right this week — two c's and two l's but only one s — it makes no sense).

"Hi."

The girls walk on.

"My hair is the same colour as hers," Becky says.

"What?"

"Me and her," Becky thumbs back towards Dayton, still bending into her car. "Our hair."

"No, it isn't. Hers is much blonder. Yours is dirty blond."

"No, it's not. It's not dirty." Becky knows her voice is shrill but she can't seem to make it lower.

"So what?" Rachel says. "I babysit for her."

"You shouldn't be. You're too young."

Rachel speeds up her walking. Her snow pants shuffle together, making a shushing noise. "I'm not too young. Why would she hire me to babysit if I was too young? You're just jealous that she never asked you."

"I'm too busy to babysit," Becky says. She fingers her newly capped tooth. The canker sore is gone now, but the cold makes her mouth ache.

"Yeah, right." Rachel laughs. "Busy with what?"

"Homework."

"I'm in your class," Rachel says. "We never get homework."

"I work on my spelling every week. That's homework. Practice makes perfect." Becky purses her lips and blows through her teeth. She knows Rachel is failing spelling. In fact, she knows Rachel is really dumb when it comes to spelling. She got "periodical" wrong. How is that possible? It's exactly like it sounds. She got "possible" wrong too. The weird thing was, she got "impossible" right.

Like most things she does, Becky finds spelling really easy.

"You piss me off," Rachel says.

"Rachel."

"Well, you do."

"Well, you shouldn't swear."

"Piss is not a swear word."

"Yes, it is."

"No, it's not. It's something you do. We all piss. Don't you? Piss. Piss. Piss."

"It is a swear word. Maybe if you learned some new words you wouldn't need to swear. Maybe if you learned some new words you'd be a better speller. My mom says that people who swear just don't have a large enough vocabulary."

"Fuck off. I can spell that," Rachel says. "Can you?"

They have trudged up to the schoolyard and they stand there now, looking around. It is empty. The climber looks stiff in the wind. The trees bend. Snow blows across the field.

The schoolyard is a movie set. An expanse of violent white,

a small climbing structure, several scraggly trees. A fence. And nothing else. When it is recess or lunchtime the yard is full of bodies, but on Sunday it is deserted and dismal. It is vacant and insignificant. A ghost playground. Rachel rubs her mittens together and walks towards the climber. Becky joins her.

"We aren't allowed on that in the winter," Becky says. "If we fall it'll be really bad."

"Why? The snow is soft."

"But they say we can't."

"Who cares?" Rachel climbs up and sits on the slide. "There's no one here. It's not school time. They don't own us. Whee," she says sarcastically — which is another spelling word for the week, sarcasm — "this is fun."

Becky rolls her eyes and looks away. She looks around for the man in the Falcons hoodie. Even though he's wearing a winter coat now, she still thinks of him as the man in the hoodie. She rubs her cheeks with her mittens. Her mouth aches. The hoodie man isn't there. He never is when anyone else is around. The other day Becky saw him walking past Dayton's house. The new woman. He was looking at her house, keeping watch on it. As if he were looking for someone. Becky stared at him for about ten seconds, studied his back. He had his winter coat over his hoodie, but he keeps the hood up so she still can't see his face. Becky wonders if Rachel has seen him, but she doesn't want to ask because Rachel will roll her eyes at Becky, like her teachers do.

He's not here now. Maybe he is invisible. Maybe only she can see him. Maybe she's just stupid.

Not as stupid as Rachel, of course. At least she can spell.

Over the fence comes a kid bundled up even thicker and bulkier than the two girls. The kid gets stuck a bit at the top of the wire fence but pulls free and drops to the snowy ground and begins the difficult shuffle towards them, struggling in the wind and snow. Rachel sits on top of the climbing structure and watches the kid's long approach, stumbling and tripping in the snow.

"Who's that?"

Becky turns and watches. The snowsuit is blue. That could mean anything. It is no one they recognize.

"I don't know."

It's a girl.

"Hey," she says, panting from the exertion of pulling her snow pants and boots through deep snow. She stands too close to Becky and looks at her. Becky stares into the new girl's dark brown eyes and says, "Hey," back. They are the same height. "You're in my personal space," Becky says, finally, and backs up.

"Yeah?" The girl turns and walks over to the climber. "I'm here to climb. I don't care about your personal space."

"You aren't supposed to," Becky says. "Climb, that is. You are supposed to care about people's personal spaces. It's impolite not to."

"Come on up," Rachel says. "You might as well ignore her. She never stops talking." The day has gotten interesting, Rachel thinks as she watches the new girl climb up the structure. The girl dangles from the monkey bars, her padded legs swishing as she swings upside down.

"Be careful." Becky knows all about concussions. Head injuries can last a lifetime. She did a project on it in school in the fall. Sometimes athletes who have had concussions years ago turn violent and kill their wives. Sometimes they die for no reason. Becky also did a project on shock and another on post-traumatic stress disorder. Becky thinks that maybe someday she could be a doctor or a psychiatrist with all she knows about these things.

"Becky, Jesus," Rachel says. "Let a girl have some fun."

"Yeah," the new girl says, her face turning red as she hangs upside down and glares at Becky.

This is one of those times where Becky should just turn around and go home. Often Becky feels that way. In an awkward situation, when someone is doing something stupid or bad, Becky knows that she should go home. She usually does. But today, she stays. She's curious to see what happens next. She sort of hopes the new girl will fall on her head. Besides, her mom and dad have been arguing a lot lately and so she doesn't want to go home and sit in that house of tension and silence.

The girl pulls herself up and sits high on top of the bars. "I come here a lot," she says. "Most weekend days."

"Where are you from?" Rachel asks. "You don't go to this school."

"Maybe I do."

"That's impossible," Becky says. "We'd know you then. We know everyone at this school."

"Not everyone," Rachel says. "But most everyone."

"I pretty much know everyone," Becky says. "I'm on the student council."

Rachel sticks her tongue out at Becky. "You don't know the kindergarten kids, do you? Or the ones who are new to the school this week? There's always someone new to the school."

"Yeah, well." The girl wipes her runny nose with her mitten. Rachel slips down the snowy slide and walks towards Becky. They stand there together and look up at the girl on the climber.

"What's your name?" Rachel asks.

"None of your beeswax."

"Fuck," Rachel says. "You're weird."

"Rachel," Becky gasps.

The new girl looks impressed with what just came out of Rachel's mouth. "Hannah," she says, as if they have passed a test and she is giving them something for it. Good girls, her smile says. "My name's Hannah."

"Fuck," Becky whispers so that the other girls almost can't hear her. "Hannah." Becky likes that name. It's a palindrome. She loves palindromes. Anna. Eve. Noon. Civic.

Rachel giggles. "Nice one, Becky."

It turns out that Hannah lives nearby. She attends the Catholic school in town. She says it's better. She says the kids are smarter. Because this is interesting, they have never met anyone from the Catholic school, and because she has promised them hot chocolate and they are cold and bored, Rachel and Becky decide to follow the girl home.

"How far is it?" Becky is looking around. They've been walking in a direction she hasn't walked before, away from her house, not towards it.

"Not far. Come on. Stop dragging your feet." Hannah walks quickly ahead of them. "Come on, come on, come on. You guys are slow."

It's a small house. With a roof over where you'd park the car. Becky says, "You have a car park," because she likes to show that she knows things. Rachel sighs. There is no car in the driveway. Hannah opens the side door and walks inside. Rachel and Becky stare at the spot she vacated and then look at each other.

"Should we go inside?"

"There's hot chocolate and I'm freezing," Rachel says.

"But we're not allowed to go into strange people's houses."

"She's not strange, just a little weird," Rachel says. She smirks.

"Come on," Hannah shouts. "You're letting in the cold air."

Letting in the cold air, letting in the hot air. Rachel pauses for a minute, thinking about her mom, and then takes one step

122

forward. Becky holds her back. Grabs hold of her arm. "We don't know her. We shouldn't be going inside. What if it's a trap? Stranger Danger."

Hannah pops her head out and waves her arms. "Seriously, hurry up."

"I don't even like her," Becky says. "Do you?"

Rachel thinks about her own house. She thinks about Charlie playing Lego by himself in the basement. Her mom and dad are probably in front of the TV watching hockey. Maybe something good is cooking for dinner. But Rachel doesn't want to go home. Becky is a drag and Rachel wants some excitement in her life. Everything seems to happen the same way every day. Winter. School. Weekends. Homework. Spelling tests. Nothing new. Nothing different.

"I'm going in," Rachel says. "You can walk home alone if you want. In fact," she whispers, "get lost. I don't want you here anyway."

But Becky doesn't want to leave. There is no way she's going anywhere alone these days. She pulls at her mouth, and then follows Rachel into the house.

The smell hits them first. Cigarettes and foot odour. It's oppressive, which is a word from three weeks ago — two p's, two s's. Hannah is standing by a dirty stove, stirring something in a pot. The stove top is like something out of that TV commercial that Becky thinks is so ridiculous. The one where the spaghetti sauce is baked on and splattering everywhere and the woman takes her bottle of stove cleaner and, with one swipe, cleans it all off. Becky always wonders to herself, when she sees this commercial, Who could ever let their stove top get that messy while they cook? How is that possible? She wants to shout, "Just wipe while you cook."

Here it is, though. Right in front of her. Proof that the commercial could actually be correct. Becky seriously doubts, however, that one swipe of a paper towel would clean this mess.

Hannah hovers over the stove. She still has her boots on and her snow pants but she has taken off her jacket. Her long, blond hair is knotted and greasy. It hangs over her back, covering her shoulders. She scratches it. Her t-shirt says, "I'm With Stupid," and has an arrow pointing to the left. Even though the arrow isn't pointing towards her, Rachel feels insulted.

"I like marshmallows in mine," Hannah says. "Do you?"

Becky and Rachel nod. They are burning up in their snowsuits but they are afraid to move. Rachel finally unzips herself and walks, tracking snow, towards a small, messy table. She moves a pair of jeans from the back of a chair and sits down. Becky remains standing in the doorway. Ready to run if she needs to. Someone coughs in the next room. Becky jumps. Rachel fidgets.

"Where's your mom?"

Hannah says, "None of your beeswax."

"I'm just asking."

"Here, drink your hot chocolate."

Rachel picks the hardened skin of hot milk off the top of her hot chocolate. She eats it. Becky feels as if she might be sick. She looks at her mug of hot chocolate on the table.

And then, suddenly, his shape fills up the doorway.

"Hey," Hannah says.

"Hey," he says back.

Rachel would never have guessed Hannah's mom could be so beautiful. Hannah herself isn't that great looking. At least not according to Rachel's standards which, because she reads *Seventeen* magazine and watches *Entertainment Tonight*, are high.

And Hannah's mom is really nice too. Not just beautiful.

It's hard to believe when you look at Hannah with her greasy hair. It's hard to believe when you look at Hannah's weird older brother. Standing there in bare feet with his hands in his jean pockets, his face all goofy and drooly. His nose running. He keeps wiping his nose with the back of his hand. When he laughs it is long and drawn out, more of a horn sound than a laugh. Hawww. Rachel squirms. And sometimes it's a low, growling sound. He laughs often.

Becky is long gone. She bolted the minute she saw Terry. She ran straight into Hannah's mom, Leah, who was coming in from outside, grocery bags in her hands. Becky picked herself up, side-swiped the car now under the car park and took off down the road. Rachel shrugged. Who knows what gets into that idiot? Just because she lives across the street from Becky, it doesn't mean Rachel has to take care of her. People think that if you can spell you're smart. But Becky proves that's wrong. In fact, there are a lot of things she can do better than Becky — basketball, for one, running, swearing.

Hannah doesn't seem bothered by her brother. She gives him Becky's cup of hot chocolate and sits him down next to Rachel as you would a child. Takes his hand and leads him to the table. Rachel guesses that Hannah is used to her brother — she must be, she lives with him — and that, with time, he won't bother Rachel either. Kind of like Rachel's brother, Charlie, who is annoying when you first meet him, but can also be kind of interesting and a little nice. Although Rachel would never admit that out loud.

"Now, Terry, it's hot," Hannah says. She blows on the cup of hot chocolate and Terry laughs and copies her, blowing so hard the hot chocolate spills over the edge. Splatters the table. No one moves to clean it up. Boy, Rachel thinks, wouldn't that piss Becky off. Becky's so afraid of mess and dirt that she would panic if she saw this.

Rachel begins to feel uncomfortable but when Hannah's mom comes back into the kitchen, she relaxes. Terry moves his chair closer to Rachel's and now she knows exactly where the foot odour is coming from. Then he puts his hand on her thigh and squeezes. Rachel jumps up.

"Oh, honey," Leah says. "Don't touch people. It's not polite."

Terry laughs. "I touch."

"You're such a retard," Hannah says.

Everyone looks at her. Rachel shudders. Her mouth falls open. Then Leah and Terry burst out laughing. Hawww.

"He is," Leah says, lighting a cigarette. "He's such a retard." Leah blows smoke up towards the ceiling. Even though Rachel wants desperately — another spelling word — to leave, even though she knows you never call anyone a retard no matter what, she thinks Leah looks glamorous. She studies Leah's profile until she's completely taken it in. Later on Rachel will pose in front of the mirror, holding a pencil. She will blow her imaginary smoke to the ceiling and laugh and say, "He's such a retard," and it will feel like sinning because retard is a word that is so much worse than fuck or piss.

"Do you wear a bra yet?" Hannah asks.

"What?"

"A bra. Do you wear one?" Hannah stares at Rachel.

"I don't know."

"Oh, you'd know, honey," Leah laughs.

"Because," Hannah says, "if you can put a pencil under your boobs and it stays there when you are standing up then you need a bra. That's a fact."

Rachel feels her face go hot. "Oh," she says. She can't think of anything else to say. She looks down at her thigh, where Terry touched her. She can still feel his hot hand.

"True," Leah says, contemplatively, "a pencil or a pen. My mother used to say that. It's one of those things that people say."

"I have to go now," Rachel says. She stands. She zips up her jacket. She starts towards the side door. "Thanks for the hot chocolate. It was nice to meet you."

Out the door, into the car park. Rachel turns back and sees Terry standing up by the kitchen table. His hands are deep in his jean pockets. He looks right at her. Leah swats his hands away from his pants and waves goodbye to Rachel. She mouths something, but Rachel doesn't catch it because she is walking quickly away.

At home Rachel goes straight into the bathroom.

"We're eating early tonight," her mother calls out. "I have hockey. You don't have to take care of Carrie. Dayton found someone else for tonight."

In the bathroom Rachel lifts her shirt and looks at her chest. Two small bumps. The nipples are large. There is no way a pencil would stay.

"Did you see the new bear?" her mom calls out. "In the laundry room? A Pig Bear. He's a pig, but he's a bear. In pig costume." Her mother laughs.

"Oh," Rachel calls back. Shut up, she thinks. A pig bear?

The phone rings.

Rachel picks up a pencil from on top of a crossword magazine left by the toilet. She grabs a roll of baby fat from her stomach and pushes it together, placing the pencil in the crease. When she lets go of the roll the pencil falls out.

"Rachel? Is Becky in there with you?"

"I'm in the bathroom, Mom. Stop bothering me."

"Is Becky with you?"

"Why would Becky be in here with me?"

"What are you doing in there? Are you okay?"

"I'm busy. Don't bother me. Leave me alone."

"Becky's mom just called. Becky isn't home yet. Do you know where she is? Wasn't she with you this afternoon? I thought you two went out together? Didn't you come home together?"

Rachel stares at the pencil on the floor but all she can see is Terry with his hands deep down in the pockets of his jeans and it makes her feel weird. He is a retard, she thinks. And then she feels nauseous. She picks up the pencil and holds it like a cigarette. She blows imaginary smoke up to the ceiling. She could easily be as glamorous as Hannah's mother.

"Rachel? Are you listening? Come out now. What are you doing in there?"

"I'm busy, Mom. I'll be out in a minute."

Rachel can hear her mother murmuring into the phone. Stupid Becky is probably wandering around lost. She'll get them both in trouble.

I may not be good at spelling, Rachel thinks, but at least I'm not an idiot like Becky. Rachel knows that this is a word that would never be on the spelling test because it's too easy. Idiot. Although Rachel also knows that you could, maybe, spell it with an It, as in Itiot. But she also knows that if it was on the spelling test she'd have no problem spelling it the way she sees it: B-E-C-K-Y.

Rachel smiles into the mirror. She puts the bra determiner/ cigarette pencil in her back pocket and leaves the bathroom.

Her mother is standing in the kitchen. She places the phone into its base and turns and looks at Rachel. That's when Rachel hears it. From outside. A screaming, screeching sound. Becky's mother calling out for her daughter. "Becky. Becky!" Rachel's mother's face goes white. Rachel's father turns off the TV and sits up in his recliner. The couch is covered with scraps of material — new bear accessories being made in front of the TV.

"Their only child," Rachel's mother whispers, as if losing one of either Rachel or Charlie would be okay, because there would always be the other. "Missing. Can you imagine? Remember that guy who came here before Christmas? Remember him? The one with the pamphlet? Oh god."

"What guy?" Rachel says. "What guy?"

"Never you mind." Rachel's mother and father look at each other.

Rachel goes to the front door and looks out across the street. Becky's mother has her hands cupped in front of her mouth and is calling, calling, calling. Looking left and right. Behind Rachel her mother begins to put on her coat and boots.

"She's not missing," Rachel says.

"What do you mean?"

"She's just lost. That's all. She just got lost. She's stupid."

"Rachel. No matter what you call it, Becky isn't home where she should be. And it's getting dark out. Where were you two this afternoon? What happened? Come out and help us find her. You can tell us where you were so we know where to start looking."

"There has to be another alternative," Rachel whispers, "another option." But her mother doesn't hear her as she rushes out the front door into the cold. "A-L-T-A-R-N-I-T-I-V-E." Rachel isn't sure if that's right or not. The snow begins to fall. Rachel hates the English language.

Grudgingly, she pulls on her boots and coat. As she comes out of the house, shutting the door behind her, she looks up the street in the direction of the school. She walks to the sidewalk. There is a figure walking towards her, coming out of the heavy snow. A teenager. He comes closer, pauses slightly in front of Rachel, and then walks on. And there, up the street, towards the school, at the end of the block, is Becky. She is walking slowly, her snow pants rubbing together, her boots thick with snow. She is staring down at the sidewalk.

"Hey, Mom. There she is."

And Becky's mother pushes past Rachel and rushes up the street towards her daughter.

Monday they are supposed to walk to school together but Rachel quickly moves ahead and ignores Becky. Both girls are grounded for going to a stranger's house. They had what their parents called "a serious talking to." Rachel is furious — she knows how to spell that. Becky refuses to talk.

"The least you could do is apologize." Rachel turns and shouts this at her.

Becky says nothing. She is still relishing the feeling of having her mother rush towards her in the snow, worried. There was something about that that made her feel so good, so wanted.

The spelling test is today. They walk on in silence. Rachel knows Becky will do well on it. And Rachel knows she isn't ready. She knows she'll make plenty of mistakes. No matter how much she tries. She always does.

To: puckbunnybrady@pik.com
From: puckbunnybrady@pik.com
Subject: Goalies and Beer

Hey Gals,

Sorry to pester you with emails so often, but we've been
having some issues with the goalies this season and we need
to reiterate our rules and regulations. All of you have signed
an accident waiver, in case of injury. Remember that? I came
around and collected them before the first game of the year.
So when you invite your fourteen-year-old son to put on goalie
gear because your regular goalie doesn't show up, and he gets
hurt, we get sued. This is why we don't let just anyone play.
We've had some complaints lately — from goalies and from
other teams. I realize you didn't win with your fourteen-year-
old son as goalie, but still, the other gals thought it was
unfair. After all, he is younger and more fit than most of us,
right? If your goalie doesn't show up, someone from your team
— who has signed a waiver — can play goalie for you. It's not
the end of the world! And, goalies, please phone your captains
if you can't make it. It's not nice to leave everyone hanging.
Be a good team player and act responsibly and with courtesy.

Which leads me to the second reason for writing this note: if
you drink beer in the change room after the game — you know
who you are — make sure you take the bottles home with you.
Last week some kids found a few bottles in the garbage cans
and proceeded to break them in the showers! I can't stress to
you enough how much trouble we got in for that — and how many
stitches there were on some of the male senior team's feet.
I know, I know, who would take a shower in those horrible,
moldy, contaminated stalls? But the men sometimes do and the
beer bottles are dangerous. It's not really our fault, you
say? Well, we aren't allowed to bring beer into the change
room in the first place! Those are the rules.

So: no extra goalies or players and beer bottles go home with
you. Capisce?

Play on!

Tina Brady
Parkville Ice Kats
Co-ordinator Extraordinaire

9

Before Jude came here, his father said to his mother, "Claire, I have always loved your hair."

Now Jude is in the arena watching the women play hockey. Wednesday night. Dead of winter.

What he doesn't get, what doesn't make sense to him, is why his father would say that now. It's rubbing it in, pouring salt on the wound, kicking her when she's down. Jude knows his father didn't mean anything by it, he just said it. He told his fuzzy-headed wife that he has always loved her hair. It was something to say at the time.

"It is already growing back, Claire," he said. "It's prickly."

"Someday it'll be long again," she said, rubbing her peach fuzz. "It's growing slower than I thought it would." Jude watched his mother watch his sister leave the room. Dinner was over. Everyone sat around looking at each other and then his father said that about her hair and then, one at a time, they all left the room.

The team is getting better. And the silly shouts and whistles and "woo hoos" have almost stopped. The occasional one here and there, but mostly they are serious and busy out there on the ice. Jude thinks he might like watching women's hockey better than men's hockey. This white team in particular. There is something about the way they play, the way they hold themselves out there on ice, the way they have attitude but in a nice way. They don't fight on the ice and Jude likes that because there is enough violence in the world. In fact, they avoid a fight. Anytime an opposing player tries to smash someone into the boards, the white team backs away. They even help the other team up if they fall. Stop and put their hands out. Pull the player up from the ice. It seems to cause the opposite effect than you would think it would. The other team becomes more and more aggressive the nicer the white team is.

Jude knows that some of them are probably moms. His mother's age. When they are in their equipment they look like anyone — teenagers or college girls. Some of them even look like boys. Jude likes to imagine his mother, if she were healthy, playing hockey. This is why he keeps coming back. He gets his women's hockey fix every Wednesday. Imagining that when his mom gets better he'll bring her here and show her and encourage her to sign up to play. Lately he's the only one in the seats. Sometimes the women's husbands or kids or boyfriends show up to cheer them on, but now that it's really cold outside he seems to be the only fan. Sometimes there is only one other guy, the one always talking on his BlackBerry. Once there was someone's mother, a much older woman, and she carried one of those foam hands with the index finger up. The hand said, "#1 Maple Leafs" on it. She waved it occasionally, but mostly she looked at the ground. She might have slept a little, nodded off.

By the hot dog vendor, in the lobby of the arena, there is always a kid playing on his iPad. Every Wednesday he's there. Jude isn't sure if he's there because his mom is one of the players or if he's there because he's attached to the hot dog vendor in some way. He's probably about seven years old but he acts like he's about three. Jude avoids him. If Jude catches his eye the kid won't stop talking to him. The hot dog vendor is a short, balding older man. He doesn't speak English. All he can say is "hot dog" and then he points to the condiments with a quizzical look on his face.

Tonight the white team is missing their best player and so they are floundering. A wave of white against a sea of angry red. Luckily their goalie is good. The defence works hard. One player ends up stuck in the corner and does a little pirouette to get out. The white team cheers. She bows. A red forward knocks her over. As if by accident, by mistake. But the white team boos anyway. The red player bends to help the white up. That's new. Shame from the red team.

Jude watches two women on the white bench talking to each other. They are paying no attention to the game, they have no idea that the other forwards are signalling to them to replace them on the ice. Jude watches their gloved hands move as they chat away, having a great conversation. They are laughing.

"Trish, Jesus, get out here."

Trish skates out onto the ice. The white player who shouted to Trish heads onto the bench and continues the conversation Trish had been having with the woman standing there shuffling her feet back and forth in her skates. And then the shuffling woman is replaced by another skater and the two new women on the bench wave their arms and talk, as if continuing where the others left off. Jude wonders if they are talking about the same thing, or if they've started their own conversation about something completely different.

In the fall when his mother was first getting radiation, Jude would skip high school and hang out at his old elementary school and watch the kids in the playground. He would watch them run in circles. Or stand around bored. Or throw leaves or skip rope or whatever they did. He wanted to remember being there. Jude wanted to feel what he felt like before he knew about things he doesn't want to know about. What it felt like climbing the jungle gym. Running with a football. Talking to girls. His mother's cancer has made him painfully aware of his body, of its limits and its end.

Then he found this hockey and, besides, it's too cold to stand outside the school anymore. It was minus fifteen today, minus twenty-five with the wind chill. Compared to that, it's warm in the arena. Also, he was missing too many classes and he knows that soon the school would call his house and then his mother would start to ask questions. Jude doesn't want anything else to worry her. He prefers the quiet mourning his mother is doing with him now. They do this in front of the TV. They sit silently, not saying anything. And Jude thinks of it as mourning her long before she is gone. As if they are having their own private funeral. Over and over. He wonders if they'll do this for years.

There has been an accident on the ice and the guy in the stands with the BlackBerry is standing up, holding his BlackBerry out and shouting, "Do you want me to call for anyone?"

One of the players skated head-first into the boards. She has a helmet on, but still she looks woozy. Jude missed the action. He was thinking about his mother. Now he's thinking about concussions. His mind wanders these days. He's turning into his dad, who is always forgetting where he put the car keys, forgetting to pick up the takeout dinner he ordered on the way home from work, or forgetting his own name. (Jude heard him on the phone one day, "My name? It's . . ." and his father went silent. Then he hung up. Quickly.)

The woman is helped off the ice. The man with the BlackBerry leaves, tripping slightly as he walks down the steep stairs, his overcoat flapping behind him. Jude watches him appear below, near the change-room doors, and then he disappears into one of them, still holding out his BlackBerry as if it's a flashlight. "I've got a phone," he shouts. "I'm coming in."

The white team stands around on their skates and looks at each other. The referee blows the whistle and soon they are skating again — a little more timidly, wary of the hard boards. The women on the bench are even more animated now. Jude watches their actions, the way they talk through their face guards. He can see the glint of their white teeth. Something exciting has happened. They flap their arms.

The thing is — they didn't tell him. Or his sister, Caroline. They didn't tell anyone — all spring, some of summer. Before the operation and the chemo Jude's mom and dad knew that she had cancer, they knew what was coming, but they didn't say anything for a couple of months.

"We didn't want to worry you until we had all the test results," his mom said.

Jude's not convinced that was the best way to go about it. Sure he would have been worried for a couple of months while he waited for the results, but by not telling him his mother had no one to talk to about it. No one to mourn with besides his father. Because, now that he knows, he's worried. He's been worried since they told him. So they didn't save him from anything. Jude knew there was something going on in the house, he could feel it in the air, he could see it in the way his mother held herself — she was straighter somehow and she kept her arms crossed in front of her chest as if always protecting herself. He could feel it in the way his father touched his mother whenever he left the room. He could hear it in the sounds of sniffing and nose-blowing coming from the bathroom.

"We were protecting you," his dad said.

The woman who was hurt comes out of the locker room and

heads back out onto the ice. Both teams, red and white, stop playing and watch her skate to the team bench. Then they all clap and cheer. Jude finds himself clapping too. He claps his hands in the pouch of his hoodie, hidden from view. Only he can hear the noise his hands make. The injured woman holds up her stick and then the whistle blows and the teams play.

One day at the elementary school Jude noticed a kid was looking at him. He'd been fading out, staring at the brick wall of the school, hanging his hands over the wire fence, thinking about things, and then he felt something and saw this girl looking straight at him. He looked back. She took off. He went back to school. Checked himself in at the office — "Doctor appointment," he said — and went back to English class. Learned about *To Kill a Mockingbird*, and thought that Atticus would be a great name for a dog.

The next time he went to the elementary school that same kid was there staring at him. It gave him the creeps. She stood there, glaring. He hid in his hoodie. The girl called the teacher over and Jude took off down the street.

His mother seems better now. The radiation is over and soon her hair will grow fully back. He is seeing it grow every day. Right now she has itchy peach fuzz. She's taking Tamoxifen, she had Herceptin transfusions, but soon everything will end. She's calmer now, almost spiritual. Like she's come to grips with it all, like she can finally think of other things. As if she's faced the devil and knows now she can fight him. Jude's father still touches her whenever he comes and goes but there are times when the whole family almost, almost, almost forgets. Times. Small, tiny, miniscule times. Or at least it seems that way sometimes, that everyone but Jude forgets.

He can still hear her sniffing in the bathroom.

The pirouette woman has done another weird spin. She was

once a figure skater or dancer, Jude is sure of it. She is graceful when she needs speed and force. She's not a very good player. Then, suddenly, the injured woman skates out to play defence. There she is. Jude knows it's her because her stick has pink tape wrapped around the blade. She lets out some sort of a war cry as she skates towards her own net, her head down like a bull running towards red. Her legs look wobbly and Jude closes his eyes because he can't watch. The woman obviously has a concussion. Jude remembers a kid on his basketball team in grade seven who had a concussion — wobbly, woozy, wild and violent, then sleepy — he remembers the kid collapsing in the change room after the game. The woman slides to a stop right before her own goalie and then, like a Victorian heroine, she faints. Melts into a puddle at the goalie's skates.

Everyone shouts at once.

There is a pink stained-glass window in the hallway at Jude's house. One of those windows that every house in his neighbourhood seems to have, pink with swirls. Some white circles and some pink swirls. The window at Jude's house has a crack in it. Something small. No one would really notice. But Jude sees it and it seems to him as if the crack has gotten bigger lately, as if it has spread somehow. If he puts his lips to it he can taste the cold air coming in from outside even though there is a storm window blocking the flow. And this is kind of how he feels about his mother's sickness. As if it's a crack slowly getting bigger, as if someday it will break and everything will shatter and the cold air will be let in.

The woman is taken off the ice on a stretcher. Two men who work at the arena and the hot dog vendor are on the ice in their running shoes. So is the guy with the BlackBerry. The weird kid is standing next to Jude. He appeared out of nowhere. He holds up his iPad to show Jude what he's doing and Jude nods. The kid is making pottery — he uses two fingers to stretch the clay into a shape. Then he paints it with his fingers and different coloured blobs that float to where his fingers go.

Jude watches awhile and then starts to walk away.

The boy mumbles sadly to his iPad.

The woman is taken off the ice.

The teams are milling about their benches, the referees talking to them. Helmets come off and Jude sees sweaty wet hair, long hair, lots of hair. Jude's father said, "I have always loved your hair," to Jude's mother.

Jude leaves the arena, his hands tucked tight in his hoodie pocket, his coat over his hoodie. He's just a short walk from home. He decides to run. He runs hard, avoiding the ever-deepening cracks in the snow-dusted sidewalk, chasing the shadow of himself through the cold night.

Pedophile Ring in Parkville

John Standon
Staff writer

Thursday afternoon Parkville Police and several RCMP officers raided a rooming house on Braithwaite Drive. Although fairly close to the Abernackie Men's Shelter, a shelter previously mentioned in this newspaper for the demonstrations against it by the neighbours on Braithwaite Drive, this rooming house is in a separate building and is not affiliated with the men's shelter in any way. The rooming house consists of paroled men serving out sentences for everything from rape, B&E and burglary to domestic abuse. There are also some homeless men living there off and on. The house consists of 10 bedrooms, two floors. Police say the sweep was carried out after an informant mentioned photography equipment, computers and printed material of a sexual nature. Police are searching for the man in whose room this material was found. He is described as short in stature (approximately 5'4") and balding. He often wears brown suits. He talks with a tic and a bit of a stutter. He was last seen on Tuesday. Anyone with information, please call the police.

10

It isn't where Claire's husband, Ralph, usually puts it. His hat. And his keys are gone too. The front hall table looks odd without his pile of things. Claire has maybe cleaned up again? But that's the way it is these days. One minute he has a grasp on things, the next minute nothing makes sense. Of course Ralph won't say anything about this to anyone. It is okay to worry about going crazy, losing things, missing things, but to admit it aloud is something that would make him horribly uncomfortable. Ralph needs his family to believe that he has some sort of control. Especially now with Claire's cancer. Someone needs to take control. Even if it is fake.

"Why are you standing there staring at the table?" Claire moves into Ralph's line of vision. On her head is a furry hat. It looks like something a baby would wear. Pink, fuzzy. It must be one of the three she got from that weird driver, the older woman who drove her to radiation that time in the fall. Jude wears his hat too, but Caroline won't go near hers. She kept complaining about lice and other things that might be mixed in with the wool. Jude and Claire just stared at her, calmly, wearing their hats. "I like my hat," Jude said, smiling, his orange-sparkly hat balanced on his head. Ralph remembers Claire laughing wildly, full-throated, her head thrown back, the veins in her neck prominent against the white pallor of her skin, her bones showing. So much weight she's lost. So much skin almost. Ralph can't figure it out. Now her skin is paper stretched tight over bone.

Ralph can't bear to look at Claire some days. The ache he feels is akin to indigestion or acid reflux — a deep splintering pain in his chest radiating up to his jaw, the feeling of no control. She is still beautiful without her hair but because of her thinness and baldness and sharpened features he feels he can see her skeleton. He sees right through her skin to what she will look like when she is dead. And this frightens him to the point of distraction. In fact, maybe that's his problem. Maybe he is losing things, forgetting things, because he's so worried about Claire? That's a very real possibility. Stress can make you forget things.

"I'm going out," Ralph says. "Do you need anything?"

Claire shakes her head. Her pink hat moves down a bit and covers the place her eyebrows would be, the place they are slowly growing in. "You're standing there staring at the table as if it's going to bite you, Ralph." She laughs. "Sleepwalking?"

"Just trying to remember what I need at the store," he says. He pats her on her fuzzy-hatted head and walks out the door. "Nice hat."

She smiles. "Gift from that weird woman who drove me to radiation. The Brussels sprouts woman."

"I thought so."

And then, as he turns away from her, "Milk," Claire says. "And bananas."

"Right."

"No Brussels sprouts. Ha ha."

Ralph smiles at Claire.

The steps are icy and Ralph holds tight to the railing. Jude
was supposed to shovel last weekend, but he forgot and then
the weather warmed slightly and the snow on the steps turned
into solid ice. No matter how much sand Ralph sprinkles on it, it
doesn't seem to matter. Teenagers, Ralph thinks. Absent-minded.
Even worse than he is. You could look Jude right in the eye, make
him agree that he heard you, and the next minute ask him again
what you said — he wouldn't know. Their minds are occupied
with sex, Ralph reasons. At least his boy. His daughter, Caroline
is probably thinking about boys. Not sex with boys. Just the boys.
But take a boy and a girl and what do you get? Sex. So, in fact,
she's thinking about sex. Just indirectly.

But how is he to know? How is Ralph to know what his teenage
kids think about? He can't even remember, from one minute to the
next, what he's thinking about. He can't even remember what it
was like to be a teenager. And why is it that when you are a teenager
you can forget things without thinking you have Alzheimer's? As
soon as you hit fifty if you say, "I can't remember," everyone looks
at you with sympathy.

Down the slippery steps and onto the sidewalk. Ralph stands
there, scratching his uncovered head. He reaches into his pocket
for his keys, remembers he can't find his keys, but finds his hat
there instead. He puts his hat on his head and begins to walk
towards town. Better for him anyway, not taking the car. Safer,
perhaps, with the way his concentration is lately. Maybe his keys
are in the car? He'll check on that later.

His head down against the slight wind, Ralph walks forward
to his destination. Not once does he look back to where he knows
Claire will be watching from the front window. Always there.
When Ralph comes home from work she is standing there in the
dark staring out. What else has she got these days but the ability
to stand in a window and look out into the world? Ralph finds it

unbearable. Although he understands it. Claire just wants to feel part of something, he guesses, even if it's really part of nothing. Part of watching the world go by. Sometimes Ralph wishes they lived on a busier street, that way Claire would have more to look at. As it is, the occasional dog walker/snow shoveller/mail delivery doesn't seem enough to occupy her. But still, every day she's there. Watching.

At the corner Ralph turns right. He wonders if maybe he's had a stroke. Maybe that's the problem. Like now, for instance, he turned right, away from downtown, when he's supposed to be running errands. It's as if his feet have a destination he knows nothing about. But then he isn't quite sure what he was getting downtown anyway. Claire mentioned two things. Cereal? Wouldn't he know if he had a stroke? Wouldn't he have fallen down or fainted or something? Ralph knows that on TV they play that commercial where they list the signs of stroke but, for the life of him, he can't remember what they are. Dizziness? Heartache? Indigestion? Confusion? Memory loss? Blackouts? Sadness?

Up ahead there are kids on the street. Standing there in the snow and cold. Talking. For a minute Ralph thinks they should be in school, but then he remembers it is Saturday. If it were a school day, Ralph reasons, he'd be at work. The kids are looking at him strangely, but Ralph merely nods as he walks past, his feet crunching in the snow.

His feet. Crunching. Cold feet. Ralph looks down. That's what they are looking at. Ralph is wearing his house slippers. In the snow. He can feel the heat move up across his face and then down his back. He shivers. What an ape. His red velvet house slippers. The silly ones Claire got him for Christmas two years ago. A matching red velvet bathrobe to go with them. He's never worn it but he liked the slippers. "You'll look like Hugh Hefner," she had said and he had laughed and Jude had said, "Who's Hugh

Hefner?" Ralph forgot to put on his boots. Ralph looks at his slippers but doesn't stop his pace. No need to let these kids know he didn't wear his slippers on purpose. Maybe that's what all men his age do. How would these kids know differently? Maybe their own fathers walk around on Saturday in their slippers in the snow. Maybe they forget things all the time. Maybe Ralph is no different.

"Freak." Shouted.

When he turns the kids scatter. He has that, at least. Ralph is big. Kids are afraid. Even if he's an aging man, lost, shuffling in slippers through the snow.

He continues on. What else can he do?

Nothing is wrong. Nothing. He's just absent-minded, distracted, worried about Claire's cancer. That's all it is. Anyone else would be like this. But now he has to somehow get back into his house without his kids or Claire noticing his footwear. And without his keys. This could be difficult.

At the next corner Ralph doesn't know where to go. Right or left. He is up by the elementary school and he can't, for the life of him, remember how to get home. Or to town. Where he needs bananas and milk. That's it. Bananas and milk. Ralph turns left. His hands in his pockets are cold. Why didn't he think to wear gloves?

This has been happening for months. This forgetfulness. A little wire in his brain, maybe, snapped. Maybe it snapped when the doctor told them Claire had breast cancer. Maybe it fizzed quickly, went taut and then snapped. Maybe that's a stroke?

Ralph is sitting on the climbing structure at the school, watching the snow blow across the field. The wind has picked up. His feet are cold and caked with snow and ice. He taps them carefully, hoping he doesn't get frostbite.

The funny thing is that he's having no difficulties at work. You'd think he would. Remembering numbers and codes, dealing with clients and proposals, the small complicated things he does every day as an engineer. He has never once set off the door alarm at the firm, for example, something almost everyone does at least once in a while. No one has said anything to him about his work habits, nothing seems to have changed, and Ralph feels in control there. But at home it sometimes takes all Ralph's energy to remember his kids' names. Jude snapping his fingers in front of Ralph's face, saying, "Dad? Dad? Are you in there?" Caroline rushing out to her friends, shouting, "I told you yesterday. I'm going to the movies." And the other night when Claire came to bed and Ralph rolled over to touch her and felt that empty, vacant place on her chest, that raised scar, he jerked violently away because he had forgotten — he had forgotten! — she was missing a breast.

There is a kid there, beside him. Sitting right beside Ralph on the climbing structure. His leg is actually touching Ralph's leg. Ralph looks at him. The kid looks back. Where did he come from?

"Hi," Ralph says and moves away slightly.

The kid nods. A strange, gangly looking kid, probably Jude's age, his hands stuffed into his winter jacket, his toque on low over his eyebrows, his nose running in the cold. Why is he sitting so close?

Ralph gets up to leave and then sits down again because he has no destination, no forward movement. Sometimes, Ralph thinks, it's as if there is lead in his legs, his arms. Sometimes he will become so incredibly tired. He will sit still until the feeling passes. Maybe he should get his blood sugar tested. Maybe that's what this is all about. But the thought of going to a doctor just about knocks him off the climbing structure. Ralph is tired of doctors. He wants nothing to do with them anymore. He understands now why you hear about doctors and nurses getting ill with diseases that could have been caught. Never getting their heart checked and then dying of a heart attack, for example. When you're around sickness all day, all month, all year, you do all you can to avoid acknowledging your own.

The kid beside him reaches out his hand and squeezes Ralph's knee. Ralph jumps.

"Hey," Ralph says. "Hey, don't do that." He stands again and backs away from the kid.

The kid jumps up beside Ralph. He opens his mouth into a scream and points at Ralph and starts shouting. "Help," the kid shouts. "Help!"

There he is in his red velvet slippers, far from his house, lost. His wife is sick and dying. His kids are growing up and leaving him. He has no keys, no gloves. He can't remember what he left the house to do. He probably doesn't even have his wallet. The kid screams louder.

"Quiet," shouts Ralph. "Shush." He wants to put his hand over the kid's mouth — the scream is piercing and hurts Ralph's ears. He wants to hold the kid down in the snow, pound on him, make him shut up. "Quiet."

"Help. Help."

"Terry." A woman comes around the corner of the school. She pauses to step on her tossed cigarette as she walks towards Ralph and the kid. "Terry, leave the poor man alone."

Ralph clutches at his heart. He holds onto it. He feels it beating hard under his jacket.

"Help," Terry shouts. "Help, help, help."

The woman makes her way towards them. "Sorry about that," she shouts over Terry's screams. "He's, well, he's just different."

"Different?" Ralph thinks, Different? Is that what they call it now?

When the woman reaches them she takes her hands out of her

coat pockets and she cups Terry's ears and stands close to him, pulling his face towards hers. He is still shouting and Ralph has no idea how she can get that close and not go deaf. The woman touches her forehead to Terry's forehead and immediately he stops screaming. The silence is pure. Ralph hears a buzzing in his head, in that vacant place where the scream once was, but nothing else.

"Phew," Ralph says.

The woman takes her hands off Terry, pulls her forehead away and Terry begins to climb the structure. He is laughing now. As if nothing happened.

"I'm really sorry about that," the woman says. "I just went around the side of the school to light my smoke. The wind is harsh over here." The woman shrugs.

Now Ralph wants to hit her. He wants to smack her in her cute nose, her pretty little face. Smoking. Before, when he was allowed to take Claire to the hospital for her radiation treatments, if he passed patients or doctors smoking outside the building, Ralph would say something. He would turn on them. Two times the security guards asked him to control himself and then, finally, Claire asked him not to come with her anymore.

"You make me nervous," Claire had said. "I'm not sure what you are going to do."

Claire has never smoked. Not once. She has always been healthy. She exercises. She lives cleanly.

The woman backs away from Ralph. He realizes his face is set in a scowl and his hands are in fists.

"Whoa," the woman says. She puts her hands up. "Hey, what did you do to make Terry scream?"

Ralph relaxes his fists and sets his face in a partial smile so he looks more friendly. "Nothing," he says. "I was just sitting here, minding my own business."

The woman turns from him and watches her kid on the climbing structure. Terry is moving along the top part of it as if he's scaling the outside of an office tower. He's only about four feet up, but he holds onto the sides and moves so carefully, a look of fear on his face.

"Listen," the woman says. She turns back to Ralph. She puts her hands on her hips and blows cold air out of her mouth in a puff. "Terry's different, sure."

"I didn't mean to —"

"You're wearing slippers," she says. She points down at his feet. "In the snow."

Ralph shrugs. He blushes.

"What I'm saying is . . . we're all a little strange."

Ralph nods. This makes sense to him. In fact, it's the only thing that has made sense to him in a while. Cutting off his wife's breast, then shooting her full of chemicals that are so dangerous they should kill her and then burning her internally and externally with radiation. None of that has made any sense. But wearing slippers in the snow, screaming, "Help, help" for no reason — this, somehow, makes sense.

On the way home Ralph sees Jude up ahead, walking purposefully. Ralph falls into step with his son. He's grateful that Jude is who he is. He is lucky to have Jude.

"What have you been up to?"

Jude shrugs. "I went downtown. Just hanging out."

"Going home?"

Jude looks at his father and nods. Then he looks down the street at two girls sitting in the snow in their snowsuits in front of a house still decorated for Christmas. He puts his head down and looks at the sidewalk.

"You're wearing slippers, Dad," Jude says. He stops and takes his father's arm. "Dad?"

"I know what you're thinking," Ralph says. "I just forgot."

"How could you forget your boots?"

Ralph wants to say, "We're all a little strange, Jude. We're all different." He wants to echo the woman in the schoolyard, he wants to make his time with her mean something, but instead he says, "I've got a lot on my mind these days." Maybe it's true that Ralph just has too much to think about. Maybe Ralph's brain is giving him a break, helping him, lessening the load. If he can forget some things then he'll have room for more things. He'll have room for life, death, memories, moments in time, images that come at him late at night when he lies in bed in the dark and listens to Claire's shallow breathing. Ralph knows that everything he forgets now — his keys, his hat, his boots, which direction to go — will not matter. Ever. All that will matter is that he lived through this period in his life with his eyes wide open. His brain will do the rest. The important things will be there.

"It's like when you and Caroline were babies," Ralph says quietly as the two of them walk down the street towards home. "Life was so complicated and fast and busy. Your mom and I sometimes forgot things. Once we even left you in your car seat inside the front hallway of the house. We shut the door, locked it, got in the car and drove around the block," Ralph laughs, "before we remembered. There you were, sleeping in that car seat, peaceful as anything, when we got back. We scooped you up, Jude, and carried on."

Jude smiles at his father's memory. "You're just getting old, Dad," he says, and nudges his father with his elbow. Jokingly. "Old man."

"Yeah," Ralph says. "That too."

They round the corner and head towards their house. In the front window Claire stands with her arms crossed in front of her chest. Watching. She is lit up from the lights inside the house and she almost glows. She has taken off her silly pink hat and her fuzzy head shines. Ralph looks at her, watches her, takes her in. His heart aches, his chest splinters again and again. This, Ralph thinks, I won't forget. He can feel his son beside him doing the same thing. Wondering, staring, filing, placing this image somewhere deep within him. Sometimes there isn't enough room in your head for all the things in the world. Sometimes there is.

Dear Parents and Guardians,

Isn't this weather ridiculous? First we have snow, then ice, then melting, then freezing, then snow again. The ground these days is an accident just waiting to happen. Literally! One step in the wrong direction and you'll land on your tush. Or worse.

I'm writing to warn parents of the hazards of our grounds, especially the south side parking lot. On Wednesday morning our lovely custodian, Mr. Berton, slipped getting out of his truck and went down with a bang. He's in the hospital with a concussion right this minute. The doctors assure us he will be fine and he might even get to go home next week. The kids in Room 201 are making him a card if you'd like to stop by and sign it. But if you do, please be extra mindful of the parking lot!

We've salted. We've sanded. We've shovelled. But to no avail. The ground is a skating rink under our feet. Children slip their way into our school. We've cautioned them but there are still some children who are running and skipping and dancing into the school. Please tell your children to walk slowly and carefully. I like to tell them to act like old men and women, to bend slightly at the waist and slip slowly along as if they can't lift their heavy, arthritic feet. The kids love to do this and they make quite a game of it.

Winter is hazardous for all kinds of reasons besides the slippery ice. Believe me. Snow shovels are sharp, for example. So are snowballs packed with rocks. And then there are the colds, the flus, the frost bite. We need the parents of Oak Park Elementary School to be super-vigilant. Work with us, not against us! Tell your child to walk slowly and don't send them to school if they are sick. Make sure they wear proper outdoor clothing: boots, gloves, hats. Remember: a lot of heat disappears out the top of your head!

Don't worry, though, spring is just around the corner!

Marge Tanner

Marge Tanner
Principal, Oak Park Elementary School

To: tomshutter@prestige.com
From: art@abernackieshelter.com
Subject: Just wondering

Hi Tom,

Just wondering if you managed to get in touch with that man
with the large scar going down his face who works at the
car wash on Braid Street? I was in there again recently. My
car gets really dirty carting around all the food for the
shelter. Just the other day I found a tomato rolling around
the back seat. It was frozen, if you'd believe! Anyway, I
thought of you. He was there. Working hard. His name must be
Michael. I could see his name tag. Were you able to pay him
back for raking?

I'm just curious. I always like to see a story to the end.
Especially if the ending is happy. Hope to hear from you.

Cheerio,
Art Spack

Abernackie Men's Shelter
Braithwaite Drive, Parkville

spring

To: dayton22@hotmail.com
From: californiajohn@hotmail.com
Subject: Kidnapping

Dayton. There are things you know about me. I have little
patience. I also never forgive. Or forget. Ever. You know
this about me. I know you do. What were you thinking? Were
you thinking at all? What you have done to me by stealing
my child is unforgivable. It is reprehensible. I will not
forget this. You took a baby from her father. This is called
kidnapping and it is punishable by the law. I don't know what
the prisons are like up there in Canada, but they sure as
fuck aren't great in California. In fact, we have the death
penalty here. That's a fact.

I have spoken to the Cress Company Finances lawyer and we are
in total agreement that you will be prosecuted to the full
extent of the law. They have offered their services pro bono
and I have retained them.

Watch out, Dayton. I'm coming.

John

...

To: californiajohn@hotmail.com
From: dayton22@hotmail.com
Subject: Re: Kidnapping

John,

I know you got fired. I know you no longer work at Cress
Company Finances. I know you were fired because you were using
— and selling? — drugs. I also know they do not have a lawyer
on staff. And, even if they did, they would not give you pro
bono service. Especially after firing you. For drugs.

I did not kidnap Carrie. I took her away from a dangerous
situation. You are not stable. Get help. My lawyer will
contact you shortly. Are you still at the same address?

Again, I am keeping all your correspondence so you might as
well stop threatening me.

Dayton

11

Jude and Claire are watching *Ellen*. She should be getting dinner ready but sitting here, tight and close with her teenage son, watching feel-good comedy feels, well, good. Claire remembers when Ellen had her own sitcom; she remembers when Ellen came out publicly and the backlash. She likes Ellen because of her past, not because she's become popular now. Jude probably watches just because his mother is watching. Although he seems to enjoy it.

Every time Ellen says something people scream.

"I don't think I could be on that show," Jude says. "I couldn't scream like that."

Claire laughs and puts her hand on Jude's leg. "Even if you won a car?" She's been trying to touch him lately. More than usual. She wants to feel his warmth through her hands. She pats his head, even though she has to reach up high to do it, she touches his back when he passes, she squeezes his shoulder when he's sitting at the table. Claire can't help herself. She does the same thing with Caroline, but Caroline always shrugs away as if her mother's touch is too much. She brushes Claire off whereas Jude stays still as if trying not to scare her away.

"I might say yay or shout a little, but that shrieking is scary. Those women holler like someone is cutting their arm off."

Claire smiles. She imagines Jude winning his own car. She imagines his shy smile, his hulking-growing-boy-shoulder-slumped look. Not too sure of his body yet, the power it will have. Then she imagines Ralph, her husband, and how he is stooping lately with middle age. How their son stands stooped from youth. Why is everyone stooped? Except Claire. She stands tall now. Facing her demons, her cancer, she has needed to stand straighter, be stronger. The more erect she is, the more body mass she seems to have. More of her to fight, she reasons.

Ralph comes into the room. "Dinner?" he says. "I'm not rushing you, but what are we having?"

Claire sighs. She gets up. Ralph sits down. For some reason he takes the remote control, as if he didn't even notice they were watching anything, and turns to the news.

"Ralph? Jeez."

"Oh, sorry." He flips back to *Ellen*. Jude rolls his eyes towards his mother. Ralph walks around in his own little world these days. Claire and Jude can't figure him out. It seems he isn't listening, hearing, thinking, seeing. He's just there. A shell of nothing. Where is he?

The things that are left unsaid in the room hang there. Elephants. Lots of them. Claire knows everyone is watching her. She knows they are thinking, Cancer. They are thinking, Tiptoe, be careful. "What do you two want for dinner?"

"Nachos," Jude says. "With refried beans. Do we have avocado?"

"Sounds good." Ralph grunts. He laughs at Ellen. She's playing some game with a bunch of shouting, excited, chubby women.

They are stacking cubes and whacking each other with soft bats. Every so often one of the women falls and everyone shrieks and giggles and screeches. So much noise on *Ellen*.

"We could write in about your cancer," Jude says. And then he goes quiet. Ralph looks at him.

"You think Ellen would give me a car?" Claire starts opening cupboards in the kitchen. Trying to find a can of refried beans. Jude turns the volume up on the TV. Claire looks out the window into the back garden. It is dingy and grey. She can't imagine that in a couple of weeks, a month, there will be lush green growth; she can't imagine that soon she'll be unable to see through the trees into her neighbours' kitchens. Seasons amaze her. Claire wouldn't want to live anywhere they don't have seasons. Nature would seem so sedentary then. But winter, spring, summer, fall, the changes are immense and powerful. One day you are walking down the street and there are no leaves on the trees, the next day you can see a shimmer, a thickness in the branches, and the next day, buds. Then suddenly the trees are full and you are walking under lush foliage, shade, green growth. It's a miracle, really.

Caroline comes into the room. She plops down with Ralph and Jude. She is wearing large slippers shaped like ducks. The duck heads are immense. Claire knows that if you squeeze the beak the ducks will quack. Jude makes room for Caroline on the couch.

"Nachos okay with you, Caroline?"

Caroline shrugs. "Whatever."

Claire begins to make nachos and Ralph gets up to help her grate cheese. There is talk later during dinner of Caroline's university applications. Like the seasons, time moves quickly. Every so often Claire tries to catch her breath but most of the time she is winded by the speed.

In his bed at night Jude wonders if he'll remember back to when he used to watch *Ellen* with his mother. He worries about this, his memories. He doesn't want to have them. But then he also wants to have them and worries that he won't remember them. How can he mourn her already if she isn't even gone yet? And the doctors say she's doing okay now. This waiting game. This trying-to-file-into-your-head-every-little-second game. He hates it.

At school there is someone. A girl. She likes him. He isn't sure if he likes her even though he knows he should. In fact, he likes her twin brother better than he likes her. She giggles a lot and puts her hand up to her mouth to hide her braces and flips her hair, whereas her brother merely stares blankly at Jude and shrugs. Both of them are funny. And have been nice to him. They know about his mother, by accident — they saw her when she had absolutely no hair back in the fall and the girl asked Jude about it. Jude confessed even though he wanted more than anything to say she had shaved her head for fun and wasn't she a dork and, god, how stupid. But the girl is getting tighter with Jude at school these days and the brother is becoming more distant even though Jude has asked the brother to do more things with him. It's as if the girl has told her brother to stay away from Jude. As if she has warned her brother, has said, "He's mine."

Jude is hanging out with her at the baseball diamond behind their school. He meets her there after last class most days and they sit in the dugout and they hold hands. Sometimes they kiss and her braces are cold. They taste like a fork, like utensils, metal ones. The taste is bizarre. It's part of her but not part of her. Jude likes it, but he also hates it.

When he kisses the girl he sometimes thinks about his mother. And about Ellen. Or about what he's going to eat for dinner. But mostly he thinks about the girl's brother. Jude admires the way the brother rolls his eyes upwards when their history teacher is talking. He rolls them up into his head and all Jude can see are the whites of his eyes, the beautiful brown has disappeared. Jude likes this. It makes him laugh. The brother is shocking, he writes "Dirty pig," next to a picture of Hitler in their history textbook and, even though it's an appropriate thing to write, it's also bad to deface textbooks. So when Jude is kissing the brother's sister he thinks about her brother. He feels hot and angry. Once Jude felt so angry that he pulled the sister's head back, pulled her by the hair, hard, when he was kissing her, and she grunted and said, "Ouch."

"Sorry," he said.

In the evening they watch *Ellen* again. She has people come on to her show and sit with her and talk about all the good things they are doing: how they are taking care of animals, or other people, or how they are stopping bullying and how they are progressive and believe in gay rights. Ellen is married to a woman. A beautiful woman.

Claire laughs and says this to Jude, and then she mentions that most gay men she knows are really handsome too and why is it that the ugly ones are straight.

"Like Dad?" Jude says. And they both laugh because Ralph is quite attractive and Claire loves him dearly. Especially now, especially with all he's done for her over the last year, the way he held her hair back when she vomited, the way he made Earl Grey tea for her with milk and sugar, just like her mother used to make, when she felt sick from the chemotherapy. The way he will go to the store at the drop of a hat if she mentions she has a headache and there is no acetaminophen in the house. Never a sigh. Never a hesitation. Ralph is great. And who is she to talk about appearances when for the last year she's been alien-looking and bony, her eyes deep set with no eyebrows, her hair gone, pale skin and rashes.

Back in the dugout Jude is kissing the girl and her brother shows up. He knows they go there to kiss, but he's never come before. What does he want, Jude wonders. To watch? The girl keeps kissing him but Jude feels bizarre kissing in front of the brother so, instead, they all sit back, leaning against the wooden dugout, and they talk. They talk about history class. They talk about sports. They talk about *Ellen* because the girl watches *Ellen* in the evenings too and she loves *Ellen* and thinks Ellen is really cool and funny. Jude and the brother roll their eyes. Jude tries to roll his eyes as high into his head as the brother does but he can't because it hurts.

"Have you seen that guy at the car wash with the scar down his face?" the brother asks Jude. "We should write to Ellen about him. I bet she'd get his story out of him."

"I think you should just ask him," the sister says. "He won't ask him what happened."

"Why don't you ask him?"

"You're the one who wants to know what happened, not me."

"But it's rude to ask him."

"Why's it rude? Maybe he wants to talk about it. Maybe he's sick of people looking at him and not asking."

"You're an idiot," the brother says.

"You're an idiot."

They argue in front of him all the time. Jude kind of likes this. It also kind of makes him angry. Mostly he agrees with what the brother says more than with what the sister says. Even though she's his girlfriend. Not officially. But they kiss a lot.

Sometimes, when they are watching *Ellen*, Jude wants to tell his mother about the girl, about kissing her. Sometimes he wants to tell his mother about the brother, about how they are twins, the boy and girl, but have nothing at all in common. How, in fact, the boy is much smarter and better looking than the girl, which is funny because you'd think they would look a little bit the same. But they don't. She is short and blond, he is tall and dark. She likes arts and French and English literature, he likes science and math and gym. But Jude doesn't. Tell his mother, that is. They mostly watch *Ellen* and talk about what Ellen says and what she's doing and how she's changing the world a little bit at a time. He respects her for that and he knows his mom does too.

"Is there bullying in your school?" Claire asks Jude one day. But before he can answer she says, "of course there is. There's always bullying in schools. And workplaces. And life. People have always bullied."

Jude hears her but he also hears what she's not saying. Or, at least, he thinks he hears that. He hears, "That's another thing I won't have to deal with when I die. Bullying." Jude always thinks he hears the unspoken stuff in his mother's words. And his father's and even Caroline's. And the brother and the sister. All the things left unsaid. Jude often wonders why people don't say what they mean. But then, Jude doesn't say what he wants to say most of the time.

What is it he wants to say?

He wants to tell the brother how much he loves him. He wants to tell the brother that the only reason he hangs around with the sister, the only reason that he kisses the sister, is because it makes him feel closer to the brother. He wants to say that when he kisses the sister he feels as if he's kissing the brother. He wants to tell his mother about his feelings for this boy in his class, but he doesn't want anything else to worry her. In fact, he doesn't want to waste her time with things like this. Instead they waste their time watching *Ellen* together, which isn't really a waste, it's more like a pause, a stop-gap measure, a way to be together without being together.

"Everyone is going to die," the brother says one day, in the dugout.

"But this is different." Jude doesn't want to argue with him, but the brother is baiting him, controlling him, playing with him. The sister has her hand high up on Jude's thigh and she's popping her gum and tracing small circles with her fingers on his leg. This is annoying to Jude even though he knows he should find it sexy.

"I don't see what's different about it. Your mother knows that her life is coming to an end eventually, but that's the same for all of us. She's no different from the rest of the world."

Jude knows this makes sense but it doesn't sit right with him. "That's not true," he says. He clears his throat. "Sure, we're all going to die, but my mom has been told that she has a limited amount of time, that there's only so much she can do about it, and," Jude clears his throat again, "and she knows how she's going to die. That's the real difference. How."

"She could get hit by a bus on her way to the store," the sister says. Gum popping. "That could happen. Or she could have a heart attack maybe."

The brother does his eye roll. "Why," he says to the sister, "do you always ruin a good conversation?"

"I don't. It was a stupid conversation anyway. And what are you doing here? We don't want you here, do we, Jude?"

Jude says nothing. The conversation has moved from him and his mother to them again. It's always about them. The twins. The brother leaves. Jude kisses the sister. Hard. As hard as he can. He cuts his lip on her braces. She puts his hand up under the back of her sweatshirt. He can feel her skin, the line of her bra, her muscles and bones. He rubs her back. Like he would rub his mother's back. He rubs in circles, comforting her, occasionally he pats.

When Claire turns on *Ellen* that night she gets a news report instead. A pedophile ring. In their city. The news flashes on the screen. Big names are involved. Local police officers even. A judge. Some lawyers. Claire stands immobile, watching. Their small city. Child porn. Numbers of computers confiscated. They haven't found the ringleader, the guy with the means and the way. Not yet. But they will. Say the police.

"Where's *Ellen*?" Jude says.

"Not on right now."

Jude leaves the room. He isn't interested in anything but *Ellen*. Claire listens to the newscaster say, "The scope of this perversion is astounding. Especially in such a small town." Claire wants to take the remote control and throw it at the TV. She wants to break something. Justified anger like this makes her glow. She feels warm and full and sharp. It's easy to be angry at these criminals. A good thing to be furious about. What they do to kids. What they do to the world. It astonishes Claire.

She wishes Ellen's show was on. She wishes she were cuddled on the couch with Jude. But then she's also pleased to be mad at something other than her body, her cancer, her illness.

"Is she on yet?" Jude is back in the room.

"No, not yet."

He leaves again.

The newscast ends. Ellen is there, on her chair, talking to a beautiful movie star about her new movie. Claire sinks into the couch to watch. "Jude," she calls out, "she's on."

Ralph comes in and asks what's for dinner.

"For god's sake," Claire snaps. "Make it yourself."

The brother has taken to watching Jude. All the time. Jude can feel the brother's gaze on his back in class or in the hallways between classes or when he's in the dugout kissing the sister. It's hot, his gaze. Penetrating. Jude likens it to a laser beam. Like radiation. He feels burnt sometimes. The sister is losing interest in just kissing. She wants more. She puts Jude's hands where she wants them. Breasts, hips, legs, thighs, between the thighs, crotch. She holds his hand there and sighs. She tries to touch him, but Jude pulls away. If the brother is there, which he often is, he snorts. He says, "Gross," and "Get a fucking room," and the girl says, "Why don't you just leave us alone?" Jude is caught in the middle. Balancing on the edge. Hanging over a precipice. Like a hang-glider with no glider, like a parachutist without a parachute, a pilot without a plane, a hockey player without a puck. Jude's English class is studying similes and so he peppers his speech and his thoughts with them.

Jude has never seen his mother mad at Ellen but today she is. Today she sits on the couch next to Jude, her arms crossed in front of her chest, and she scowls at the TV. Her legs are crossed and one foot is furiously pumping up and down.

Ellen's guest needs a new kitchen. She's lost her job. Her kitchen is a mess. Ellen is having one made for her and, for some reason, this bothers Claire. She doesn't know why. She looks over at her own kitchen, the stained and cut-upon counter, the broken tiles on the floor, the splattered backsplash, and she is angry.

"What did she do to deserve a new kitchen?" Claire asks.

"She wrote a letter to Ellen," Jude says. "It's as easy as that."

"Not fair."

"Life's not fair." Jude looks at his mother. She looks at him. They laugh.

"I'm supposed to say that to you," Claire says. "That's the kind of thing I say to you all the time."

"I'm just imitating you," Jude says. "Because I know that's exactly what you'd say to me."

"Well, it's not. Fair. Life."

"Nope."

Ralph is in the kitchen filling up a pot with water. "Pasta," he says. "I think we'll have pasta tonight. Sound good?"

She doesn't show up at the dugout. It's cold. A sharp breeze. Jude is there by himself. Wondering. Thinking. Should he stay here or go home? And then, suddenly, the brother drops down beside him. Sits close.

"She's not coming?"

"Not today. She felt sick or something."

"Great," Jude says. "I'll probably catch it and then give whatever she has to my mom and then —"

Jude is rambling.

The brother reaches over and grabs Jude's head. He turns Jude's face towards his own, looks at Jude, fierce, and stops Jude's words with his mouth. Hard. Jude recoils at first, pulls back, but the brother smashes his mouth against Jude's, keeps Jude there, stuck to him. He is stronger than Jude and Jude can't pull away.

And Jude's heart is racing, his heart, his heart, his heart . . . his mind has stopped. His heart pulses and beats and pounds until Jude can't feel anything or think of anything. Jude doesn't want anything for the first time in his life. There is nothing. Just the brother's lips and tongue and hot mouth. Everything else has gone black. The world seems simple. As if everything in it has been erased. No dugout, no girl, no metallic tasting braces, no *Ellen*, no mother.

Jude's mother kisses him goodnight. She comes into his room and sits on his bed. He has his laptop on his lap and it is hot and he's working on his history essay in bed. She sits there, staring at him.

"How are you doing these days?"

Jude looks away from his laptop and into his mother's eyes. Into her concern. "Fine?"

"Good. That's good."

"How," Jude asks, "are you doing?" But he doesn't want to know, he doesn't want the answer to this.

And his mother senses this, because Claire is aware, she is smart, she is sensitive. "Great," she says, happily. "I enjoy our *Ellen* time together." She ruffles his hair.

"Me too." Jude smoothes his hair back into place.

"We should dance more," Claire says, laughing. She stands up from the bed and dances towards the door. A crazy dance, a funny dance, an Ellen dance. Swaying her hips and bending her legs. Arms in the air.

Jude laughs. He rolls his eyes back into his head.

"I'm practising for when I get on *Ellen*," she says, and she dances out of the room.

Ms. Maisy Crank
Build-Your-Bear™
Madison, Wisconson

Dear Ms. Crank,

I am writing to see if we can come to some sort of amicable agreement regarding Build-Your-Bear™ and my business, The Bear Company. I have read and reread the letters you have written me and I have to say they've put me in a tizzy. I'm quite stressed, actually. I'm sure you didn't intend this and I'm sure you didn't realize that I'm just one person in my house in a sewing room. You probably think that I have staff! Or even an income that makes up for the amount of work I do! Well, I don't. I have nothing, really, but my bears. And my family, of course. But nothing else. If you go ahead and sue me or make me stop working I don't know what I'll do. Probably break down. Probably go into a deep depression. Probably just give up. Now, do you really want that to happen? Is that what you are trying to do? Destroy me? Because, honestly, Ms. Crank, that is what will happen.

I make my bears with love. I make them to order. I do what people ask. I also do what comes to mind. I'm quite creative. In fact, right now I'm working on a female hockey bear. She has little hockey skates and the full equipment (even a stick!) and she has long hair that flows out of her helmet. I play hockey — yes, hard to believe at my age — and so, you see, the inspiration comes from me, from my life, from the things around me. I'm not trying to steal anything from you. I do not have a store where kids can stuff their own bears. I do not have boxes and boxes of accessories for my bears — each tiara, tutu, briefcase, for example, is made specifically for that particular bear. And each bear is made specifically for a particular person.

Please, Ms. Crank, stop your Cease and Desist. Stop sending me these letters. Stop harassing me. I'm just a poor woman in a small sewing room. The stress is overwhelming me.

In good faith,

Patricia (Trish) Birk
The Bear Company, Canada

12

Tom is at work when Maria calls. He is thinking about the woman in the coffee shop this morning who asked him if he liked cream and when he said, "Sure," she laughed as if he had said something particularly suggestive. She even licked her lips. Tom is trying to figure out what she meant by it all. Cream in his coffee? He likes cream in his coffee. "Sure" isn't really that suggestive, is it? Tom sometimes feels so out of it, as if everyone else in the world is participating and he's on the sidelines, watching and not taking anything in. It seems to him that he doesn't understand the little innuendos. Maria says that he never notices when a woman looks at him, but Tom has never seen a woman look at him — not in the way Maria says they do. Something happened when he got married or when Becky came along, something turned him from being aware of the sexual energy out there to being aware of nothing. He feels as if he's gone through the last fifteen years as merely a big lump of unformed clay. In the last several months, however, Tom is noticing more. Not understanding more, just noticing more. So when the phone rings and it's Maria it surprises him out of his thoughts.

"It's Becky," she says. Tom stands at his desk and looks around the open office, at the workers, like bees, all huddled in their grey cubicles, typing on their computers, talking on their phones, shuffling papers. His mind clears and sharpens. He can hear his own breath.

"What happened? Is she okay?"

"You need to come home. Now."

This is the moment every parent dreads and yet expects. Something has happened to their kid, they need to go home. Now.

"What? What is it?"

"It's Becky. Just come home, Tom. We'll talk about it when you get home."

"But, Maria. Is she okay?"

"Sort of."

"What do you mean?" Tom is frantic now, imagining his daughter's legs broken, her hand cut off, her head split open — or worse. He imagines she's dead or missing. It occurs to him that missing is much worse than dead. He's never thought about that before. You would think each horror would be equal, but the thought of her missing stops his heart. The office seems to go quiet all around him. Tom can't breathe.

"Calm down, Tom. She's home from school. I just need you to come home and talk with her. With me. All of us. She's done something bad."

Tom puts his hand on his heart. "You could have said that, Maria. You could have said she was okay. You could have mentioned she was at home."

"I did say she was okay. I don't know what the problem is, Tom. You're overreacting."

"No, you didn't. You didn't say she was okay." He pauses. "I'll come home now." Tom hangs up the phone hard and gets his coat off the hook on his cubicle wall. He walks towards the elevators at a fast pace. He tells Rick he'll be back later in the afternoon.

Even though Maria said Becky is home, Tom can't get it out of his head that she's gone, missing, hurt. He wonders where Maria's sense is, where her brain is, where her soul is — she reacts and acts and shouts and complains. She is always making his heart speed up — and sometimes this is good, but most of the time this is bad. If Tom didn't work out sometimes, if he didn't take Dog for a walk occasionally, he's sure Maria would shock him into having a heart attack. Someday it will happen.

Mary-Beth, from Human Resources, is in the elevator when it opens. Tom smiles at her as he walks into the box. He smiles tightly. He's still mad. He doesn't know Mary-Beth well but it occurs to him that he feels different when he sees her. His back straightens slightly. He feels warm. She smiles back at him and then turns to the front of the car. Tom sidles in behind her and watches her body as she stands there staring at the numbers. He looks at her straight back, her long legs, bare and sleek. None of those nylons Maria always wears. Her legs are tanned as if she's been somewhere south. He looks at her ass in her tight skirt. Round. Full but toned. And he knows that if she turns around — he saw it on the way into the elevator — he will see her substantial cleavage. Tom isn't a breast man, but these breasts, well, she wears clothes that highlight them. Maria, on the other hand — Tom's temples pulse when he thinks of her — has little cleavage. She's tight and toned and muscular. No soft curves. Mary-Beth turns towards Tom, as if she knows he's watching her, and she smiles again. She brushes her hair off her shoulders. The doors open. "Bye, Tom," she says, and leaves the elevator.

Tom is shocked that she knows his name. He has to think to close his mouth.

Tom enters the house, throws his keys in the bowl in the front hallway. Dog comes to greet him. Sniffing and groaning, his back legs almost collapse from the wiggling excitement. Other than Dog, there is no one around. He hears nothing.

"Hello?"

"Tom, we're in here."

Back towards the kitchen. Tom follows Dog, who follows Maria's voice.

They are sitting at the kitchen table. Becky hunched over, her coat on. Maria is wearing her yoga pants and coat. Her hair is in a ponytail.

"What's going on?"

"Sit down."

Tom gives Becky a sympathetic look, but she doesn't look up from the table.

"I was at yoga," Maria begins. "I was doing a class at lunch, taking a break from work." Tom nods, but he's not listening and he's aware that he's not listening. Instead, he's thinking about Mary-Beth in the elevator. He can't help it. The comparison between her softness and Maria's sharp angles is astonishing. He's never thought of Maria this way before — all edges and dangerous points — but now he can't stop thinking this. "And the school called. Mrs. Tanner wanted me to come pick Becky up immediately."

"Mrs. Tanner?"

"The principal, Tom. Don't you know anything that goes on around here?" Maria sighs. "Marge Tanner? She's been Becky's principal for years. We talked to her just recently about the person Becky kept seeing. The man she thought was watching her, remember?"

"Oh, yes. The principal. What did you do, Becky?" Tom can't imagine what she could have done. Look at her here. She's huddled up, leaning heavily on the kitchen table, looking so sad and sorry. Is that a tear? She might be crying. He wants to reach out and touch her shoulder but he knows Maria will be angry if he does. "Maria, what did she do?"

"I didn't do it," Becky says. "Not like they said I did. They just hate me. They hate me because I'm always cleaning."

"Her pants," Maria says. "They said she had them off when they found her."

It isn't as if Tom would act on any of the images in his head, on his emotions and imagination — Mary-Beth in the elevator, the woman with the suggestive cream reference — it isn't as if Tom is guilty of anything. But, in these last several months, these things that have been happening to him have made him feel alive again. These small images — the Mary-Beths of the world — they keep popping into his mind. Half-dressed, seductive, wonderfully soft and sweet women. Who want what Tom has. Whatever that is.

"Her pants?" Suddenly he's paying attention. "Off? What do you mean? Who said this? Who found her?"

"There's this guy," Becky says. "At the school. They hate him like they hate me."

"The principal said that the kids said that Becky initiated it."

"Mom, I wouldn't do that." Becky begins to cry. She stands and goes to the kitchen sink and takes the sponge out of the draining rack. She wets the sponge, squeezes it out and begins to wipe the counters.

"Becky, sit down."

She keeps wiping. "They lied. They all lied to Mrs. Tanner and she believed them."

"I'm not sure . . . ." Tom begins.

"They said he was licking her," Maria shouts. A little scream. She puts her hands up to her face when she says it, covers her mouth. Her eyes are so wide Tom thinks they might fall out of the sockets.

"What? Where? Who?" Tom stands up. "What?"

Becky cries. She wipes and cries. "I didn't do anything. They're lying."

"Other children saw this. They told the principal."

"Where, Becky?"

"In the field behind the play structure," Maria says.

"But it's cold," Tom says. "Weren't you cold?" He doesn't know why he says this and the minute he says it he wants to take it back. Maria stands and puts her hands on her hips.

"Tom," she says.

"What happened to the boy?" Tom asks.

Becky sobs loudly. She crumples to the floor. "I didn't do anything. Don't you believe me? They are lying. They are all lying. They hate me. They hate him."

"Maria, what's going on?"

"They are lying to hurt me. They hate me. I didn't do anything."

"The boy was suspended," Maria says quietly. "And Becky has been suspended too."

"She's only twelve years old, Maria," Tom says. "Twelve years old."

At work the next day Tom is on the lookout for Mary-Beth. He sees Susan leaning over Simon's desk, talking to him. From the side, she is stunning. She notices him looking at her and turns and waves. Tom waves back.

What is happening to him? For years he has noticed nothing. Now he can't stop noticing things. As if a switch has been turned on. A light bulb in his brain. In his pants.

Pants. Becky said it didn't happen and Tom wants to believe her. But why would the kids at school lie? She says they hate her. They hate the boy. She says they are mean and evil. Tom can't imagine, though, that they would know what oral sex is and how to explain it to a principal if they'd never actually seen it happening.

Maria, in bed later, confessed to Tom that she can't imagine Becky with her pants down. "She's terrified of dirt, of germs," Maria said. "Can you see her doing that?"

"How do we prove that she didn't?" Tom said.

Becky is home every day with her mother. Maria has had to take personal days at work. Tom comes home each day to their anger, their individual silence, to Becky's shame. He rushes back to work each morning. So relieved. Becky is to stay home for two weeks. Maria says she doesn't know how much more of this she can take. Tom might have to take next week off, she says. Her work won't let her be away this long. She says they should move schools. Or even move houses. She says they should get rid of Dog because he's always needing to be walked and she can't walk him because her back hurts when she walks too far. She says they need a new kitchen countertop because Becky has worn the finish off it with her incessant wiping. She says he's not paying attention, he's not listening, doesn't he care?

And, at work, Tom is surrounded by perfume. Mary-Beth in the elevator. Susan in the hallway. Ruth in her cubicle, braiding her hair, her arms high behind her head and her tank top sleeve open enough for him to see the cup of her armpit, the swell of her breast. Tom remembers back to that fall day when that man with the scar down the middle of his face helped him rake his lawn. He remembers how impressed he was with the confidence in the man, the ability to ignore the stares. Tom thinks maybe he did learn something from that day about how humans perceive themselves.

Because the more he smiles at women at work, the more they smile back at him. The more he feels they are sexy and beautiful and individual, the more they seem to feel that way about themselves, and the more they feel that way about themselves, the more Tom thinks of himself as something they could want or need or even like. Because he is sure they are looking at him differently now. As if he's giving off a scent that's even stronger than their perfume.

He hasn't had the nerve to go down to the car wash and pay the scar-faced man for the raking job. It seems to him there might be a statute of limitations on how long you can go between paying for work that has been done. And his statute is long gone. The whole thing would just be shameful now. So shameful that he hasn't had the nerve to answer Art Spack's emails from the men's shelter. So Tom ignores the emails and hopes they will go away.

Maria is giving Becky talks. Talks about sex. Talks about boys. Talks about self-respect. Talks about self-control. Tom tries not to listen but sometimes he can't help it. Sometimes he wants to take Becky in his arms and tell her everything will be okay. Sometimes he wants to tell her not to listen to her mother. Sometimes he wants to leave the house. So he takes Dog for walks and runs. He disappears into the night. He leaves for work early in the morning.

It is Becky's first weekend after being suspended, and Tom has to work on the Saturday. Maria is incensed.

"I've spent the whole week with her," she says. "The least you could do is take the weekend off and do something with me, with her."

"I can't get out of it. Human Resources scheduled me this weekend. We all have to take turns. This is my turn." Tom doesn't tell Maria that he could easily have switched weekends with someone. He doesn't know why he doesn't tell her but he's pretty sure it has something to do with how angry she has been lately. With Becky home Maria can't go to work and when she can't go to work she can't do her yoga and when she can't do her yoga her back aches. When her back aches she becomes angry.

"I'm in pain," she says. "I'm always in pain."

Tom is at work. Saturday. It's quiet. He's the only one on his floor and so he wanders around to all the cubicles, looking at the photos and other decorations people have put up. There is a picture of Susan with a baby. He didn't know she had a baby. There is a picture of Simon with his arms around another guy. The guy could be his brother. Or maybe Simon's gay? Tom doesn't know. He doesn't really care except for the fact that he feels bad that he doesn't know these people who surround him every day. Tom needs to open his eyes to more than the beautiful women around his office. He needs to start seeing the world he lives in. Really seeing it. Getting to know the people around him.

It's when he's thinking this that she comes around the corner. Mary-Beth. Of course. Tom thinks, Of course. He can't help himself. It's as if this was planned. There she is, on a Saturday. Mary-Beth. And Tom. Alone in the office.

"Hi," Tom says.

"Oh, hi Tom," Mary-Beth says, startled. "I didn't know you were working today." Mary-Beth moves towards him. "I didn't know anyone was on this floor. I was going to raid the fridge, see if there was any juice up here." She smiles. She is wearing tight jeans, flat shoes, a t-shirt that is scooped at the neck and hugs every part of her. Tom stares.

"I'm sure we have juice," he says. "Here, I'll get you some."

Mary-Beth follows closely behind.

Is he reading into this? Is he imagining this? Is it part of some weird fantasy? Something he's seen in the movies or on TV? Should he stop and turn and kiss her? Should he push her against the fridge, the counter, the table? Should he run his hand down her back as she bends towards the fridge? What should he do? Should he do nothing? Anything? Something?

Mary-Beth takes the juice he hands to her. She pops the lid off and sips. "Thanks," she says. And then she turns and walks away from him. Tom watches her ass, the way her legs move, the flip of her hair. She stops and turns back to him. "Have a great day, Tom," she says. And she's off. Gone.

That answers his question.

Maria is pacing in the kitchen when he comes home. Tom opens a beer and takes several long swallows. He burps. Maria scowls.

"Marge called."

"Marge?" Tom asks.

"The principal. Becky's principal. Marge Tanner. Jesus, Tom, where do you live? What are you thinking all the time? God, Tom." Maria slumps down into a kitchen chair and glares at him.

"Sorry, *that* Marge. What did she want? On a Saturday?"

"It seems that a bunch of the kids felt bad. It seems they were lying. That it was all made up. They lied about Becky and the boy. In particular, it was two girls, Veronica and Sharon. I don't know them. I've never even seen them. I don't know how," Maria sighs, "how they even know about oral sex. I mean, they are only twelve. What kind of girls are these?"

Tom sits down hard. They were lying. Of course they were lying.

He looks up and Becky is standing in the doorway to the

kitchen. "I told you," she says, quietly. "I told you they lied. You didn't believe me."

"But why?" Maria throws her hands in the air. "What did you do, Becky, to make them lie about something like this?"

Becky sucks in her breath. Tom hears this. He pays attention. He stands quickly. Smacks his beer down on the table. It foams over. "Don't you dare, Maria," he says. Pointing his finger hard at Maria, stabbing towards her with his finger, stabbing the air around her. "Don't you dare blame her."

"Pardon me?" Maria looks shocked.

Becky, leaning in the doorway, looks at her father. He looks back at her. She smiles slightly and turns and leaves the room. He can hear her thump up the stairs. Dog follows behind. Tom hears her bedroom door shut. He hears her TV turn on. He hears her DustBuster start up.

"What was the meaning of that?" Maria says. But she is red-faced and it is not from anger. She is ashamed. Tom knows that Maria is aware of what she has done, of what she has said. Tom knows he doesn't have to say anything. For the first time Tom knows exactly who he is and where he stands. He might not like himself very much right now, he might not like Maria very much right now, but he does know that he's a different man from who he was several months ago. He's a man who is awake to the world around him. He is a man who is suddenly alive and full of all the confusing stuff that alive people are full of — emotions, feelings, soul. Tom finally feels as if he is something. And the funny thing is, he didn't know before that he wasn't something. He didn't have a clue that he wasn't whole.

To: dayton22@hotmail.com
From: californiajohn@hotmail.com
Subject: I know where you live

Dayton,

That's it. I've had it. I'm coming. I'm going to bring Carrie
back home. Now.

John

Dear Dad,

Hey, Dad. How are you? I haven't written in a long time, I know. So sorry. Things have been crazy busy with work and home life. Maria and Becky and Dog send their love. I hope you've been enjoying Florida this year. How are Mom's migraines? The warm weather probably clears them up.

Listen, the reason I'm writing is that I've been remembering something from my childhood lately and I was wondering if you might clear it up for me. Did Grandpa Mel keep a collection of postcards of circus freaks in his basement? On the shelf above the workbench? I keep thinking about them and I hope I've not remembered incorrectly. I remember going through them as a child and I've been wondering lately, well, why? Why did he collect these postcards? Where did he get them from? Antique shows? I know he collected a lot of things, but these postcards weren't displayed like most of his collections, they were hidden in an album and up high. Was there a reason for this? If you have time, I'd love to hear more about the postcards.

Thanks, Dad. Say hi to Mom for me.

Love,

Tom

Dear Tom,

Your mother sends her love. Her headaches aren't any better but, even so, we've decided to stay into summer this year. Maybe the intense heat will make them go away? I don't know. Your mother wants to stay down until the beginning of August. I've been playing a lot of golf when it doesn't rain and when my sciatica isn't acting up. Of course, I also have that damned arthritis in my fingers. Can barely hold the golf club somedays.

I don't remember any postcards of circus freaks. You must be thinking of someone else or maybe a book you read or a movie you watched. Why would your grandfather collect something weird like that? He was a proper, respectable man. You'd do best not to mention this to your mother. Unfounded rumours such as these, when the man is already dead and can't defend himself, would kill her.

Your mother wants me to ask if you're ever going to come down and visit? Remember last year when you said you would come down and see us? Well, we've seen not hide nor hair of you yet. We wouldn't mind seeing our granddaughter once more before it's too late. Your brother, as you know, brought down his brood this year. We enjoyed showing them off to everyone here. Now that we're staying later this year you have plenty of opportunity to come visit.

Your mother says you need to put flowers on Aunt Betty's grave on Easter. Don't forget. She loved Easter.

Sincerely,

Dad

13

Leah is on the ice. She bends forward at the blue line, waiting for the puck to drop. In her mind she sees the puck hit the ice and bounce back towards her. In her mind she sees herself smack it hard towards the goal. But it doesn't and she doesn't. Leah's team gets the puck and off they skate toward the red team's goalie. Leah follows. Her mind is elsewhere. Back with Hannah, earlier today, after school. Back with Terry as he melted down after dinner. She held him tight until he calmed. She smoked on the back porch for an hour after, just to calm herself. Leah wonders what they are doing now, her kids, but then sees the puck sail past her and she turns and follows it, shaking her head. It bothers her that she fades-out on the ice. Leah wonders if she has attention deficit disorder because she can't seem to pay attention to anything these days. But then, Leah thinks, she's always been like this. Even as a kid. Her mind whirls around, hundreds of miles per hour. Always thinking. Mostly about nothing important, but always on.

"Behind you, behind you," someone shouts.

Leah is on the puck but a red player hooks her stick and yanks hard. Leah falls. She can't believe the woman didn't say sorry. Perhaps she isn't aggressive enough for this game.

"Good try, Leah," someone shouts from the bench. "That is Leah, right? Is that her name?"

Leah doesn't say much in the change room. The other women talk back and forth but Leah changes quietly and listens. She knows that they think she is new to the game even though she's been playing for years. Leah just hasn't got any better. She started seven years ago but she's so quiet and she hasn't improved at all and so they all think she's brand new every year. And she's so shy she's never made any connections in the change room. She comes in from the parking lot reeking of cigarette smoke, knowing she's not like anyone else here, and she puts on her jill and shin pads and socks and hockey pants and she sits on the bench breathing hard in her own small world. Leah knows it's not that they don't like her. It's just that when they try to talk to her she feels herself backing off, looking down, moving away. She can't help it. She knows they feel this too. All these women seem to come from a world different from her own.

Meaning: for one thing, none of them smoke and, even if they did, she would bet anyone a million dollars that no one on her team works at Walmart.

When her kids were young Leah would bring them to the rink to watch her play. They are older now and not interested in seeing her games anymore. Which is probably good. Terry fell that one time from the seats. He was leaning over the railing and he flipped over somehow and landed below, near the change rooms. Luckily he landed on his side, not his back or his head — although Margie, at work, said in a half-joking way that if he had landed on his head it wouldn't have mattered.

Meaning: he's stupid anyway.

186

Meaning: he's brain damaged.

Leah skates over to the bench to wait for her next shift. Margie is as stupid as Terry, if not stupider.

Terry's not stupid, Leah's caseworker would say, "He's challenged." Or "He's special." Or "He's just different."

Different, Leah thinks. My ass. The anger Leah feels about Terry's situation is almost as fierce as her love for him. Leah thought that her anger would be gone by now. He is, after all, fifteen. But it's a burning anger, a violent-unfair-temper-tantrum-furious anger. Why him? Why her? It's not fair for either of them.

"Nice shot. That was good, wasn't it?" One of the women on her team is chatting to her on the bench. Leah smiles and nods her head in the helmet. The helmet bobs a bit. She stretches her jaw out into the chin pad and moves her helmet up and down using her chin. Some games her helmet seems too tight. Some games it wobbles. The woman who is talking to her smiles nicely out of her face mask. Leah can't remember her name. Trisha? Tasha? She comes with that skinny woman from California, the one who looks haunted and sad.

Leah feels haunted and sad.

Margie, at work, is haunted and sad. But that's because she's married to an asshole who has been off work for three years because of a work-related "disability." In quotes. "Disability."

Meaning: he lifted a box and pulled his fat back.

Meaning: Margie works full time at Walmart and lifts boxes every day — big boxes — over her fat stomach. She bends her short little legs to lift, carefully, and then she goes home and takes care of her lazy husband, who spends all day watching TV.

Leah goes back out on the ice. At least Margie has a husband. Leah smiles to herself. That's a joke, she thinks. Thank god she's not married anymore. Leah never had to take care of Carl, in fact she rarely saw him, but maybe if she had taken care of him she would have noticed what he was up to. Problem with marrying a guy who is always on the road? You can't ever know what he's doing. Or, more correctly, who he's doing. When he says he won't be home for three days, you think it might just have something to do with work.

"Leah, take it up!" Leah has the puck on her stick and she's moving up towards the red team's blue line. Over the blue line. She's not even off-side. She's near the net. Takes a shot. It hits the post.

"Good try. Woo hoo." This from the Tasha/Trisha woman who is playing defence beside her.

Leah instinctively looks up into the seats, she looks up half-expecting to see her kids there. As if maybe they did come to watch her. But the seats are almost empty. Except for one man, a handsome man. Watching the game from afar. He's hidden a bit in the corner. Leah doesn't think anyone else has noticed him there. And there's the guy with his BlackBerry, paying no attention but always there. And that kid in the hoodie. Leah wonders if his mother ever washes it. Same hoodie every time, hands in his pouch.

When Terry would climb and squirm and move around at the rink, Hannah would sit nicely, properly, in the seat and cheer Leah on. She used to wave when Leah looked up. Once she made a big sign that said, "Go Mom Go!" in pink letters and glitter glue and she flapped it around furiously. She would talk to other people in the seats. She would try to watch her brother. But she was young then, six or seven, and Terry was ten and larger and would take off in the opposite direction, scattering hats, gloves, coat throughout the arena seats. Hannah couldn't keep up. And Carl left before Hannah was born, so he was no help. Now, eleven and fifteen, Hannah and Terry are at home alone while Leah plays hockey.

Meaning: Terry's roaming the house touching things, touching himself, crying, agitated, or happy, singing to himself, always moving, and Hannah is watching TV, occasionally keeping an eye on the oven to make sure Terry didn't turn it on, her ears alert for any noises she doesn't understand. Like the time she heard the lawn mower start up in the garage.

"It's a hard enough life," Hannah sings when she is in a good mood. She dances often, little spins and twirls in the kitchen. She's a happy kid, despite everything.

Leah pulls her ponytail and laughs. "You've got it made, baby," she tells Hannah. "Compared to my life, yours will be just swell."

But Hannah is right. Leah shouldn't leave Terry with her. She's too young. It's not fair.

Meaning: life is not fair.

"Shit, I missed." One of her own teammates crashes into Leah. "Sorry, sorry."

"No problem," Leah says, stumbling into the boards.

Her mind won't stay in the game tonight. She's fractured and confused. It's these short shifts — two minutes on is ridiculous. Leah finds that once she's finally playing well, at about a minute in, she is pulled off to sit on the bench again. Off. On. Leah would rather stay on until she dropped. Get in the zone. Become one with the game. She's noticed lately that when she is in the game she breathes funny. She pulls air through tight, half-open lips, closed teeth, makes a sucking noise.

Red scores on the white team and they crash their sticks along the wall in front of the bench, bang them hard, shouting, "Woo hoo."

In Texas, Leah thinks, they'd say, "Yeehaw."

In Texas they might shoot you if you scored on them. That's a joke. She wonders what they'd say in California. She should ask the skinny, blond, sad woman. "Right on." Or maybe, "Too cool."

Why is Leah thinking about Texas? Because that's where Carl went on his last "work-related trip."

Meaning: he stayed here, in town, in the Days Inn on Belevedere Street, and screwed one of the many women he was seeing.

In the change room earlier Leah heard the other women talking about their kids. Some neighbour whose kid cleans all the time — and she thinks this is a problem? Another kid who can't put down the basketball, even when it's snowing. One kid who should be getting all A's at school but never tries hard enough and so comes home with B's. According to his mom, according to the teacher, the kid is a literal genius. One woman talks about her neighbour's dog, which is always barking. She wonders aloud if she should open the back gate of her neighbour's house and let the dog run away one day. Shout, "out of here," and pat the dog on the butt, watch him run. The California woman laughs, she agrees. She says she lives right across the street from the dog and she actually saw it disappear this morning, "So you don't need to worry, Trish." She says the woman who owns the dog pulled her back out when the dog took off and had to lie down on her kitchen floor almost all day. Although she feels sorry for the neighbour, she hates the noise the dog makes and she too hopes the dog never comes back. Leah doesn't know much about dogs but she could talk about Hannah. She never does, however. There isn't much to share. In school Hannah does okay — not an A student, but she isn't failing either. She's nice to kids, she's nice to teachers. Actually, the only thing wrong with Hannah is that she's too nice. Too trusting. Bringing people home. And stray cats. Talking to everyone on the street. One day, Leah thinks, someone's going to walk off with Hannah. And Hannah will go peacefully with them. Happily. Probably hold the guy's hand.

Leah thinks that Hannah will probably find this missing dog and adopt him.

The California woman and the Trisha woman are getting better at hockey. They are new to the game this year and Leah has noticed improvement. The other new woman still can't skate that well, but she handles the puck heroically.

The handsome man in the seats stands and begins to walk down towards the glass. A few women on the team notice him. The new woman who is weak on her skates notices him and almost falls over. Not that it matters, but when you thought you were alone as you played it makes you slightly self-conscious to see that you were being watched.

Terry scares away anyone Hannah brings home anyway. The ones who come over after school, the few friends Hannah manages to make. He thumps himself down in a chair in the kitchen and rubs at his crotch or picks his nose and Hannah's friends up and leave.

Leah's caseworker says that's because he's lonely.

Meaning: don't you know a boy needs his father?

Leah doesn't know why her caseworker seems to hate her so much. She's just trying to get help for Terry. Leah can't understand why this woman is making her jump through hoops for it. Leah thought the woman would take one look at Terry and make sure he has the proper help at school.

"Can't you see he needs help?" she asks. The woman just nods her head stiffly and looks around Leah's overcrowded living room. She takes in the ashtray, which Leah just cleaned, and the TV, which, sure, is always on — Leah likes background noise. Sue her. Then the woman sniffs. She sniffs.

Leah is at the net and the puck is between her skates and there are three red players on her. The white goalie is shouting at Leah to move away, that she can't see. Move? But isn't she helping? Making sure the puck doesn't go in their net?

What the goalie means is: Leah is always in the way.

Leah takes the puck around the back but a red player comes out at her, crazy-large, and Leah swears the woman's eyes are on fire. She smashes hard into Leah and Leah's stick becomes stuck in the goalie's net. She can hear her team shouting. It happens so fast, but somehow the crazy red player takes Leah's stick up in her arms like she's holding a baby, and tosses it hard at the boards. The stick almost hits the referee. He stands there, looking amazed. Leah's team boos. And, as Leah is struggling to pick up her stick with her huge hockey gloves on, like trying to pick up a penny from the floor, or like trying to turn the page of a book with dry-fingers, the insane red player scores.

Meaning: she doesn't, not even for a second, turn and say, "I'm sorry." What kind of a woman is she?

And this, this makes Leah mad. Mad at herself and her wimpiness.

"Fuck," Leah says under her breath as she comes around to the front of the net. The goalie pats her shoulder.

"That should've been a penalty," the goalie says.

And where is Carl these days? Terry's father. Leah would like to know that herself. Just for the money, though, not because she ever wants to see him again. He owes her a lot of child support. Right when they figured out something was wrong with Terry, something was different, Carl up and left. Went out on the road, to "Texas," and never came back. Yeehaw. Leah used to like to imagine that he was killed somewhere, that she hadn't heard from him because he was brutally murdered, but inside Leah knows he's probably off somewhere with a new family, a new kid, this one normal. She never even got divorce papers, but she doesn't have the money or energy to track him down.

Hannah's father is a different story. Leah sees him every day in Walmart, stocking the shelves, helping Margie pick up those heavy boxes. He stocks the shelves with no sense of urgency, as if his life is clean and clear. Leah guesses it is. After all, he doesn't know he's got an eleven-year-old girl. He knows nothing except that he had drunken sex with Leah after a work party eleven years, nine months ago. He knows that this happens once in his lifetime. He knows that Leah let him in once, and will never do that again. Sometimes Leah wonders at his stupidity. After all, he saw her pregnant, he signed the card given to her from the staff when she gave birth to Hannah. Leah supposes he can't add, she supposes he never finished high school. Or maybe he does know, but doesn't want to know. Leah doesn't want to know anything about him. His name is Hank. He is thirty-six years old. He's been working at Walmart since he was twenty-four. Since he finished university. He might still live at home with his parents. Leah doesn't know. Who the hell pays to go to university and then settles with working at Walmart? Someday Leah knows Hannah will have questions and she'll have to come clean but, for now, she really doesn't care.

The man at the glass is staring hard at the California woman on Leah's team. Leah is on the bench with her and she says, "Do you know that guy? He keeps looking at you."

The California woman swivels her head away from the game and looks across the ice at the man. Time stands still. Leah can feel it actually stop. She can hear the intake of breath from the woman beside her. It's as if there is always a ticking in her head and suddenly it went silent. The woman beside her stiffens.

"You okay?"

"Oh god," the woman says. She drops down on the bench. "Oh my god."

Leah doesn't know what to do. Does she go back on the ice or sit with the woman?

"What is it, Dayton? Are you okay?" Trisha/Tasha comes off the ice.

Leah takes her position on the ice. The man behind the glass walks down the hallway, towards the change rooms, and then Leah loses track of him as she concentrates on the game. Dayton stands at the bench, white-faced. Trisha/Tasha stands with her.

Boyfriend trouble, Leah thinks. Good thing Leah doesn't have that.

The game is over. They lost. But they are still boisterous and happy in the change room. Two women open beers. The cans explode all over them. They sip and laugh.

But in the corner near Leah, the California woman, Dayton, sits in her hockey gear and stares at the floor. Trisha/Tasha is beside her. Leah watches them as she undresses. It is as if Dayton can't move a muscle. She sits there, a statue, sweating in her gear, while around her everyone is moving, undressing, talking, laughing. She is completely still. Whoever that man was, Leah knows he's trouble. Will Terry be that? Will Terry be trouble for some woman in the future? Or will he never have a woman? Never have a future.

Leah stands to leave. She lugs her hockey bag behind her, grabs her stick from the corner. And, as she opens the door to go, she hears it. Everyone in the room, every single player on her team, says, "Good game, Leah." She smiles shyly and heads out into the hallway, her bag scratching up against the walls.

The season is almost over.

They know her name.

As Leah leaves the arena Dayton's handsome and bad boyfriend smiles at her. He opens the door for her. She struggles with her bag to get out, says, "Thanks." He laughs. He says, "Good game," in a warm way, his voice low and quiet. And, if it weren't for the reaction she saw from Dayton in the change room just a minute ago, Leah would have told anyone that she would have let this handsome man, this smooth talker, this "he's trouble" man, run his fingers down her cheek and touch her neck. She would have let him kiss her lightly on the lips, move across her jawbone and suck on her earlobe. She would have. He was that handsome. And, after all, strange things do happen every day of the week.

To: puckbunnybrady@pik.com
From: puckbunnybrady@pik.com
Subject: Season Wrapping Up!

Hello Hockey Ladies!

As you are well aware, the season is almost over. It has been
a super season despite the robbery, which was never, as you
know, solved. All the teams this year played with spirit and
fairness. The complaints were down this year by a lot. And
goalies — holy crow, goalies! You were amazing. Thank you
for calling ahead if you couldn't make your games. Thank you
for filling in for each other. Hockey isn't hockey without
goalies. Remember those games last year when we had to turn
the net around and shoot off the boards? Ridiculous, and
definitely not fun.

This is a reminder to hand in your jerseys to your team
captain on your last Wednesday night — three weeks from now.
We'll wash them for you for next year, no worries about that.
Also, our pub night is going to be March 23rd this year.
We're doing it after March break for those of you who go away
with the kids for the school holiday. Free pizza and beer.
How can you resist? I look forward to seeing you all there.

Again, thanks for another great season.

   Tina Brady
       Parkville Ice Kats
       Co-ordinator Extraordinaire

To Mrs. Rathbin
c/o Cancer Society Volunteer Driving

Dear Mrs. Rathbin,
Hello. This is Claire Smythe. I don't know
if you remember me. You drove me to radiation
one day last fall. It was in early November. You
gave me some lovely knitted hats and you talked
to me about Brussels sprouts. I just wanted to
tell you about a month after our drive together
I found an article about Brussels sprouts and
cancer. It talks about the benefits of Brussels
sprouts to the body's DNA. I'm assuming you
knew about this and that is what you meant
when you brought up Brussels sprouts. At
the time I was confused, but now I think I
understand. I guess I really wanted to just say
thank you for the hats. I've worn mine most of
the winter and my son, Jude, wears his all the
time too. We've come to love them. I'm sorry I
didn't write to thank you sooner.

Sincerely,
Claire

14

Michael isn't sure if he became this way because it was expected of him or if his face makes him this way. If the scar running straight through the middle, from forehead to chin, is the outer representation of his real, true, deep internal self or if it's just a marking on the surface and he is simply this way. His mother tells him it's the way people treat him.

"With a face like that it's expected of you. The world turns on you when you look like this."

Michael is at the local pool hall after work. A place called Barney's. It's owned by the mayor. The Toyota dealership is also owned by the mayor. As is the Suds'n'Such car wash, where Michael works. Michael doesn't know the mayor personally, but sometimes he feels he does. His mother says the mayor's got his hands in the honey jar. His mother says that's why the mayor's so fat. "Soon he'll own the whole city," his mother says. "He's swallowing it up."

When Michael is at work and he gets out from the cars lined up inside the car wash, when he wrings out the cloth he is using to dry the windows, or when he spritzes the dashboard and then hands people their receipt, he knows they will step back. He waits for it. They will cringe. Shiver. Sometimes it's violent. Sometimes imperceptible. He expects it. When people don't react, when they seem to be able to control their emotions, then Michael feels awful. He feels hurt. He can't explain why he feels this way. If anyone other than his mother ever asked him to explain there would be nothing he could say. Michael doesn't like people's reactions, their stares, but he is so used to getting them that when they don't happen it's almost as if he is disappointed.

"Don't be silly," his mother says. "Buck up. Get some spine. You have one life given to you, Michael. Only one life. Be strong."

At the pool hall the locals know him. They still react. But they know his face is coming. Or maybe they are too drunk to really care. And it's dark. Michael can sit at the bar in the corner, under the burnt out light bulb and melt into his beer. He can watch without being watched. He can think about it all. About good and evil, about fate and his face and his mother, who is getting old, and his car-washing job and what his life would have been like if he didn't have this face. And the more Michael drinks, the more he ponders. His mother says, "Don't dwell on what you can't change, Michael." But Michael dwells. He wallows.

People never ask Michael what happened to his face. They'd be more likely to ask him about the embarrassing tattoo of a cross on the back of his neck that he got when he was really drunk and angry years ago. He's not even religious. Michael can't figure out why they don't ask about his face. They look away, turn from him, but no one ever says, "What happened?" Except kids. Sometimes kids will ask but their mothers will pull them away from him before he can answer. Kids can be the most aware, they can sometimes even be sensitive, but they can also be the cruellest. Staring at him. Pointing. Saying, "Eww." Michael's seen and heard it all.

After he's had a couple beers Michael really wishes people would ask him to tell them the story of his face. Then he would tell them and he would watch their faces for reactions. He would start, "Once upon a time" and finish with "the end," even though the story is still continuing. And if they didn't believe him he wouldn't care. At least they would know. Michael's mother says that no one ever wants to hear bad news, but Michael isn't sure that's true. Sometimes people are so interested in the bad news they forget the good. He hears it all the time. People talking about crime, wars, illnesses and disease. They become animated and their eyes light up. People can't get enough of bad news.

When he has finished his beers Michael tends to walk through the residential streets and look in the lit-up windows of people's houses. With the beer inside him he doesn't feel bad about this. It's only the next day, sober, when the guilt washes over him. Because peeping in windows is something people would expect someone with a face like Michael's to do. With a face like that, they'd say, of course. And this is what it comes down to. This is why Michael doesn't know if it's his face that makes him do the things he does, or if he does these things because of who he is inside.

What Michael does: he creeps into backyards and looks into windows. He presses his face close against the windows, leaves his breath behind. He moves things, a rake, a watering can, a snow shovel. He steps on flowers or steals the pucks from a backyard hockey rink. He knocks softly on doors and then escapes before anyone can answer. He punctures soccer balls, volleyballs, basketballs. He takes a spring or two from trampolines. He opens shed doors, leaves them vulnerable. And then he walks home through the quiet nights, his hands in his pockets, his soul a guilty flurry of disgust and grief. His mother tries to wait up for him most nights, but falls asleep in her chair listening to the radio. Michael will throw an afghan on her and climb the stairs to his attic room. Exhausted. Spent. Sorry.

But tonight he is sipping Bud Lite by the end of the bar and the bartender is pretending to clean the counter but instead watching the hockey game on the TV over the mirror. This is probably happening in hundreds of bars all over the world. Bartenders wiping. Hockey on the TV. Drunks lined up, pretending to enjoy their beers when really all they want is to get enough beer in them to feel nothing.

"Creak," says a voice beside Michael. A little man in a mud brown suit sits down on the creaky stool next to Michael. "I can't help but notice you're alone."

Michael is looking the opposite direction, but now turns his face slightly towards the man. Shrugs. Sips his beer.

"Tap, tap," the man says, tapping on the counter. "Bartender. Snap. Snap." The man snaps his fingers. "One beer please. Sigh." He sits back, his legs dangling off the high stool. "It all depends on how you get their attention," the man says. "Snapping your fingers works, but some find it offensive. What do you think?"

"Huh?" Michael says.

"Well, look at you. You're awake." The man laughs. Loud. A guffaw. "Ha ha," he says.

Michael turns full on and looks at the man. The man is bothering Michael so, Michael reasons, why not bother the little man. His face, all of it, inches from him. The man backs up a bit, leans off his stool. His eyes wide open, he stares at Michael's face. Then he blinks once, twice, three times and turns back to the beer just put in front of him and says, "My goodness. Fresh, cold beer," as if he hadn't ordered exactly that and was surprised. He sips the beer, the foam on his upper lip.

Michael turns back to his beer. Holds his finger up to order another. Stares down deep into his almost empty glass.

The little man swings his feet back and forth. He whistles a quiet tune. Unexpectedly, he slaps Michael on the upper arm when someone scores in the hockey game.

"My, what a day," the man says. "Did you have the same kind of day I did? No, you don't need to answer. You look like you had the kind of day I did. Women. Phew." He dramatically wipes his hand over his brow. "Women." He pauses. "I think it might be time to wear the brown linen suit I bought at Value Village two summers ago. This one is hot."

Michael notices that the suit is two sizes too big, but that doesn't matter. Feeling philosophical after his beers, Michael thinks that not everything is about looks or the ability to impress by clothing or appearance. It is merely about comfort, it has always been about comfort. The man hums.

"Not like my boarding house," the man says, "where the heat stays off most of the winter and seems to pop back on come summer. Pop. Where my temperature is never right. Never comfortable."

Michael isn't sure if he's interested in this man's day or his clothes or the temperature or if he's had too many beers, or if he's just interested in the fact that someone, after seeing his face straight-on, is talking to him — that he isn't a dark shadow in the bar again tonight — but he feels a slight warmth moving through his body. Annoyed, yes he is. But also a bit touched. He gave the little man his face — dead on — and still the man continues to sit close, knock into him even, laugh, talk. As if Michael's face is nothing special. Just what Michael wants it to be. So Michael clears his throat and asks. He can't help himself. Later on he'll wish he had said nothing, but now, with three beers in him and this strange man, Michael feels sociable: "What about women?"

"Ah," the man says. "The fairer species. Women. The word moves around my head, almost soothes the sounds of this bar. In my boarding house I have a hot plate, a microwave, a printer and a laptop. I have worked hard for these things. I lock my room when I leave so no one else will come in and steal what I have worked so hard for. I sell the things I make. It's hard work. It's dangerous work. Once a kid bit me. But it's worth it. Women."

Michael snorts. All women have ever been to him is distant. Not fair. Not mysterious.

"The loveliness of some does outweigh the hurtfulness of others."

"Are you a poet or something?" Michael asks.

"Well, nice of you to notice. But no, not a poet. Not quite. Not really. More of a . . . hmmmm, a, shall we say, hmmmm, a salesman." The little man waves his arms in the air as if he's catching an insect out of the sky. "I used to do art. When I was still growing taller and hadn't stopped so short, har har," he laughs. "Back then my mother and father and brother, they liked my work. They saw my work as worthy of fridge magnets. They saw my work as art." He pauses. "And then they tried to change me." He taps loudly on the counter with his right index finger. Stabs the counter.

"You okay, there?" The bartender is paying attention to this little man now. His strange movements when everyone else in the bar is still and sullen. "How are you doing?"

"Nice of you to ask," the man says. "Just fine. Just fine." He whispers to Michael, "Manny says that I'm acting strange. I heard Manny say it the other day, to the new guy down the hall in the boarding house. He said, 'That fucking guy in 2B, he's fucking weird.' And that meant me. I'm in 2B."

The bartender raises his eyebrows and looks at Michael. Then looks away, just as fast, as if he'd forgotten what he would be looking at.

"So you're having trouble selling things to women?" Michael asks. Four beers now. He's emboldened. He's feeling like talking. He doesn't feel this way often. Sometimes the guys at work ask him things. He talks to his mother when he's home. But that's about it. Michael clears his throat.

"It's that particular street," the man says. "There's something about it. Edgewood."

Michael leans back. Edgewood. Back in the fall Michael helped some guy rake leaves on Edgewood. He doesn't know what got into him. He was walking past the house and there were so many leaves and the guy looked tired. There were girls out front, beautiful young girls. Michael was feeling good. He was feeling helpful. He wanted to be near this guy and the girls. They reminded him of easier times. When he would help his father do chores. Before the accident. Besides, earlier that week he had been in this guy's backyard and he was still feeling guilty about it. He had moved the girl's basketball across the yard. He had piled up some sticks that had fallen off a tree and put them in a formation that resembled the beginnings of a campfire. He had picked up dog shit with two sticks and placed it atop the fire. Michael was feeling bad about it so he offered his help and the guy took him up on it.

"And there's no wood," the man says. "There can't be an edge of a wood if there's no wood."

Becky. That was her name. The guy's daughter. The guy called out to her once or twice, and Michael picked up her name and carried it with him.

"Anyhow," the man says, wiping the condensation of his beer off the counter with his sleeve, "the street just screams for what I'm selling. All those women, those little girls. They could really use what I am selling."

"What's that?" Michael asks, but the little man continues on as if he didn't hear. The bartender places two more beers in front of them.

"So I walk up and down all those front walks today. Yesterday. The day before that. I went once before Christmas but that didn't go well. Clomp, clomp, clomp. Back and forth. Sometimes they answer the door. Knock knock. Ding dong. Sometimes they don't. I try to shake their hands. 'Shake shake,' I say. But most of them will not shake my hand. As if I'm a dog. As if I'm asking to shake a paw. Ha ha. I wear out my good suit walking to and fro. I wear out my good shoes. I'm stiff and sore. It rains on my head. Splish splash. And no one takes me up on anything. No one wants to hear about what I'm trying to sell. In fact, they get mad at me and slam the door in my face."

"Most people work during the day," Michael says. "I'm surprised anyone is home."

"Oh they are. The women. Some of them. They are there, holed up inside their houses. You think this is a fair and equal world? You think feminism changed things? These women are still inside their houses, waiting for their husbands to bring home the money. Ha ha." The man stretches, his arms in the air, his mouth open. He yawns. "I've had it with this job. I've had it. Just worn to the bone, I am. Worn right out. Exhausted."

Michael doesn't know what to say to this. His eyes are blurry from too much beer. He can't see straight. He focuses on the TV and occasionally gets a glimpse of a hockey player skating down the ice. Women, he thinks. Hockey on TV. Women. Girls. Home. All the time. This makes sense to him, but also doesn't make sense. When he walks that street during the week it feels deserted, empty. The kids are in school, the women and men at work. Only the dogs are there, behind the curtains, getting into the bathroom garbage, sleeping on the sofas, resting their chins on the windowsills and looking out.

"I don't know," Michael says. "I think the women work too." Michael mentions that he's been on that street, that sometimes he goes into the backyards and checks things out, and no one is ever home. He doesn't know what makes him tell the little man this

— it's something to be ashamed of, not something to brag about — but he feels like talking after all this beer, he feels like sharing some part of his life. Telling this man about the things he does feels dangerous and makes him feel alive.

"Did I tell you that I occasionally take a train and then a bus and then I walk past their house at night. I sneak into their backyard. My parents. My brother is gone now. I don't know where. My mother and father watch TV alone in the living room. I walk past the house in my old city and I think of those fridge magnets holding up my art. My work proudly displayed and I know that they have no idea how famous I've become. How much I sell my work for. The guys in the boarding house. The doctor and dentist over in the next town, the mayor even. Everyone loves my work. My images. And my pamphlets, they educate. They educate people about the kids."

Michael doesn't know what to say.

"Now that I've told you my story," the man swings his legs back and forth under the stool, "you have to tell me yours. How, my good friend, did you get a face like that?"

There is sudden silence. At least Michael hears it that way. In fact, only the bartender stops wiping and looks at the little man, but it seems to Michael that the whole bar shuts down. Even the TV is quiet. It seems as if everyone has turned towards Michael, waiting for the answer.

"I mean, really. A face like yours. There has to be a story behind it. Right? Am I right?"

"My story?"

"Uh huh."

"My face?"

The bartender looks at Michael. Michael looks right back at him. The bartender looks away.

And it's not as if Michael doesn't want to tell the whole sordid story about his face, about his father and his drinking, the steel snow shovel.

But suddenly the room feels so close and sticky, so hot and cold at the same time, so loud and quiet, that he pushes back his bar stool, jumps off and stumbles towards the door.

"Hey," the bartender shouts. "You need to pay me."

Michael shuffles back to the bar.

"Don't leave," the man says. "Don't leave now. We were just starting to have fun."

Michael pays his bill, turns from the little man, from the bartender, and heads out into the night. He pulls his jacket around him. Shivers. It's raining slightly.

"The world isn't anything like you think it'll be," Michael's mother is fond of saying. "It's always a disappointment, no matter how you look at it." She should know. Look what she got for a son. Look what she got for a husband. "Roll with the punches," she says. "Take it in stride."

Michael rounds the corner, rain falling, covering his face, soaking his shoes. The worries, fears, the life he's led. For what? A snow shovel. A drunk man. An accident. Because that's all it was. An accident. It could've happened to anyone. And Michael wishes it were more than that, he wishes his story was as terrifying as his face. He wishes that his tale had impact and punch. A lesson. Instead, he is back there again, standing behind his father, ten years old, a cold evening. His father brings the metal shovel up, ready to dig down again into the soft snow, and he stumbles slightly from the drink. Michael has crept up, ready to scare his father, ready to dump snow on the man's hatless head. But the shovel comes down behind his father and there is nothing more Michael remembers about the evening. He doesn't remember the blood. He doesn't remember his father screaming, the ambulance, the police.

"Up and left us because he couldn't take the guilt, Michael," Michael's mother says. "Not your fault."

But it is Michael's fault. Because if his face didn't look like this then his father wouldn't be constantly reminded of that evening, of that sharp snow shovel.

"At least he sends us money," Michael's mother says. "That's something."

Thirty-three years old. Twenty-three years of this now, to be exact. Plodding through life with this face, this accident, this failure. His father gone. His mother lonely.

"Hey, behind you." The little man is running up towards Michael. He is shorter than Michael figured now that he sees him standing. "Wait up. Breathe. Breathe." The man takes deep breaths as he says this. "Listen," he says. "We all have our burdens to bear. We all have those things in our lives that tell our stories, that make us who we are. Phew, I'm panting. I can't get my breath. Pant pant. Ha ha. But it behooves me to tell you, my kind sir, that your burden is no deeper than most. In fact, my burden goes all the way to China. Ha ha." Here the little man leans into Michael's frame, bends double, smacks his hand on his knees and laughs. He points down to the ground. "All the way to China. In fact, all I've ever been is myself and they are telling me that I myself am not all right? Is something wrong with me when all I am is myself?"

Michael shrugs off the man's hand and continues walking away. "You're drunk."

"And I'll sell you that burden," the man shouts as Michael walks on. "I'll sell it to you. You're a grown man. You'll want it. Women don't want it. They push me away. Shove me away. But you'll want it for a price. I know you will. Wait."

Michael says, "You are crazy."

The man says, "I might be. In fact, Manny says I'm fucking crazy. Oh dear. Maybe I am. I'm not sure. I've heard that word used before when it comes to talking about me. But I like my room, my hot plate, my microwave, my laptop and my printer. I like my suits. My life. I like my life. I want nothing to change. Sometimes I think about my mother and father. I want to know what happened to my brother. I love the kids, the children. I do them no harm."

Michael doesn't stop.

"Wait for me."

Michael turns on to Edgewood Street. Before he realizes it he is standing in front of the basketball net across from the house he raked the leaves at last fall. Tom's house. Becky's house. He stands under the net and he looks at the house there, raised a bit on a hill, empty of leaves, one small patch of snow left over, melting quickly in the rain, and he sees something move in the upstairs front window. The curtains are closed but Michael can see a finger poking out between the blinds. And then a face. The girl. Becky. Looking out at him. Michael draws his coat tightly around his frame and moves back, out from under the street light.

Up the street, slowly, comes the little man. "Oh, I'm out of breath," he says. "Pant pant."

"You said that before."

"Wheeze? Wheeze?"

The girl pops her head back inside her room. The blinds close shut when she takes her finger out.

"You might want to leave me alone," Michael says. He is still looking up at the window, searching for the girl's face. The little man says nothing. Michael feels sober now, as if he hadn't had a single beer, as if he hadn't even gone into the bar after work and met this strange person. In fact, if the little man wasn't there in front of him right now Michael would think that, perhaps, he'd just gotten off work and was heading home to have dinner with his mother. But there he is, bothering Michael. Right there in front of him. "I'm not feeling very generous right now."

"Oh my," the man says.

"You might want to keep your distance."

The little man backs up, his hands up as if he's being arrested.

"You've hurt my feelings. You've made me want to cry," he says. "Oh my. It hurts. Tears tears."

"Shhhhh." Michael walks quickly down the street, in the direction of his mother and his own home, which is over the railroad tracks and at the end of a busy intersection. The farther away from the little man Michael walks the less he can hear him and the better he feels. It's almost as if the little man is filling himself up with all of Michael's evils, Michael's fears and insecurities and unhappiness. It's as if his gradually louder, but also diminishing voice is giving Michael's feelings the release they need. Michael doesn't have to do anything but walk away from it all. Go home to his poor old mother, to his attic room, to his job at the Suds'N Such, to his beers at Barney's. This bizarre little man in the mud brown suit, with his deep burdens that he is unable to sell, with his craziness, has somehow diminished all that Michael carries within him. All the mixed-up feelings. All the remorse. Michael has left the man now, he can't hear him whining anymore, and he is walking away.

This scar on his face, Michael thinks, may not be as deep as he thinks it is.

Suddenly Michael stops. He thinks of that girl, Becky, in her window peeking out. He thinks of the little man in the brown suit and how, when they were talking in the bar, he told the little man about going into the backyards, he told the little man about how he snoops and watches. Knock knock, the beginning of a joke that's not really funny. Michael turns. Waits. What did the man mean about the children? Then he begins walking back, back towards the man, towards Becky, towards the backyards that he haunts, past a stray dog who lumbers by him in the rain, back to where he was coming from.

Build-Your-Bear ™

Your way is the right way . . .
Come Build, Come Play, Come Love.
Your Bear.

Dear Ms. Patricia Birk,

I am writing to apologize for my threatening letters regarding your bear-building business, "The Bear Company." I was not made aware of your situation when I began writing to you. My informants make sure I know about any competing business, but they don't always give me the full details. I had no idea you were sewing out of your house and that your yearly income was so low.

I'm wondering if you'll forgive me for upsetting you.

I'm also wondering if you think there is any way we can work together to help each other? Occasionally we get orders for birthday parties, bears made-to-order. A mother might want twenty or so Little Mermaid Bears, for example, for her child's party loot bags, and she might not want to come into our store in the mall and make her own — she might not have enough time in her busy day, rushing around doing errands and having tea with other mothers. Maybe there is a way we can commission you to do these kinds of orders?

Please let me know how you feel about this, Ms. Birk, and, again, I apologize for my mis-information. I'm so glad you took the time to write to me. Please ignore any further letters from my lawyers. Sometimes it takes months before they realize I've called off the dogs — ha ha.

Sincerely,

Maisy Crank.

Maisy Crank
CEO and Head Bear of Build-Your-Bear™
Madison, Wisconsin

Dear Dad,

How is it possible that you don't remember the circus freak postcards? He had a whole album full of them. I'm not imagining this. I'm sure of it. I'd like to know what you did with them.

Love, Tom

Dear Tom,

He was a disturbed man at the end. Son, please do not mention this again.

On another note: when are you coming to visit? Your mother wants to know if it's that wife of yours who doesn't want to come down to Florida. If so, can you come with Becky on your own when her school is out for summer break?

Sincerely,
Dad

15

Maria was bending down, purple robe held tight, reaching for the newspaper, when it happened. The paper, wrapped in a pinkish plastic bag slightly damp from the morning rain, tossed on her front porch every day by Trish's son, Charlie, who lives across the street and who couldn't throw straight to save his life, fell from the untied bag and landed in a puddle. And right before it happened she was thinking, Today is the day. She was thinking, Today is the day and she was bending towards the paper and then the dog bolted out of the house and she bent just a bit further to try to reach for his collar and then it happened and she thought, Today isn't the day. And she thought, Damn it. She thought, Why does everything always happen to me? She laughed a little, her barkish laugh. One quick, painful one. She tried to call out for the dog but he was long gone.

Some of this is what Maria tells Tom when he comes home from work.

"I was bending. Just bending down."

"Uh huh." Tom has his head buried in the refrigerator. Maria can only see his long legs, clad in khaki. She can see his brown shoes, which he forgot to take off at the door. From her position she can see the wet tracks he has made, barely visible footprints, slightly muddy. "Don't we have any beer? Did you drink the last beer?"

"I bent over, the paper fell, and here I am."

"Here you are," Tom says.

"You forgot to take your shoes off."

Tom looks down, then up again at the fridge. He finds the beer at the back of the refrigerator, behind the pickles and the sour cream — sour cream that is, Tom thinks, definitely more than sour now, how long has it been in here? He twists open the beer and takes a deep swallow. Then he opens the sour cream container and sees all the green mould. He studies it for a minute and then puts the lid back on and, without thinking, places the container back in the fridge. He turns to look down at his wife.

Maria is lying on the kitchen floor. Watching him.

"There are bits of food down here, Tom," she says. "You wouldn't even believe it unless you were lying here. I thought I was so clean, but there is food everywhere. Crumbs. And hair. And dust. Mostly crumbs. I've been picking it up all day but I have nowhere to put it so I drop it again."

"Don't let Becky lie on the floor then." Tom smiles. He is rifling through the mail. A few letters. Bills. A magazine about cottages.

Maria smiles.

"Have you taken anything?"

"Robaxacet," Maria says. "In fact, truth be told —"

"Truth be told?" Tom laughs.

"I'm a little high on it." Maria giggles, slightly.

"Hence lying on the floor?"

"Hence?" Another giggle. Gone is her barkish laugh.

Tom reaches down and takes the newspaper from the floor and tries to open it. The pages have stuck together. Everything looks melted. Sports, News, Life, Arts and Entertainment, Wheels, all combined into one big gluey mess. Dry, though. It has been sitting here all day. Whole sections of the world crammed together.

"I'm cold," Maria says. "I've been in this robe all day. I haven't been able to move."

"You should have called me."

"I thought about that but what could you have done? I just need to be still. Remember the last time? Just lying still is the only cure."

Tom shrugs. He glances down at Maria, in her purple robe, the belt cinched tight around her tiny waist, and he says, "Where's Becky?"

"Rachel's." Maria nods in the general direction of the phone. "She left a message on the answering machine. I guess she thought I wasn't home from work yet so she went to Rachel's after school."

"Ah." Tom settles on the stool behind the counter with his beer and his mail and his stuck-together newspaper. "No dinner then, I guess?"

Maria sighs. "You'll have to make it." She stares up at the ceiling. She now fully understands the saying "stiff as a board." She is cold. She is high on muscle relaxants. She wants to fall asleep.

"Where's Dog?" Tom says. He looks up. Looks around. "I haven't seen him since I've been home."

Becky cries, "I can't believe you lost Dog." She hasn't stopped crying dramatically since she returned from Rachel's. She's been flinging her arms around and the flinging heightens the drama. Every so often she mentions the issue from school, the bullying problem, every so often she shouts, "You are always trying to hurt me." Maria thinks she's a blur of colour and light. The sun has almost set. Maria is still on the floor in the kitchen. Tom has ordered pizza and they have eaten it sitting down with Maria on the floor, handing her slices one at a time. She has a straw for her milk. Tom offered to carry her to the bedroom but Maria feels that if she moves her back will split in two. She will break.

"I really have to pee," Maria says. "I managed to pee at lunchtime, but I had to pull myself there. I'm afraid to go, though." Maria looks at her pizza slice. "Maybe after I eat you can drag me there?"

"Well," Tom says. What else should he say? He isn't sure. "Okay."

"You can put a rug under me, like I do when I move furniture. And pull me there. Slide me." Maria smiles.

"Mom, what about Dog?"

Maria thinks they really should have named the dog. They call him "Dog" or "Dogster." They talk about The Dog. They couldn't agree on a name. He is old now, eight, and he's never had a name. They thought it was cute and original not to name him. But now it only makes Maria sad.

"After we eat we'll go out and look for him," Tom says through a mouthful. "After I drag your mother to the bathroom by her hair." He smiles a little but no one thinks he is funny.

Maria has an idea in the fog of the pain killers. "Maybe he's in the backyard. Maybe he came back and is outside waiting for us to let him in?"

Becky stands up from the towel she was sitting on to keep clean, washes her hands in the kitchen sink and then walks to the back door, opens it and yells, "Dog" out into the evening. "Where are you, Dog? Come home, Dog."

Maria doesn't tell them about Dayton. She doesn't tell them how Dayton saw her from across the street, saw Maria, her robe open, her body hanging out there for all to see, almost falling, stiffening up and leaning forward, clutching her back, screeching in pain, she doesn't tell them how Dayton came across the street quickly and steadied Maria before she fell. She helped Maria into the kitchen, stretched her out on the kitchen floor, straightened her robe and tied it tight around her waist. She said, "I have to get Carrie. Just a minute. I'll be right back," and she ran off out the front door and across the street and found her young daughter somewhere in her house and then came back. When she came back she was carrying the baby on her hip and she had her purse over one shoulder. She had Maria's newspaper as well. The baby was fiddling with the strap of Dayton's purse and cooing.

"Oh dear," Maria said, "We don't even really know each other that well and here you see me half-naked lying on my kitchen floor."

"Neighbours," Dayton laughed. "That's what we're for." Carrie burbled a bit.

The women nodded at each other. Maria nodded at Carrie. She swore the baby nodded back. Everyone was calm and quiet. Everything was silent as if there was nothing odd about this at all.

Tom helps Maria get comfortable. He helps her to the bathroom by dragging her there. She struggles as he lifts her to standing, and after she pees he helps her back down to the floor. He slides her back to the kitchen where the floor tiles are heated. He has turned them on now and Maria feels the heat in her back. "Why didn't you remember that earlier?" Maria says. Tom shrugs and brings her blankets and pillows.

About time, she thinks. He's been home from work for more

than an hour. He plumps the pillow and tries to roll some blankets under her for comfort but it hurts too much and so he just lays them over her and tucks her in a bit. He gives her another Robaxacet and some water with a straw.

"Are you sure you don't want me to carry you upstairs?"

"I think I want to just lie here," Maria says. "It really hurts to move. Maybe later you can help me get on the couch in the TV room. The floor feels nice on my back now with the heat on."

Becky is pacing beside her mother.

"Don't step on me," Maria says lightly, as if it's a joke, but she really means it. Becky is getting close, back and forth, back and forth, her tread heavy.

"Hurry up, Dad." She won't look at Maria.

"You'd think, Becky, that you actually liked Dog," Maria says. Tom glances at her. "I mean you're always complaining about him shedding and his dirty paws and the way he smells."

"I love Dog," Becky shouts, staring straight down at her mother, her feet inches from Maria's head. "You let him go and you didn't do anything about it. I love him. You always do this kind of thing. You're always hurting me."

"I didn't let him go on purpose."

"But you could have phoned Dad. You could have phoned him at work and he could have come home and looked for Dog."

Tom says, "She has a point. Why didn't you call me?"

Maria sighs. "I'm stuck here. I don't know."

"But you got to the bathroom. You said you got to the bathroom once."

"That was an emergency."

"And the dog isn't?" Becky is crying now. "Sometimes I hate you."

"Teenagers," Maria says and Tom looks at her but quickly looks away. "What? I'm the one who's hurt here. It really hurts to move.

You guys don't know. You've never had back problems. Every little movement —"

"We'll find him, Beck. Don't you worry."

Becky puts her coat on, stamps awfully close to her mother, and heads out the door behind her father. Maria can hear them calling "Dog" up and down the street. Another reason they should have named him. How will he know that he's the dog they want?

Maria isn't certain why she didn't think to call Tom. Well, she is certain, actually. She didn't call Tom because she had forgotten that Dog got out. Dayton distracted her and, for the day, Maria actually forgot she had a dog. Because he doesn't have a name, Maria thinks now, he doesn't exist?

"For god's sake, try harder," Maria tells herself. But it comes out, "Fer gut sake, dry hearter," because the Robaxacet is starting to work. That's another reason she didn't call Tom. The Robaxacet. Lovely, melty, liquidy pill.

Dayton moved from California last fall, which made Maria both envious and sad. Maria would like to go to California someday. In fact, she never goes anywhere. She'd like to get out of this town once in a while. It really doesn't matter where. Dayton said there was a complicated husband, a bitter breakup — Maria isn't sure now if she mentioned a divorce. Little Carrie has no father anymore. That's all there was to it. Something about moving here to get away from it all. To get away from him.

One thing Dayton did mention that stuck hard in Maria's head, that made her see red — Dayton has been playing hockey in that league with Trish. This fact made Maria horribly envious and sad. Mostly envious. Why didn't Trish didn't ask her to play? They've known each other for years. Maria was not quite sure why she hadn't been asked. It made no sense. According to Dayton, Trish's daughter, Rachel, has babysat Carrie when they play hockey — this fact made Maria the most envious and sad. Becky and Rachel are the same age but Becky is much more mature. The thought of that little twerp Rachel babysitting anyone's child made Maria uncomfortable — more uncomfortable than she already was, lying on the floor in her bathrobe.

"But don't you think she's too young?" Maria asked.

"I'm just down the street at the arena," Dayton said. "She can always call me."

"Do you carry your cell phone when you play hockey? When you're actually out on the ice? I mean, what if something happens when you're out on the ice?"

Dayton looked at Carrie, looked at Maria and said, "No. I guess I don't. But Carrie is asleep when I play hockey. I didn't really think —"

"Well, it's none of my business, but that Rachel girl can be a real handful."

"She seems lovely," Dayton said, "but I don't really know her like you do. And, besides, I sometimes use an older girl, Caroline."

"Oh, I could tell you things about Rachel. She plays with Becky and she's quite bossy, quite controlling. She does things sometimes that make me so mad. Sometimes she steals things from our house. Our food. She comes over and eats all our food and puts the empty containers back in the fridge or in the cupboard —" Maria stopped talking and blushed. She realized that she sounded shrill. It was just that Rachel and her mother, Trish, well, it was just — Maria wasn't asked to play hockey. That's the crux of it. Why wasn't she asked?

So Maria felt left out of everything, lonely. Even with Dayton there beside her she felt lonelier than she'd ever felt in her entire life. And, lately, Maria has been feeling very lonely. Tom is distracted at work. Becky hasn't liked her since that incident with the school and the lying kids who bullied her. That's why she threw her back out. Stress.

Maria has been so angry lately. Every time she thinks of anything she sees red. The world sucks. The people around her suck. Everything sucks. But then, after that red-hot anger disappears, Maria feels nothing at all. She has no opinion and doesn't care. It's one way or the other — hate or indifference. There is no in-between. Maria finds it exhausting. She wonders often if this is peri-menopause. Maybe that's what it is. Hormonal fluctuations.

Dayton was sitting on the floor near Maria. She leaned her back against the wall. Carrie was sitting on her lap, looking at Maria, sucking her thumb, her baby fist pressed hard against her nose. She is a cute baby, Maria thought at the time. A sweet-looking thing.

"How well do we really know anyone?" Maria said. "And she's a child. I shouldn't say mean things about a child."

And that's when Dayton started to cry. It shocked Maria at first. Even though Dayton has lived across the street for months and months, they've never really said more than "hello" and "nice weather" and so they don't really know each other. And here Maria was, lying on her kitchen floor in her bathrobe with someone she just met and the woman was crying. Carrie took her finger out of her mouth and screwed up her face to cry. But then, just as quickly, she plugged her finger back in and stopped.

"I'm sorry," Dayton sniffled. "It's just — "

"Oh, I completely understand," Maria said. But she didn't. She had no idea why this woman was crying in her kitchen. Maria thought, I should be crying. I'm hurt. I'm lonely. I have no friends who ask me to play hockey. My kid doesn't like me. I'm angry all the time. My husband —

"It's just."

"Yes, yes, yes. No problem at all."

This went on for a bit. And then Dayton wiped her eyes, blew her nose, and got Maria a Robaxacet from the bathroom cabinet. She left a little while later. She had to put Carrie down for her nap.

Now Maria tries to roll over. The dark has completely set in. Tom and Becky have been gone for about an hour. Maria heard their voices carry down the street and disappear. She heard them come back for the car, and then drive off again. "Dog, Dog, Dog . . ."

Fucking dog, Maria thinks. What about me?

The kitchen tiles are filthy. Hair everywhere. Is that an olive slice from the pizza under the dishwasher? A hair clip beside the chair leg? It's amazing what you see when you get down to the level of the mess.

So many things to worry about. A woman alone on her kitchen floor. A dog with no name lost out in the dark. A stranger crying in your kitchen. This is when Maria realizes that she never called in to work. She missed a whole day of work and she didn't call in and they didn't call her. No one called. All day. Except Becky, when she was at Rachel's after school.

Didn't they wonder where she was? Didn't anyone worry about her? Or miss her? There was supposed to be a meeting today, Maria remembers. About a new insurance policy her company is considering. Better drug plan. Better dental. Maria wasn't there and no one noticed. Maria starts to get teary just thinking of it. She would have liked to have given input. She would have liked to have said something about orthodontists and prescriptions. Especially if pain killers were covered. And maybe physiotherapy coverage. Or massage.

On the news the other night there was a story about a woman who had died at her desk in her cubicle at work — a heart attack. She had died on Friday morning and they hadn't discovered her until Saturday afternoon. For an entire day the woman slumped dead over her desk and no one noticed. The weekend cleaning staff discovered her. Imagine leaving for home on Friday and saying, "Have a good weekend, Betty," to a dead woman. How many people walked past, oblivious? It makes Maria wonder why she even has a job.

Well, money. Of course. That's why. She sometimes enjoys what she does. But it's definitely impossible to live off one income these days. Two incomes barely make ends meet.

"We're home." Tom is standing at the back door. Becky looks defeated. "No luck."

"He'll come back," Maria says. "I'm sure of it, Beck. He has his collar on." But she isn't sure. In fact, she's sure he's gone for good. Dog. Out in the real world. On an adventure. They've had him for eight years but, for some reason, Maria doesn't even feel sad that he's gone.

"I can't believe you, Mom," Becky says. She is deflated. Her eyes are puffy. "I can't believe you lost our dog." She kicks past Maria and heads up the stairs to her room, stomping all the way. Her door slams and then Maria and Tom hear her DustBuster start up. Becky cleaning. This is part of the reason why Maria thought Becky wouldn't mind that the dog was gone. He is, after all, loaded with dirt and hair and dead skin. He sheds everywhere.

"Poor Beck," Tom says. He runs his hand through his hair. "I bet he will come back, though. Dogs do that, don't they? Remember when Frank and Trish lost their dog on the bike trail, and when they came home after looking all day for him he was sitting on their front porch?" Then he turns on the TV and settles in to watch something. After about half an hour Tom says, "can I get you anything?" Tom turns the volume up on the TV so he can hear over the DustBuster. Maria lies there, waiting for something, for someone, for anything.

Late at night was the worst, Dayton told Maria. When the dark settled in and Carrie was asleep. When the trees outside scraped against the windowpanes. "That's when I'm afraid," Dayton said, "that he'll come for me. That he'll come and take Carrie back."

Trapped there, on her kitchen floor, an imprisoned woman, Maria could only blink in response. What more could she have said to Dayton? Of course he will come. He wants his daughter back, doesn't he?

"You'll figure it out," Maria said. "I'm sure once the lawyers get involved it will all be figured out."

Dayton shook her head. "That's the problem," she said. "He isn't communicating with my lawyer and I don't think he even has a lawyer. He's crazy, Maria. I don't know what to do."

"Restraining order?"

"I took his child." Dayton began to cry again. Carrie joined her this time. And then Carrie found her thumb and became silent. Maria wished that Dayton would use her own thumb, plug her own mouth.

"Oh dear," Maria said.

Dayton waved her arms in the air. "John just hurt me so much. I needed to get away. I wasn't thinking. I didn't think the whole thing through."

Maria didn't like this story. Not when it was being told to her and not after. In the late afternoon, as she lay on her kitchen floor alone, after Dayton had gone home, she felt as if someone were sitting on her chest. She felt sick and scared and angry. Men who cheat on their wives. Such unfaithful cowardice. Why not just leave? Why cheat? Women who steal their babies into the night. How did she get Carrie out of California without her father's consent? Maybe she forged his signature? Why not just go the legal route? Why not ask for help? Surely someone would help, even if you had to pay them to help you? The Robaxacet was working and Maria felt disoriented and confused. She wondered if Trish knew about this — about the cheating ex named John. Left in California. Maybe if Trish had known about this she would have thought twice about asking Dayton to play hockey. Or, at least, Trish would never have let Rachel babysit for a woman whose ex-husband cheated on her, for a woman who stole her child away from the child's father. After all, it takes two to tango. Right? Isn't that always the case?

Maria would never let Becky babysit for Dayton. Not for a second. Dayton and her history. And who knows what kind of man she'll take into her life again. She's attractive. She's young. Surely the house will be swarming with boyfriends soon enough. And they'll probably cheat on her. She'll become more unstable, insecure, get more boyfriends — the cycle will go around and around and around. Maria could see it. Maria spent the day thinking about it. That poor girl, Rachel, sitting over there in the dark on hockey nights while Dayton skated away on a team Maria should have been invited to join. If Trish had only asked Maria to play hockey with her she would never have put Trish's daughter in moral danger. Right? Bad influences. Maria isn't sure, but this sounded right in her mind. It's not as if she didn't like Dayton. She was nice to come rescue her when her back went out and her baby was well behaved and quiet. Just the kind of baby Maria appreciates.

And then Maria fell asleep.

This has happened before, this back problem. Maria thinks she has a weak spine. The doctor says she has osteoarthritis but she doesn't believe him. He says she has bone spurs that press on the nerves in her back. How can she have bone spurs? After all, she's young. Healthy. Once, every couple of years, she has to lie still for four days, take muscle relaxers and stay completely still, and then, after those four days, she will get up and the pain will be gone. A miracle. Three days doesn't work. She isn't sure about five days, as she's never tried it, but four days is the cure.

Tonight Maria lies alone on the TV room floor off the kitchen. She didn't want to move, no matter how Tom begged her and told her that he would carry her gently to the couch, that he wouldn't jar her spine. The couch is too soft. The floor is hard and unforgiving. Just what her back needs. But tomorrow Tom will carry her up to their bedroom and she will lie there. Tonight she wants to lie on the TV room rug and not move until morning. Tom carries her into the bathroom for the second time, Maria screeching in pain, helps her in there and then makes up the TV room floor with a stiff yoga mat, a pillow, quilts and blankets. He places the phone and a flashlight beside the mat and settles Maria in for the night. He then kisses her forehead like she has watched him kiss Becky's as he tucks her in for the night. She listens as he climbs the stairs to their room to stretch his long frame out on the empty queen-size bed and fall into oblivion. Tom works hard. She appreciates that. He may not notice things sometimes, but he is a good man. He would never cheat on her. She knows this. She is sure of it.

Alone on the TV room floor, the house dark and creaking around her, the fridge humming, the light on the microwave blindingly green, Maria begins to worry about Dog. She hears rain hit the windows and she imagines him out there in the blackness, under a bush. She imagines him hungry and sad and confused and wet. And then she thinks of Becky upstairs. Becky who wouldn't come down again to say goodnight but instead stamped around on the second floor, smashing her feet into the floorboards, pounding out her frustrations on top of Maria's head as if she wanted to come through the floor and crush her mother's skull. Sometimes

227

Maria wishes that Becky was dead. Gone. Away. Sometimes she thinks about how great her life would be if her kid disappeared. Then she begins to cry.

Maria didn't know why Dayton told her that story about her ex-husband, John, and how he had many affairs culminating in one big one. She didn't know why Dayton wanted her to know about it. Maybe it was because Maria was trapped on the kitchen floor. She couldn't run from the story, she couldn't stop it from being told. She had to hear Dayton through to the end. Maybe Dayton had no one else to talk to. This thought made Maria wistful. Even though Dayton is playing hockey with Trish, she is just as lonely as Maria. Usually women don't confess their weaknesses, and a cheating husband is definitely a weakness. The women Maria knows do everything in their power to hide the fact that their marriages aren't all that they pretend them to be. They talk about other women they know, they chastise, they say that their child/husband/pet/parent would never behave that way. Inside, though, they all have problems and they are all terrified of the truth.

Luckily, Maria doesn't have problems. Not really. A few things here and there. A back problem. She doesn't really enjoy her job. And Becky. With her cleaning and her moods. With the fact that she doesn't actually like her mother. That's a problem. Other than that, though, Maria is A-okay. Hunky dory. Peachy keen.

Tom is slightly less attentive than he could be. A little distracted. But nothing to worry about . . .

"All he has to do is tell the police I took Carrie without telling him where I had gone." Dayton's eyes were vacant, empty, glazed. Maria wondered if her new neighbour was on drugs. Wouldn't that just kill Trish? Her kid babysitting for a drug addict?

"But he's Carrie's father," Maria said. As if that made all the difference. "Shouldn't he be allowed to see her?"

"You don't understand. She's my baby," Dayton said, shrugging. She held Carrie up then and both women studied her. A chubby, beautiful child. Big eyes. A smile that melted hearts. Carrie bubbled up some saliva and laughed a bit. The women laughed.

"She's his daughter too, though. Right? His daughter. I think firmly that both parents —"

"No. This is different."

"But it takes two —"

"I said no."

Dayton stared at the floor tiles and that was when Maria noticed all the dirt and hair, that's when she noticed the crumbs and how many crumbs there were on her kitchen floor. What was Dayton seeing on the floor? The way she was staring. So intently. Maria wasn't sure.

The noise wakes her. She was dreaming about a handsome man. He was bending down, offering his hand to her, and she was going to take his hand and rise up from the floor. She's not sure what she would do once she got up, but she sees his face in front of her still. Really handsome. Chiselled features. Blue eyes.

The noise again. A scratching over there, by the back window. An outside noise or an inside noise? Maria isn't sure. She lies there waiting for it to happen again. Listening hard. Nothing.

And then again. There it is. Scritch-scratching. Like a mouse. Oh god, a mouse. What if there is a mouse in the house and it runs over her, runs over her face, into her hair. Oh god. But no. Not a mouse. Maria listens. It's outside. At the back door, not the window. Rain? A tree branch? Tapping at the window?

Dog?

Why, Maria wonders, did Tom give her the phone? It's not as if she can phone him on the same line in the bedroom. Why didn't he give her the walkie-talkies they got for the ski hill so Becky could go off with her friends and they could call her into the lodge for lunch? The friends Becky never made at the ski hill, preferring instead to spend her time cleaning her ski mask with the little squeegee they got her for a stocking present at Christmas. But the phone? What was he thinking? Maria picks the phone up and looks at it. She drops it beside her. The scratching continues.

Oh Dog.

It's a matter of will power. A matter of mind over matter, actually. What's the matter? Maria will try to pull herself across to the back door. She will try to open the door and let Dog in. Maybe she can roll herself. She can do it.

Or she can call loudly for Tom or Becky.

"Tom."

"Becky?"

"Tom."

"Toooommmmmmmm."

Nothing. The house is too spread out. The kitchen isn't below anything but the upstairs office. Tom is a deep sleeper and Becky is at the front of the house. They are both too far away to hear. And even though Becky and Tom always tell her she is loud, they don't really mean it. Maria's voice is faint and delicate.

Scratch.

Maria uses her legs to slide herself across the floor. Her bathrobe is so thick, it makes all movement difficult. She propels herself with her legs. She tries to roll. Moving her arms is not an option. When she moves her arms her back breaks. Even moving her legs makes her feel like she's about to die. So she keeps her arms down straight at her sides and moves her legs back and forth as much as she can. The hardwood parts are okay, she gets across them rather rapidly, faster than she thought she would, it's when she hits the carpet again near the door that the problems arise. She gets stuck on the carpet and finds it difficult to slide anywhere. Her purple robe, thick and piled, is like Velcro on the carpet.

The pain is surreal. It's intense but then moves through her and disappears. And then intense again, a sharp, shooting, angry pain. Her hips take the pain, her neck, her feet — even her feet, her toes, her ankles — feel the pain as it vibrates through her. Sometimes it feels as if she is paralyzed in one area, but then that area frees itself of the feeling and the stabbing feeling comes back three-fold. Maria begins to cry. She is, after all, still young. Why should she have this pain? Why is her body doing this to her?

Maria wonders if Dog will stay there. She wonders if he'll be there in the morning, but she doesn't want to take that chance. Does she? Becky is already so mad at her. She rests a bit, thinking about it. She clears her mind. Stops her tears. Sniffs.

Scratch. And then a thump, like a knock. Just one.

Can dogs knock on doors? Perhaps she just imagined it. Another scratch. Yes, it was a scratch, not a knock.

Dayton said one more thing before she left. Dayton said, as she balanced Carrie on her slender hip, as she looked down at Maria on the floor, her long blond hair framing her face, she said, "I keep thinking I see him in the neighbourhood. I keep thinking that he's been creeping around the house, looking in our windows, waiting. That's crazy, right? I mean, it's been eight months."

"Waiting for what?" Maria said. "What would he be waiting for? Why wouldn't he just knock on your door? Come get Carrie?"

"Waiting for the right moment, of course. To steal my baby.

He said he was going to get Carrie. I don't expect him to do it legally." Dayton flicked her hair over her shoulder and left. She called out, "I'll lock the front door on my way out," and Maria heard her walk across the front porch and disappear.

All Maria could think about, after Dayton left, was: if she's so worried that her ex-husband is stalking her, why does she leave her baby with a pre-teen babysitter and go out to play hockey? Huh? Does that make sense to you? Maria asked herself.

Maria thought, that long, cold, sore afternoon by herself on the floor, that maybe some women got what they deserved. Not in any self-righteous way, of course, she wasn't trying to be self-congratulatory because she has such a great life, and she certainly didn't want Dayton or Carrie to come to harm but some mothers just don't know how to have a good relationship or how to raise their kids. It's a matter of give and take. It's a matter of communication. And, really, if you thought about it, any woman who won't let the father see the child, well, she should be punished in some way. Shouldn't she?

The scratching continues. Poor Dog, Maria thinks. Out there in the cold and wet and dark. Poor, poor, anxious old Dog. And here she is, drugged out on pain killers, thinking that Dog is knocking on the door. Crazy crazy.

Maria pushes herself across the rest of the carpet, towards the back door, towards Dog and his pitiful scratching. All day she's been lying on the floor. All day she's been cold and sore and now she is almost there, almost to the dog at the back door in the dark. Her back is burning from the carpet. Becky will be so happy when she wakes up and sees Dog lying beside her mother on the TV room floor, keeping her mother warm. Maria will make sure they look good together, she will make sure it looks as if she went to the ends of the earth to get Dog and that Dog is grateful and loves Maria and can't lie anywhere but beside her, nuzzled in, nestled in, breathing deeply and contentedly.

When she finally, miraculously, gets to the door the scratching stops. Maria listens and then she props herself up as high as she can get, groaning wildly as the pain shoots into her back and hips and arms, a stiffening, cracking, breaking pain, and she manages to click open the lock. She collapses back before she can turn the knob on the door.

Just breathe, she tells herself. Breathe. She closes her eyes. But the pain wells up and coats her brain. There is nothing but pain. It's unbearable. Maria sees spots. Red spots, white spots. And then a cold breeze rushes in and covers her already chilled body, a cold breeze shoots across her and she feels as if she has been dipped in the freezer. Maria cries out.

Can Dog open doors?

But then there is there someone standing there at the open back door, just over her, looking down at her broken body.

"Dog?" Maria says, and then, just before she passes out from the pain, she hears, "Mom?" coming from behind her, from the kitchen.

And then she hears Becky say, "Who are you?"

Maria had said to Dayton, before Dayton started to tell her about the ex-husband, "I couldn't play hockey anyway, even if Trish had asked me, even if I had wanted to. I really didn't want to. Hockey isn't my thing. And Trish would have asked me if she thought I could have. But, seriously, can you imagine me playing hockey? Not with this back." Maria had laughed and motioned towards her back with a nod of her chin. "You'd have to slide me off the ice, wouldn't you? I mean, I'd fall and my back would give out and then where would the team be?"

And, instead of saying something like, "Oh, we could really use you on the team," or "I'm sure Trish would love to have an extra player and we'll call you next year," or "We just didn't think of you and we're so sorry," or something like that, Dayton had merely looked at Maria with a curious expression on her face. She had looked at her long and hard, judging her almost, and then she had said, "I guess you're right." There was pity in her eyes and Maria cannot abide by pity. She. Can. Not. Be. Pitied.

That small sentence. That look in Dayton's eyes. That's what did it. That's what made Maria forget about Dog all day long. That's what made Maria lie on her kitchen floor for so many hours, thinking about her life and her loneliness and the fact that she never seems to get invited to anything, the fact that everyone seems to be jealous of her when they don't even really know her, when they don't know at all how she feels or who she is or what she is going through all the time. All. The. Time. Those small words from this new neighbour seemed to break apart the fact that Maria has known Trish for twelve years. They seemed to dissolve what Maria thought of as a friendship. Or at least a neighbourship.

Neighbours, she thought. Neighbours.

16

The way the whole situation sped out of control, the way it rapidly devolved, wasn't something Dayton's ex-husband, John had planned on. Not that John had planned much in the first place. But once it ran out of control there was nothing he could do to stop it. He also didn't intend for there to be others involved: a small man in a brown suit, a man with a vicious scar straight down his face and a tattoo of a cross on the back of his neck, a women's hockey team, random neighbours, babysitters, a frightened girl, a missing dog. What started out as a rain-soaked, cold, dark night, turned into . . . What, precisely? Yes, John intended a few things — to steal his child back and to scare his wife. But not in that order. He intended to frighten her the way she had frightened him. One day she was living with him and his child, the next day she was gone. His daughter. Gone. Of course his intention was to terrify her, in the same way she had terrified him. But he didn't mean for the rest of it to happen.

John was blindsided by the two men first. And then the dog. The girl and the man. The darkness, the confusion, the commotion and sudden lights, the footsteps all around. As if the sky was illuminated by searchlights directed at him. The whole world watching.

On the plane on the way over, John exchanges a glance with the woman two rows up from him. She is reaching to put her briefcase in the overhead bin and her shirt rides up, exposing a small butterfly tattoo high up on her hip. John stares. The woman glances over at him and smiles. She smooths her shirt down and sits back in her chair. Later, John buys her a drink. Sends it up the aisle with a stewardess.

There are a lot of things John gets away with because of the dimple on his chin, because of his polished, whitened teeth, because his suit fits so well and his hair is greying at the temples. Just the right amount. Those Touch of Gray commercials — he should be the model. He gets away with more than most. At least more than most of his friends and colleagues. It's the confidence, the swagger, the poise. That's what John has been told it is by friends after they've had too much to drink, by women who hit on him. And he thinks they must be right. Because he does get away with a lot more than most people. One woman told him he looks a little like George Clooney and, she said helpfully, that should explain everything.

This is why, when Dayton took off with Carrie, John was thrown for a loop. It's not that he can't do without Dayton: their marriage was reaching a natural end — she was unhappy and boring, he was bored — or even Carrie, although, truth be told, he did miss her more than he thought he would. John has always known he has no interest in babies. He told Dayton that before they had Carrie. It's not that he can't do better without them, it's that they left him. No one has ever left John before. He doesn't mean to seem self-centred and egotistical, but it shocked him that they left. And the way they did it was violent — Dayton didn't move down the block, she disappeared. With her passport, with Carrie's passport, with all John's savings.

For a couple of months after they left John tried not to care. He told himself he was better off without them, that eventually he could find her if he tried and file for divorce and move on with his life. Marry again. Hell, even have another kid. In the fall he was busy with work. Christmas came and went and that bothered him a bit. His daughter's first Christmas and he hadn't bothered to send her anything. Slowly John was feeling lonely and missing her. But then things started to go insane at work. Strange things began happening to him, because of him; once or twice he overslept for a meeting, once or twice he forgot to return a client's phone call, once or twice he drank too much at lunch and made a fool of himself. Then there was that party at Tsar's, the one with the cocaine in the bathroom, the one with the escorts and champagne. The one he couldn't afford but picked up the bill for anyway.

So things were slipping and John thought about what the connections were, if there were any, between Dayton stealing Carrie and his slow decline. And there were connections; he could see a lot of them. The fact that the house was always messy and when he hired a cleaning service they didn't show up half the time. Or when they did, they did a half-assed job. The fact that when he came home at night there were always dishes in the sink — his, of course, but still. There never used to be dishes in the sink. And the fact that Carrie's bears and baby toys were still taking over the living room and John couldn't be bothered to move them, instead tripping on them, bruising the soles of his feet on them. Fucking toys. Toys he didn't need. When he brought women home they would glance at the toys and he could feel them pull away. No woman likes to imagine George Clooney with a baby.

So here he is in an airplane, high above the world, following the trail of some slimy detective who charged too much for his services but quickly, easily found Dayton and Carrie. It wasn't that hard. They used passports to fly into Ontario and then the detective followed holes and gaps and sightings and such. Traced the credit cards. He did his job. Whatever that was. And here is a woman with a butterfly tattoo just up ahead and John's got a drink in his hand so things aren't all bad.

John wonders if — had he not been fired — he would be here at all. But then he pushes that thought out of his head — of course he should get his daughter back. And get back at his wife. How dare she steal from him? John wants to do to Dayton what she did to him. He wants to steal Carrie into the night, take her back home to California, leave no trace of her for Dayton so that there is that intense moment of panic when you think your child and wife have been stolen out from under you. Because, even though John quickly realized that Dayton had left on her own cognition, she didn't even leave him a note. Because, even though John figured it out within about twenty minutes, for those twenty minutes his heart beat so quickly he thought he might die. He had no idea where they had gone.

At this point, on the plane, John has a bit of an idea as to how he's going to go about it. Getting his daughter back. An idea. Not a plan, but a tiny bit of an idea. But he hasn't yet thought about what he's going to do with her when he gets her back to California. He hasn't yet realized that he'll have to take care of her in some way or another. There is nothing in his plan past getting Carrie back. Once they get back he has no idea what to do. Especially without a job. And his credit cards are maxed. John hasn't thought it through enough to worry about what Dayton will do when she finds out her baby daughter is missing. It hasn't even occurred to him that Dayton might not take only twenty minutes to come to the conclusion he came to, that Dayton might actually think Carrie has been kidnapped. And he hasn't thought through the kind of trouble he'll be in — because, in fact, he is intending to kidnap his daughter. Sure, he's going to take her away from her original kidnapper, but John doesn't let the idea enter his brain that maybe, to the outside world, he'll be just as guilty as Dayton.

But that doesn't matter right now. The butterfly woman is standing because the seat-belt sign is off, and she's coming his way. She thanks him for the drink and proceeds to the back of the plane to use the washroom. When John follows her, she smiles at him. But once they're in the line up for the bathroom she turns away from him and stares straight ahead. He tries to make conversation but her attitude is stiff and unyielding, her arms crossed in front of her chest. John gives up. That's another thing that has changed — he gives up so easily these days. After she uses the bathroom, he enters and the smell of her perfume is all around him. A floral scent, mixed with the urine smell in the air, that together make him think of funerals. John gags a little and then sneezes. Right now he thinks it's the scent that makes him sneeze, but later he'll realize he's getting a cold.

Settling back into his seat, John thinks that maybe there are alternatives to his situation. Maybe Dayton will have changed her mind, maybe she did this to test him, maybe he can talk to her and she'll agree to come home with their daughter. Even though, when he finally started contacting her, her emails were nothing but nasty and tight — like her — maybe she has realized that life is not easy alone, that she needs him to cope. She needs him to support her. But John shakes his head. He knows this isn't true. And he doesn't really want it to be true. The woman is a bitch. She has always been one. Never trying to fit in in California, never trying to assimilate. All his colleagues' wives did. Assimilate. Why couldn't Dayton? Was she too good for them? For the clubs they joined?

For the Mommy-and-Me classes? For the cosmetic surgery?

"It's not like it's a matter of life or death," the woman ahead of him is saying to her seat-mate.

"Well, death, if you think about it," the seat-mate says.

"No, but really."

"Really, honestly. Honestly." John looks at the man who is speaking. Bald head, his shirt collar skewed and stained, his hands moving quickly over the empty tray in front of him as he eats and talks. The woman is no better. Her shirt collar is stained too, making John wonder what detergent these people use. Her earrings dangle below her chin; her hair is so short he can see her scalp. There is dandruff on her shoulder. Black rimmed glasses with rusty screws.

"I just wouldn't do it if I were you," the woman whispers. "Not now."

"But, Rita, it's a matter of —"

"It's not. It's really not. Harold. It's not."

John puts on his headphones and pokes at the movie monitor in front of him. Every time he pokes it, the seat ahead of him moves. The woman finally looks back at him. Glares through her black-rimmed glasses. John smiles, shrugs. What can he do? The screen isn't sensitive enough. It's not his problem.

He arrives. The rain splashes. Cabs slosh water over people waiting on the sidewalk. He has to get from here to there, from the airport to where Dayton lives. Without him. In a house. The detective said a nice house, on a nice street, with a huge tree out front.

"Who the fuck cares about a tree?" John said.

"But it's huge. Like . . . HUGE." The detective uses his hands, spread out in front of him, to signify this.

"That big?" John mocks. "That's really big."

But when he is standing in front of that tree later, when he looks up into its eerie, naked branches, when he tries to imagine putting his arms around the trunk and then realizes that it would take five men to wrap around it, he knows the detective was right — it is a big tree.

To get from the airport to Dayton's house John has to take a cab downtown and then a bus. An hour and a half–long bus ride, through the night, John sleeping off and on, his head banging the window, and then he's there. Still with no real definite plan. Nothing. Even his tiny ideas have faded. All he is, all he has, is his emotion. And that emotion is mad right now. It's revenge. His tiredness doesn't help matters. It has been a long, long day. Why the hell would Dayton chose to move to this small city? So far away from the real world. What is it about Parkville and how did she even know about it? John figures she moved here because it's the end of the world. A dinky, stupid little place.

Walking through the deserted downtown of this dirty, ugly city — no palm trees, no sparkling lights or patios full of beautiful people — he thinks maybe Dayton has been punished enough. He laughs at himself, because stealing a man's child, well, you can never be punished enough for that. If it had been the other way around, if he had taken Carrie and moved to Canada, he'd be in jail right now. It's always a different story for men. Of course taking Carrie back is not at all the same. He's bringing her home, not stealing her away.

Walking softly towards Dayton's neighbourhood, John starts to think about things — for example, he realizes he never called anyone. He never reported his child missing. So he isn't sure what would have happened to Dayton — he's pretty sure it would have been something, but nothing as impressive as what would have happened to him. If roles were reversed. Which they wouldn't ever be because he's not so stupid as to do what she did. John shakes his head out. He's so tired he's thinking himself in circles. But men always get the short end of the stick on this kind of thing, don't they? Steal the kid away from its mother and you go to jail immediately. The mother steals the kid and gets a slap on the wrist. It's really not fair. In fact, the reason he got fired was probably because they needed more women in the company. It probably had nothing to do with him but everything to do with his gender.

His hair is soaked.

His coat is soaked.

His feet are soaked.

All of this, John says later to explain his mood to the cops. He says all of this to explain how it could have happened, to let everyone know that, really, John's not such a bad person. Deep down. He was merely tired, frustrated, wet. His wife stole his child. Remember that, he wants to shout to everyone. Remember that she did it first.

John sees a well-lit building up ahead and decides to go inside to get dry. Somehow he finds himself inside an arena, the only thing open that he passes on his walk towards Dayton. A coffee. A hot dog. He could use the washroom. It's lit up inside, warm and inviting. John buys his food, his drink, uses the washroom and then stands by the window looking in to the arena. There, on the ice, are women. Mature women. Playing hockey. John smiles. Things have changed since he was a kid.

John decides to take a load off and go in to watch.

He doesn't see her right away. Right away he focuses on another woman, one who is head and shoulders better than anyone else on the team. But then someone shouts "Dayton," and John knows, feels it, knows for certain that there is his wife. He can't explain it, considering she'd never shown any interest in hockey, but he doesn't even have to see her blond hair coming out from the back of her helmet, her tiny body in that huge amount of gear, before he knows it's definitely her. Besides, how many other Daytons could there be in this town?

John instinctively looks around for his daughter. Of course she's not there.

He sits up in his seat and watches her, watches the game.

When she finally notices him he knows it immediately. Her face pales. Her body stiffens. She stares, mouth open. After the game John walks slowly out of the arena, opening the door for a sweaty woman as she struggles through, carrying her hockey bag and stick. Back to where he was headed. His plan has now changed. She saw him so taking Carrie won't be as good revenge. There won't be that twenty minutes of terror for Dayton. Instead, John will wait for Dayton at her house. And then he will take Carrie. Straight from her arms.

The tree is there. Gigantic and old and powerful. A nice house set back from the street, the front yard all tree. The lights are on downstairs. No car in the driveway. John moves silently around the house, scoping out the backyard, the windows (curtains on all of them), the tree. And then he starts walking around the street, checking out the neighbours' houses, peering from the sidewalk into some of the lit-up windows. He walks to the house next door and sneaks a look into the back through the wire gate of their fence. Their curtains are open and John can see a man sitting in a reclining chair in front of the TV. John startles. Stops dead in his tracks. Until he realizes the man is fast asleep, leaned back, his feet up. The TV plays a hockey game and John watches for a bit before he moves on, down the street, towards the corner. He can see the glimpse of a pool through a spotty hedge in one person's backyard. The rain falling on the winter covering. He glances at a swing set behind another house. From where he stands it looks rusted and half broken. Dayton's yard, in contrast to her neighbours' yards, is empty. No toys, no barbeque, no chairs. Nothing. Although winter has just ended. Or maybe she never goes outside?

Across the street and up. John is walking back and forth, wearing down the sidewalk. Back towards Dayton's house, but on the other side of the street. Waiting for her. Some of these houses have fences and a dog barks fiercely at one house when John passes. He can see its shadow in the front window. He's walking slowly, ducking into the shadows whenever a car passes, when he hears them coming up the street. Later John realizes how stupid he is. Who cares if anyone sees him now? Dayton has seen him. His plan has changed. In fact, the more people who see him, the better his chance of getting Carrie back. But he hears people coming and so, not thinking clearly, tired from the long flight and the time change, from the day that seemed to stretch out forever, John ducks up the side of a house across from Dayton's and crouches in the bushes. He waits within inches of the fence, feeling trapped by his predicament, by the huge house beside him, by the rain that is still falling.

"Oh, I'm out of breath," he can hear a man say.

Two men on the street. They pause in front of the house John is hiding behind.

"You said that before."

John peeks around the bush and sees the two figures. One standing stiffly, looking up into the high reaches of the house where John is hiding, the other, a short man in a brown suit, scurrying around him.

"You might want to leave me alone," the taller man says. John can't see his face, but his voice is deep and angry. "I'm not feeling very generous right now."

"Oh my," the other man chirps. He claps his hands. John pulls his head back. It would look bad, if he comes out from behind

244

the bush now. If he stands and heads down the driveway, waves hello, and keeps going. They might know he doesn't live here. John waits.

"You might want to keep your distance."

The other man says, "Oh my. It hurts."

"Shhhhh." And then John hears footsteps recede.

John only hears one set of footsteps walk away. The smaller man is still out front, making snuffling noises. Drunks. John leans back against the brick wall of the house. His coat scratches the bottom of a window pane, and the noise feels loud. He feels exposed.

From inside of the house he hears someone shout, "Mom" or "bomb" or "Tom," and this startles him.

So this. This. This is how it happens: John tries to stand up without being seen (because, he tells the cops, he's trapped by the drunk man out front. But when the cops say, "Why were you hiding in the first place?" John has no answer), and so he stretches his body up slowly and peers over the bush and then he sneezes. Suddenly a dog comes tearing towards him and slams into him and John screams a little (because the dog startles him), and his scream is a bit high-pitched (he does, after all, have a cold), and then there is a little man with a brown suit standing right in front of him and John screams again. That is how it happens. He, John, did not go in through the back gate and open the back door, the man in the brown suit did. He, John, did not take the girl, the man in the brown suit did. He's sure of it. And yes, the girl went with the man easily and yes, the man smiled at John as he passed him and yes, John was immobilized by the dog, who didn't need to bite him or, if the dog did need to bite John, the dog could have let go of his leg, let go of the death grip — John was sure he could feel the dog's teeth on his ankle bone, holding on. John says this later as an excuse for why he didn't go after the little man in the brown suit leading the girl away. After all, John's wife stole Carrie from him. His small daughter — no, he's not sure exactly how old she is now, but she's still a baby. Just a baby. After all, John was not thinking right about everything — he hadn't been thinking right about everything since Dayton took the kid. Plus he was jet-lagged. And tired. And wet. And in pain. Remember: he was in pain. The small man opened the door. Not him. He never even went in the backyard. And, besides, why was it even open? Shouldn't people lock their doors at night? What kind of a town is this?

John would like to know that. He knows he looks suspicious and, no, he has no idea which direction they went down the street. It wasn't until the man with the huge scar on his face showed up that he finally realized the little girl had been taken from the house. It seemed so natural. She just walked past him with the man, holding his hand. There didn't seem to be a struggle. In fact, he tells the cops, he was so busy trying to kick the dog off him that he didn't see much or think much at all. But he knows what the people who live here feel like, after all, his wife stole his baby from him. When a kid is missing, that's the worst thing . . .

It went like this: first he ducks beside a bush at the side of the house to avoid the two drunk men, then he sneezes, then the dog whams into him and takes hold and he screams, then a small man in a brown suit walks calmly by (not helping him with the dog) and opens the back gate as if he lives there. Then the girl comes out with him and then they leave. All the time John is stuck to the dog. Of course the noises start then, shouts from Dayton and her friend as they come home from hockey and see him hobbling down the driveway bleeding. And then you come, John tells the cops. And they discover the girl is missing. That's the story.

"Why were you hiding in the first place?" the cops ask again.

John learned quickly that nothing in this neighbourhood is normal. A women's hockey league, for god's sake, that should have tipped him off. And then that little man hanging out with that scar-faced man. Loitering. Drunks. Kidnapping all around. John thinks later that Dayton's neighbourhood is shit. It is certainly not a good street for his daughter to grow up on, and he's pretty sure that if things had gone better that night he could have used this information to sway the judge to his side if there ever was a custody battle.

The funny thing (something John muses on in the future) is that the two men, the screaming neighbours, the cops, even the dog, the hours of questions in the rain and then the police station, the missing girl, that wasn't even the worst part. That wasn't so bad. It was what happened after all of that. All that after-stuff that landed on him, with the police, the court, the judge, all that crap that took his baby away from him. Permanently. Forever. Dayton won, didn't she? That was worse than anything.

While the man comes past John with the girl, the dog has hold of John's ankle — first his pants, then quickly and viciously, the ankle itself. The skin, the bone. The dog gnaws and bends and cracks. John is hitting at the dog with his fists, smacking and punching it. And later it's not the terror of the dog attack but it's the image of the scar-faced man as he came down the street towards where he was hobbling towards Dayton and her friend, where they were standing out front shouting. That man's face haunts John. In the night, in the rain, in the dark, with the light from the street shining down, the man looked as if he were wearing a mask. As if he had stepped from the stills of a horror movie. His mouth was open but was warped by the crack down the middle. The shadows distorted everything.

John can feel the warmth from the blood on his ankle (he is sure his ankle is broken). He lunges out from the bush and into the driveway.

Dayton is there, getting out of her car, shaking slightly, pale in the streetlight. Her friend (Trish, he later finds out) starts shouting, already calling 911. Then the man, his face split in half, barrels down the street towards them. Everyone soaking wet. Shouting. The cops come. A girl is missing.

A girl is missing.

That girl. He saw her go.

The bottle of pills John has to take later for the pain in his ankle has a label: "Take With Food." What John finds interesting, in his drugged haze, is that the picture signifying "Take With Food" is toast. Toast and crackers. Little square crackers, drawn in white over a black background. Four small dots on each one of them. And a slice of bread, that distinctive shape of it. Toast and crackers. Take With Food. This fascinates John, which is good, because otherwise he'd be in agony. He wonders why the label doesn't have a glass of milk on it — usually recommended to soothe the stomach if pills are strong. The little crackers make him smile. They are cute with their little dots, the kind of crackers he got on his tray in the police station when they offered him some soup after all those hours of questioning him. Soda crackers, he thinks they are called, and he doesn't know why they are called that and he ponders it for hours.

At first the parents thought the scarred man had taken their daughter. Tom, the father, came screaming down the front porch in his boxer shorts, no shirt, and began attacking him. The police held him off. The mother was taken off in an ambulance. Something about her back, about fainting, about pain, maybe a slipped disk.

Tom said, "You were stalking her. At school, in the playground, at home. Standing outside our house, looking up at her window."

The scar-faced man said no. Denied everything. Mentioned the little man in the brown suit. But no one believed him because he looked like that. Until John stepped in and mentioned the little man in the brown suit and Trish began screaming hysterically, saying something about pamphlets and pedophiles and bears. Then they believed him. Then they believed both of them.

The police said they were going to find him. "Don't worry," they said. "He can't have gone far."

The scar-faced man's face was horrific.

John saw it, his face, one last time in the police station. The man was being led through a hallway to be questioned. His face in the harsh fluorescent light even worse than in the shadows.

The dog wasn't put to sleep. Although he should have been, considering the permanent damage he did to John's ankle. John will always walk with a limp now. George Clooney with a limp. But John was a trespasser, they said. The dog was merely protecting his family.

"You see," Dayton says. Later. "You see why I had to take my daughter and leave you? Do you see?"

John was hoping that when he finally saw Dayton he would be much more distinguished, much more manly and in control of the situation. He didn't expect to be bleeding and crying a little, limping into the back of a police car. Lights flashing.

The neighbours on the street stand together. The rain is hard, cold, unforgiving. Dayton walks up to him, then. She approaches him and leans into the window of the police car and says, "You get this." She puts her hands up and signifies the entire street, the houses, the world, the sky, the rain. "You get this. This here. You get what you deserve."

John sits in the police car awkwardly. He can hear the radio blasting in and out — "suspect sighted," "shelter," "no girl."

Afterwards, after they let him go, after they are satisfied that he had nothing to do with it, and when he is finally boarding the plane back to California, storing his crutches with the stewards and then limping back to his seat, John thinks, "She's wrong. I didn't deserve any of this." When the plane takes off and begins to climb it feels to John as if his foot is going to explode, as if the broken bone is splintering and is going to stab him in the brain. Kill him. Instantly.

But not quickly enough.

John isn't sure what happened to that missing girl, but he is sure that he never got to see his daughter that night. He went all that way, he suffered through all of that, and he never laid eyes on his child. His baby girl remains missing for him.

Parkville News
Columnist, C.L. Douglas
On the beat since 1965

After the arrest of the Rooming House Pedophile (as he was immediately labelled following Judge Snider's media publication ban yesterday), the director of the Abernackie Men's Shelter, Art Spack, who had met the accused several times when the Shelter men got together with the Rooming House men, has been quoted as saying that the man was "quiet, kept to himself and wouldn't kill a fly." Despite this assurance, Rebecca Shutter, 12 years old, is still missing. She has been missing for 30 hours and counting. Rumour has it that the accused isn't aware of the girl, has no idea what the police are talking about and "didn't do anything." We have heard that he will plead not guilty and is currently being held without bail. There will be psychiatric tests, of course, and I, for one, would like to see if there is a connection between his behaviour and the Tourette's-like symptoms he displays. It's a chicken or egg situation. Does this man's difference make him commit crimes or does he commit crimes because he is different? This makes me wonder about the other characters (again, because of the media publication ban we cannot publish the names of those involved), the man whose face was split in half from an accident with a snow shovel when he was young, or the California man who was intending to kidnap his own child back from her mother. What role did they play that night? Stay tuned for the most interesting trial Parkville has ever seen.

A fundraiser is being organized at the Local Legion 21 by Rebecca Shutter's friends. Please help by donating what you can or by registering to take part in the searches. Yellow ribbons are also available for your trees. The more volunteers, the better. *Parkville News* has already donated $1,000 and our staff has committed to volunteering on a rotating basis. Please do your part to help bring Rebecca Shutter home.

17

Becky hadn't planned for it to happen this way. He was so weak and clammy and snivelling and, well, sort of funny. It wasn't at all like she imagined it would be. He reminded her, actually, of Mr. Bean. Last year, in French class, Becky watched *Mr. Bean's Holiday*, where he wins a trip to Cannes and bikes around and falls in love and generally screws up a lot of things. Becky thought it was funny, but the rest of her class thought it was stupid. Becky doesn't have any idea what she was supposed to learn from the movie, although some of the actors did speak French occasionally. Mr. Bean mostly grunted. The way he does. The man in the brown suit was like Mr. Bean in that he screwed everything up. He couldn't get the kidnapping right. He let go of Becky's hand about five minutes into the kidnapping and then he started to cry a bit and pat her on the head and Becky mainly felt sorry for him as she ran quickly away. She forgot to feel afraid. In fact, she had been waiting for so long for someone to kidnap her, for all fall and all winter, that the whole thing felt completely inevitable. It was like capital-letter-F Fate. Like those commercials you see for online dating sites. The ones where the man and woman connect online and then meet at a fancy restaurant and say that it was "meant to be," as if it was magic. Becky didn't, however, expect the kidnapper to be the brown-suited-Mr. Bean guy. She thought he would be a scar-faced man wearing a hoodie that said Falcons on it. For god's sake, this man was shorter than Becky. And weaker. And slower. He clip-clopped down the street after her (actually saying "clip-clop" as he came running), but couldn't catch her even though she was wearing her slippers in the rain. "Wait," he snivelled. "Wait for me."

Becky saw him at the back door. No, not true. First she saw her mother on the floor right beside the back door. Becky had heard her mother call out and she had come down the stairs in her slippers. There was her mother, all tangled in her bathrobe, lying near the back door and the man in the brown suit was standing there, the door open, and Becky said, "Who are you?" and the man smiled at her, a creepy smile, and Becky's mom seemed to fall asleep or faint or something, her head hitting the floor hard. Becky moved forward — to help her mother, she thinks later — but the man put his hand out, thrust it towards Becky, and Becky was terrified and kept thinking, "This is it. It's finally happening," and she took his hand and they walked out together into the rain. Becky doesn't know why she took his hand but she thought that maybe it had something to do with the way her mom has been treating her lately. Becky thought a few things at that moment — so quickly that she didn't know she was thinking these things — and one of them was that maybe her mom would be nicer to her if she had been kidnapped. Maybe then she would see how much she needs Becky, how much help Becky is to her with her cleaning and such. It was kind of a told-you-so moment. One Becky later regretted. So she took his hand and walked out with him, sort of wishing that he'd have kidnapped her a little more forcefully, dragged her or something, a little more dramatically. She should have something to show for this, something other than a gross sweaty palm. This walking out, holding hands, just seemed weak to her. Becky wondered who the other man was, the one by the bush at the side of the house, but Dog came — Dog! Safe! Home! — and was attacking this man as Becky walked away with the brown-suited man — with Mr. Bean — and all she could think was that this was Fate. Finally happening. All those months of waiting for it and, blammo, the time had come to be kidnapped.

Fate and her mom. All she could also think about was her mom and what she would think when she found out Becky was gone.

That day in the snow, after she left Rachel at Hannah's house with the hot chocolate and the weird brother, Becky went back to the school to think. She huddled on the play structure, trying to keep the wind off her face, her nose buried in her collar, and she thought about Stranger Danger and the guy who was stalking her and she thought about how old she was — twelve — and how she was either too old or too young to feel so afraid of everything. So, later, when Terry — the weird brother — came up to her and sat down next to her, she made a conscious effort not to scream or move or run or freak out. Becky sat there, with Terry bumbling away beside her, talking and scratching his private parts and fiddling with his nose, which was leaking in the cold, and she didn't move. Later she went home and everyone else was afraid. Because they thought she was missing. And it was a nice feeling to have everyone worried for her, even if she did end up getting grounded. But even though she did that, stayed there with Terry on the play structure, got used to him and his strangeness, she was still scared of things. Her tooth, the dentist, the men she sees everywhere, dirt. Everything.

But she's not afraid of Terry anymore.

Now they sit together in the baseball dugout at the back of the field at the high school. The first night it's raining and wet and cold and Becky is afraid when Terry leaves her and goes back home and she is alone. The first night, the night she escapes her kidnapper, she can't stop thinking about the man in the brown suit and worrying that he'll find her. She worries that he might change his mind and really kidnap her this time, not let go of her hand, rape her. Because that's what they do, these kidnappers. But the second night the rain stops and it's a bit warmer and she's getting used to being by herself in the dark. Terry keeps her company for a while. The brown-suited man never appears. She thinks about her mom. If she stays one more night, she thinks, she'll be cured of all the fear that wells up inside her. If she stays one more night, her mom will have been punished enough. In the daytime Terry comes and goes between his classes, and when he is with her they watch the teenagers head into the school and no one seems to notice them. Terry brings her an old sleeping bag to put over her pyjamas, to keep her warm. Becky figures they blend in, with their dark clothing, with the green sleeping bag, to the forest green of the dugout.

"It's odd how it happened," Becky says again. She's been saying this over and over.

Terry nods and uses the penny he found to carve things into the bench. A turtle, a lion, an elephant. His carvings look like the petroglyphs they've been reading about in school.

"I ran away from him and you were outside your house and we bumped into each other and here we are."

"Why aren't you going home?" Terry asks. And it feels as if he's asked that same question thousands of times. Because he has.

Becky doesn't know. She shrugs. Terry keeps asking this, but Becky isn't sure how to answer him. It's like she's been hit on the head, she's brain-damaged, she has a concussion or something.

Becky doesn't want to get up from the dugout and go home. How do you explain it, how do you explain your mom and everything that has happened lately and how you just want her to love you, need you, want you. You want her to pay attention to who you are, Becky thinks, not try to change you. Not be ashamed of you. You want her to love you for who you are, not for who she wants you to be. How do you tell someone like Terry all of this when you don't even get it yourself — because how can a mom be ashamed of her daughter? Becky knows that if Terry didn't come see her she'd be home already, but having him here with his tics and moans and grunts and things, even for an hour or so, makes her feel like she's protected. Or protecting. She's not sure which. He makes her safe while she figures it all out.

"My mom lost Dog," she says.

Terry barks quietly. Becky smiles.

"She also never believes me."

"Sad," Terry says.

"I was kidnapped."

"Me too," Terry says. "I was kidnapped."

"No, you weren't."

"I was."

"No."

"Yes."

"Okay, whatever." Becky sighs. "You were kidnapped too."

"A girl was kidnapped," Terry says. "On the news. On TV."

"Well, I was too," Becky says. "Me."

"You were kidnapped."

"Yes." Becky hears her stomach growl. Terry is bringing her food. He shares his lunch. He brings her a few granola bars or a jar of peanuts from home, but he tends to grab small stuff, as if he's not thinking about her when he's at home. He brings small, insubstantial stuff that makes her hungry minutes after she's

256

eaten. And she keeps having to remind him to bring water. If he keeps this up she'll dehydrate and starve by tonight. Although she doesn't mind the dehydration. She hasn't had to pee for hours. Ever since last night after Terry left when Becky crouched out in the field in her slippers in the dark, terrified more of the dirt than anything else.

Why can't she go home now? She's had enough.

Why won't she go home?

Becky begins to cry. Terry says, "There, there," and pats her on the head, reminding her of the man in the brown-suit and the way he patted her head while he was crying. His patting also reminds her of her mom and dad and suddenly Becky wants her mom more than anything. And her dog. And mostly her father. She wants a bath. A clean room. New PJs. Food.

A bell rings at the school. Becky needs to get home.

Maybe she's in shock? She studied shock at school. Did a huge project with a bristol board and a PowerPoint presentation. About how your heart beat speeds up and how you get irritable and confused and withdrawn. She's withdrawing from others. So she may be in shock. She's also tired and can't think. Becky thinks that Rachel is an idiot. Rachel thinks that everything they are learning in school doesn't matter, that you don't need to pay attention or listen, but it's times like this, in the dugout, when Becky is grateful she listened, grateful she read the book about World War II and learned about emotional shock. How else would she know what's going on in her mind? Even if she is confused.

Even if she's not in shock, well, she can tell everyone she's in shock. Maybe then she won't get in trouble for taking off, hiding out?

Obviously Becky didn't plan any of this. How could she have? Even though those girls at school eventually confessed after that incident, after Becky was suspended, Becky knows that still no one believes her. In fact, sometimes Becky doesn't believe herself. She'll think one thing and then wonder if she's just making it up. Maybe what she thinks about things isn't the right thing?

"Bye." Terry gets up and leaves. Like that. He infuriates Becky, but this is also what she likes about him — he does what he wants when he wants. And doesn't seem to care one way or another.

An hour later, as she's shuffling towards home in her muddy slippers, Becky sees a few yellow ribbons wrapped around trees. They look pretty in the grey day; they brighten up the trees.

She will tell them she was confused. She will tell them she was in shock. Or she will tell them she was kidnapped, that he took her to his lair and had his way with her. No, maybe not. But that he took her somewhere. Because she was kidnapped, wasn't she? Wasn't that the way it happened?

Exactly like in the winter, they see her and they all come running. Like in the winter, she feels warm inside seeing them rushing towards her. But this time police run too, and a few men in suits (not brown!), and even Rachel comes at her, crying. They all stomp down the street towards her — why is Rachel crying? — splashing through a few of the puddles left over from the morning shower. Dog bounds towards Becky, and Becky's mom hobbles stiffly forward, wearing a back brace, sobbing. Calling, "Becky, Becky." There are yellow ribbons everywhere, the whole street is decked out in them, even the huge tree in front of Dayton's house has three or so ribbons tied together to make it around the trunk. But it's Becky's dad who surprises her the most. He stands still, on the top step of the porch, his mouth open, tears slicing down his cheeks. He doesn't come towards her, he stands still and cries quietly and stares hard. As if he's seen a ghost. His mouth open.

And beside him is the scar-faced man. Standing up there, on the porch, with her father. The kidnapper who isn't a kidnapper. The truth that was a lie. Standing there, looking at her, an odd half-smile on his face.

Dear Dad,

Thanks for all your letters regarding Grandpa's postcards. I'll forget about them. I won't mention them again. I just find it weird, that's all. I remember them, but then I don't remember them. But, then again, I've never been good at remembering what I think I remember. If that makes sense. Hmmm. As I've learned lately, life is weird. Weirder than you'd think. I mean, anything you can imagine happening, Dad, isn't half as strange as what will happen. Believe me. Take my word for it. And there is nothing you can do about any of it — about life, about life being weird. I'm not sure what I'm trying to say except for the promise that I won't bring up the postcards again.

On another note, Maria, Becky and I were thinking of coming down after school is out to visit you. When is the best week? I know it'll be hot but Maria loves heat and Becky would love to use your pool (is it chlorinated? Cleaned daily? Is she allowed to wear flip-flops in it?). I think I can take two weeks off the beginning of July if that works for you and Mom? I'm glad you've decided to stay for a bit this summer. We could really use the break. Let me know. It would be great to have a nice holiday.

Love,

Tom

Dear Parents and Guardians,

As you might have heard, Rebecca Shutter has, thankfully, been found. After a harrowing almost forty hours, her parents found her unharmed, although a little tired and dirty. We, at Oak Park Elementary, encourage you to talk to your children about this fantastic outcome, as it may help dissuade a few fears. We all know that our children are very susceptible to fear — a prime example is what we learned this fall from the Stranger Danger Week. And remember what happened to the kindergarteners after we did those fire drills? Dozens of them couldn't sleep for weeks according to their parents. We all know our children see the things that are going on around them, but we also need to know that their minds might not process the information the same way we adults do. Rebecca's disappearance and then reappearance probably wreaked havoc on a few sleep schedules, believe me. So, share! Talk! Discuss! Explain! Your child needs your counsel right now.

On another note — it's spring. Almost officially. I saw a few plants pushing through my mulch just yesterday. This means: stay off the area around the shade structure! We want to win the Best School Garden prize again this year, don't we? If we trample the flowers, we won't win. The garden is to be admired, not picked, so please discourage your children from bringing home the flowers. Also, if you notice any funny business in the shade structure — especially on weekend evenings — please don't hesitate to report it. A few broken beer bottles last weekend led to stitches on Monday morning for one of our Grade 2 children. Think also of what one stray lit cigarette may do to the wooden structure! It stops my heart cold. Of course we know that it isn't our children who are doing the damage. We teach our children responsibility and respect, don't we?

Keep up the great work, parents. Happy spring.

Marge Tanner

Marge Tanner
Principal, Oak Park Elementary School

P.S. The high school counsellor, Mr. Davies, has made himself available to any parents or children who need to speak to him about anything. Please call the high school for more information.

To: mariashutter@victory.com
From: puckbunnybrady@pik.com
Subject: Hockey registration

Hey Maria,

Great to hear from you about registering for hockey! We open
the registration in early July so head on into the site and
sign up then. Make sure you mention which team you'd like
to be on if you have some friends you'd like to play with,
and also what position you play. Don't worry if you've never
played hockey before, though. We're mostly a laid-back bunch
of ladies and we have many new players every year. Make your
cheque out to The Parkville Ice Kats. Thanks.

Looking forward to meeting you in October.

        Tina Brady
                            Parkville Ice Kats
                            Co-ordinator Extraordinaire

18

Jude has brought his mother to the arena on the last Wednesday night of the season.

"See, look." Jude takes his mother's arm and leads her towards a seat.

She squints out onto the ice, wishing she had her glasses on. "All women? My age?"

"Yep. And they aren't too bad either."

Jude sits down. Claire sits beside him. She looks up to where she can feel heat coming down on her — small metal heaters suspended from the ceiling directed at the seats. "Nice," Claire says, pointing.

"Sometimes they don't have them on, though," Jude says. "Then it gets pretty cold."

Claire adjusts her furry hat. Yesterday she got her first haircut since last spring. One year without visiting the hairdresser. Ralph said that at least they are saving on haircuts.

"And shampoo and conditioner," Claire had said. But now her hair is growing in nicely. It's a different colour than what Claire remembers, lighter almost, or less shiny, more dull. But then Claire hasn't had shiny hair since Caroline was born. That's the thing about women — they give birth and transfer all their youth, their soft skin, their shiny hair, to their kids. Caroline's hair glows in the light sometimes.

"See, what I'm thinking is that next year you sign up to play."

"Me?" Claire looks at Jude. "Me?"

Jude smiles. He nods. "Yes, you. Why not?"

"Where do I start?" Claire asks. She laughs. " I can't even skate."

"You can learn."

"But I don't even know how hockey works."

Jude is silent.

"Don't be disappointed. It's just that I've never thought about playing hockey. It's never occurred to me."

"Well, you should think about it."

Claire watches the women on the ice. She knows that Dayton and Trish are playing but, for the life of her, she can't tell who is who.

For the life of her.

You kill me.

I just died.

Claire has spent a year siphoning phrases like this out of her speech. Bit by bit. Getting rid of "he was so funny we all died laughing" or "that jog was so long it killed me."

It's amazing what disease does to language, Claire thinks. To thought.

"I'm just saying," Jude says. "What would it hurt to try?"

"Why do you care, Jude? Why do you want me to play hockey? What if I hurt myself? What about concussions? You hear about concussions in the news all the time. Long-term effects. You don't even play hockey, Jude. You don't. Why should I?"

Jude looks at Claire. "Mom."

"Sorry."

Claire doesn't know why she's angry all the time. No, that's not true. She knows why she's angry all the time. But she doesn't know why she would take it out on her son. Or how to stop it. How to stop being angry all the time.

"It's okay," Jude says. He leans forward in the seat, elbows on his knees, and studies the players. White vs. Blue.

"Do the teams have names?" Claire asks.

"I don't know."

Claire nods her head. A white player looks up into the seats, sees Claire and Jude, and waves.

"That must be Trish."

"Yeah," Jude says. "Must be."

There is nothing on the ice that interests Claire. She can't even see the puck without her glasses on. So she looks around the arena. They are the only two in the seats. There are some men and kids standing by the boards. A few people look out over the arena from the windows near the snack stand. They shovel fries into their mouths as they watch. The smell was overpowering when Claire came in — grease, fried meat. Other than that, the place is empty and boring. Claire would rather be in front of the television right now. Or with a good book. She should have brought her book. She doesn't know why Jude asked her to come tonight. What was the point of it? Claire is cold. She wiggles her toes in her boots.

"It's just that —" Jude stops talking, looks down at Claire's boots.

"What?"

"Nothing."

They watch the game. Claire can't figure it out. It makes no sense to her. Especially when sometimes the referees blow the whistle and everyone stops for what seems like no reason. She wants to ask Jude to explain it to her but she feels bashful and shy around him. Is he in love with one of the players? Why else would he watch women's house league hockey on Wednesday nights? And where was she when he was here each Wednesday? Why didn't she notice he wasn't home? How did he get here? Walk? In the winter? In the snow?

"Every Wednesday you come here?" she asks.

"Uh huh."

Claire has spent the entire year focusing on herself, her body. She thinks it may be time to focus on something else. Although she doesn't know how to do that. Yet. She doesn't know how to think about something other than life and death. Her life and death.

"You could always sign up for hockey, try it, and then quit if you didn't like it. I'm sure you'd get your money back."

"It's not about the money, Jude. It's the fact that I don't play hockey." Claire can't figure him out. What does she have to do to make him understand that hockey doesn't interest her?

"Fuck," Jude whispers.

"What? What did you say?"

"Nothing."

"I don't know why you're being like this." Claire wraps her arms around her torso. She's so cold. She holds on tight.

"I don't know why you're being like this," Jude says. At first Claire thinks he's mocking her, but then she gets it. He's upset with her behaviour.

"Because I don't want to try to play hockey? What gives you the right —"

"I just want you to sign up for it. I want you to try. What's wrong with trying?"

Jude stands up. He walks up the stairs towards the door that leads into the seating area.

"Come back, Jude," Claire sighs. "Come here."

"I'm getting a hot chocolate. Do you want one?"

Blowing on her hot chocolate, Claire watches the game. Jude is standing at the back. He says his back hurts sitting. He is slurping his hot chocolate and watching the back of Claire's head. She can feel it. It's as if his eyes are burning a hole in her scalp. She wishes she had more hair to protect herself from his fire. Suddenly he comes down and sits beside her.

"This is the last game of the season," Jude says. "It starts in October and goes until mid-March. That's pretty good."

"Long season," Claire says. "Listen, Jude. Why are you mad that I won't play hockey? What does it matter? Look, that woman just got hurt. Look at her. What if that happened to me?"

Jude watches the woman pick herself up from the ice.

"She's not hurt, she has lots of protection. You won't get hurt."

"But do you want me to take that chance?"

Jude stands again. He looks down at his mother. "Yes," he says, quietly. "Yes."

Sometimes Claire wishes that she would die. Now. Right now. This whole waiting for it, this whole suffering, there's nothing good about it. She has spent a year fighting. As far as she knows, as far as she feels right now, as far as her body and her doctor are telling her, she's doing okay. So far so good. So far. Like a ticking bomb. Inside her. Tick, tick, tick, tick. Any minute she could explode. Any second a doctor will call her in, settle her into a seat, perch on his desk and tell her the news.

So what Jude's trying to tell her, if Claire thinks hard, what he's trying to say is "next year." There will be a next year. And she should jump right back into life. That any sort of delay she had last year, any sort of interference — because cancer is an interference — should be put aside. Claire should just march on up to the hockey arena in her skates and equipment and start playing hockey. Sure. Why not?

Fuck him, Claire thinks. And then her eyes tear up and she can't see the game. She can't see her hot chocolate. She can't see her son.

Jude puts his arm around Claire and they sit together in the stands, under the little heater, watching the game. The white team scores. Neither of them move. Trish waves up from the ice again. She shouts, "Woo hoo."

"That's what I like the best," Jude says. "The woo-hoo's. The cheers they have. The laughter. They are always laughing and shouting 'woo hoo.'"

"Woo hoo," says Claire. "Kind of like Ellen."

"Woo hoo."

They laugh.

"Listen," Claire says.

"It's okay, Mom," Jude says.

"No, listen. I don't know. Maybe I could think about it. Playing hockey. Would you come watch me if I played?"

"Every game," Jude says. He grins. He doesn't tell her about the concussion he saw when that woman slammed into the boards with her head, or about the strange kid in the stands who plays with his iPad and talks to himself. Jude doesn't tell her about everything he's seen on and off the ice this year. He doesn't tell her about how he used to skip school and stare at kids in the playground of his elementary school. He doesn't tell her about seeing his dad wearing slippers in the snow. Or about that guy in the brown suit who gave him a pamphlet with pictures of naked kids in it, the one who was eventually arrested. Jude saw him on the news. He wants to protect his mom from all of this stuff. Protect her from the world, but open her up to new things. Jude doesn't want her to be scared anymore. About anything.

After the game — white won, this pleases Jude — they stand in the lobby of the arena waiting for Trish to come out. Claire wants to congratulate her and to apologize for not keeping in touch, for having let their relationship — whatever kind it was — slide. Just because someone drives you crazy, just because someone can't finish a sentence without rambling and giving so much detail you want to pull your hair out — if you had hair, Claire thinks — that doesn't mean you still can't be friends. When Claire first got diagnosed with cancer she let go of all the friends who bothered her. But now Claire realizes that real relationships are about the give and take, real relationships and friendships and family come with a price. Often a steep one. Trish is not easy. But it's worth paying that price. Sometimes. Most of the time.

"Hey," Trish says.

"Hey."

Dayton is there too. The women came together in one car. They both smile openly at Claire. They are sweating and Trish's face is an unhealthy purple. Dayton's eyes shine.

"Caroline's at your house?" Claire asks.

"Yes. She's wonderful with Carrie," Dayton says.

"I can follow you home and pick her up on the way," Claire says.

"Sure."

"How are you doing, Claire?" Trish shuffles her huge hockey bag from one shoulder to the other.

Claire shrugs. What can she say to that question? Her medications have stopped. She's done it all, doped up on chemo, burned with radiation, operated on. What can she say?

"Fine, great, thanks. How are you?"

"You played a great game," Jude says to Trish. "I really like watching you guys out there. You're good."

Dayton and Trish laugh delightedly.

"In fact," Jude says, "I was just saying to my mom that she should join hockey. She should play with you next year."

"Yes," Trish says. "Yes, definitely. Yes. We'd love it if you played."

The women laugh.

"I can't even skate."

"You'll learn," Dayton says. "You can learn. I learned how to play hockey."

There is a lull in the conversation. Claire is surprised that Trish isn't filling every second of silence with blather.

"I'll give you lessons," Trish says. "I'll teach you over the summer. I think the arena still operates over the summer? I need to teach my neighbour, Maria, too. I can give classes." Trish squeals a bit with delight. "This will be such fun."

"And I'll teach you how to put on your equipment," Dayton says. She laughs. "That's the hardest part of playing hockey. It took me ages to figure it out."

Jude stands tall. He watches his mother talk to these women. He looks outside and sees the cool, crisp night, the darkness, the lights from cars and buildings, the dry parking lot, every inch of snow gone now. Every Wednesday night he was here. Now it's over. Spring is just around the corner.

"We sign up in July," Trish is telling Claire. "Make sure you request the white team on your form."

"July? Okay. Sure," Claire says. "I just might."

"Bye, Leah," Trish says to another woman who appears in the lobby, lugging her hockey bag and stick. "See you next year." The woman passes by them, smiles shyly, waves with her stick. Leaves. When she gets outside she pauses to light a cigarette.

Trish turns back to Claire and Jude and Dayton and she says, "It's good to have something to look forward to."

This thing she says, this small sentence, "it's good to have something to look forward to," sums it up for Claire. The sentence reveals quickly to her that this is what cancer does to you, that this is what growing older does to you, that this is what life does to you — it slowly robs you of something to look forward to. There is no "next year," or even "tomorrow." Only now. In the moment.

This could be bad. Or this could be good. Depending on how you look at it. Sometimes it's good to live right in the moment, to live second to second, without any plans. Then again, Claire thinks as she leaves the arena with Jude, then again it might be good to have something to look forward to. Like hockey.

"So?" Jude says to Claire.

"Why not?" Claire says. "As long as there's nothing else on my schedule that it interferes with."

Jude laughs.

Claire punches him lightly on the shoulder.

As they get into the car Claire sees a man with a horrible scar on his face pass through the parking lot on his way to somewhere. The glow from the parking lot lights him up. He is walking purposefully. His head held high. His face there for all to see.

Claire puts on her seatbelt, starts the car, turns on her headlights and drives away from the arena, into the night.

Notes

A version of "1." was originally published as "Leaf Day" in *The Winnipeg Review*, June 2011.

A version of "2." was originally published as "Knock, Knock" in *The New Quarterly*, Winter 2012.

A version of "9." was originally published as "Cracks," in *The Toronto Quarterly (TTQ8)*, Fall 2011.

A version of "14." was originally published as "Backbreak," in *Joyland Magazine*, July 2011.

The myths about breast cancer come from the Canadian Breast Cancer Foundation website (http://www.cbcf.org/central/AboutBreastCancerMain/AboutBreastCancer/Pages/Facts-and-Myths.aspx).

Acknowledgements

This book would not have happened without a large group of incredibly supportive people. First and foremost, my husband, Stuart Baird, and my children, Abby and Zoe, for inspiring me (and putting up with me) every minute of every day. My friend Heidi den Hartog, who, along with Stuart Baird, taught me more about courage than anyone could imagine. Margaret and Edward Berry, David and Nicola Berry and Alec and Joshua, Beverly and David Baird — family. My friends — Jennifer Wales, for titling this book (I still owe you that bottle of wine) and for forcing me to sign up for hockey, and Karen Kretchman, who still keeps me in shape (all these years).

From the bottom of my heart, my team of readers, thank you: Jonathan Bennett, Susie Maguire, Charles Foran, Hilary McMahon, Heidi den Hartog, Chris Bucci, Stuart Baird, Edward and Margaret Berry, Chris Casuccio. Your input was invaluable.

My agent, Chris Bucci. Hopefully this will be the first of many books we work on together.

ECW: my brilliant editor, Michael Holmes (because he couldn't resist a book that has hockey in it). It has been an honour to work with you. Thanks to Rachel Ironstone, cover designer extraordinaire, and Jennifer Knoch, my sharp-eyed copy editor. Thank you also to Crissy Calhoun, Erin Creasey and Sarah Dunn.

Thank you to the Ontario Arts Council for a much needed Writers' Reserve Grant.

And finally, the Peterborough Ice Kats White Team, 2010–2014, past and present players. Senior Ladies Leisure League Hockey doesn't feel as ridiculous as it sounds when we're out on the ice together. Go, white team, go.

Michelle Berry is widely published in Canadian literary magazines, national newspapers, and anthologies. She teaches creative writing at both the University of Toronto and Trent University, and she is a mentor at Humber College. Two of her previous four novels have appeared in the U.K. as well as Canada, and she has published three collections of short fiction. Born in California and raised in Victoria, BC, she lives in Peterborough, Ontario, with her family.

get the ebook free